GEORGE LESTER

MACMILLAN

For Jordan <3

Published 2020 by Macmillan Children's Books
an imprint of Pan Macmillan
The Smithson, 6 Briset Street, London EC1M 5NR
Associated companies throughout the world
www.panmacmillan.com

ISBN 978-1-5290-4211-5

Copyright © George Lester 2020

The right of George Lester to be identified as the
author of this work has been asserted by him
in accordance with the Copyright, Designs and Patents Act 1988.

1 3 5 7 9 8 6 4 2

A CIP catalogue record for this book is available from the British Library.

Printed and bound by CPI Group (UK) Ltd, Croydon CR0 4YY

ONE

The music is so loud I can feel it pulsing through the floor, the rhythm creeping up through my feet and running through my entire body.

'Do you want me to go over it one more time, or have we got it now?' Miss Emily calls out from by the sound system, not turning round as she pulls her mass of curly black hair into a ponytail. There is not a single soul in this room that will ask her to go over it again. We *j'adore* her, we *j'can't* get enough of her, but we know when she just wants to crack on.

I'm sweating. The whole class is sweating. I look in the mirror, which also appears to be sweating, to see my light brown hair stuck to my forehead, my pasty, ghost-white face absolutely dripping. I look a sight. There are many girls (even some of the boys) in this class who manage to make it look more like a glow than anything else, but I am not the one. Priya, for example, is standing next to me in a sweat-soaked grey crop top and leggings, but the pop of highlighter on her cheeks hasn't moved.

'Robin, how far will we get before she turns it off and screams again?' she says, untying and retying her hair.

'First chorus,' I say.

She snorts. 'We won't even get through the first verse.'

'Give us some credit.'

'Where do you know it to?' she asks.

'I know the whole thing,' I reply.

She raises a perfectly drawn eyebrow.

'End of the first chorus.'

'Same.' She laughs.

'Front and back lines swap over!' Miss Emily calls out as she starts the music again. We have about sixteen counts before this is going to turn into absolute carnage and while I see in the mirror that my mask of confidence has slipped to reveal the panic behind my eyes, Priya swaggers to the front and hits a pose so fierce I swear the room actually quakes from the sheer level of fabulous she exudes.

Priya is bigger than the other girls in our jazz class. They tried to give her shit about it once upon a time, but after they saw her dance it was all over. What could they say? She dances rings round every other person in the class, but is never cocky about it. She just lets the work speak and knows her damn worth. Every day I try to be a little more Priya. It definitely helped during auditions.

'You coming, or are you chicken?' Priya calls out, eyeballing me in the mirror.

I hurry to the front just as Miss Emily starts clapping and shouting, 'Five, six, seven, eight!'

And we move.

It's like I can see the music around me as I dance, drifting on the air, sparkly, metallic, glittering before my eyes with every step. The dynamic changes, and we all shift with the music, like it's controlling us, or we're controlling it, and it feels like nothing else. It's the same rush I get when I sing, when I act, any time I'm performing. I'll go from wanting to chew my own hand off rather than step out on to the stage, to getting my absolute life in a matter of seconds. Once you take that leap, the pay-off is sheer joy. It's like flying, I swear.

That is until Emily shuts off the music.

'Once more from the top!'

We all know that's a damaging lie – it won't be once more. We're tired, we're sweaty, but there isn't a single face in that room that doesn't have a smile so wide painted across it you'd think it would split in two.

'What did I say?' Priya says as we leave the dance studio half an hour later, our faces glistening, the cooler air of the corridor a welcome alternative to the humidity of the studio.

Even Priya looks to have got a proper sweat on tonight, so she might be human, after all. Thank goodness for that.

'You were right, you were right,' I reply.

'And you didn't know it to the end of the first chorus—'

'I knew it when there were people in front of me doing it,' I interrupt.

'The ultimate test,' she says. 'So long as you didn't do that at your LAPA callback, you'll be fine.' She looks at me expectantly, like I've been keeping news from her.

'I've not heard,' I say. 'Believe me, if I'd heard, I'd be in here screaming my tits off about it.'

'You're going to be fine,' she says again. 'Dan and Tyler don't have a patch on you.'

'But I'm not just up against them, am I?' I say. 'It's everybody else in the country that—'

'We're not doing this again,' Priya says. 'Let me shorthand it for you. You'll go into a tailspin about not getting in, I'll remind you how good you are and that there is only one Robin Cooper in the freaking world and you just so happen to be a-ma-zing.'

I can't stop the smile spreading across my face. September is so full of possibilities that I can hardly stand it, but until I get a yes (or a no) from LAPA (London Academy of Performing Arts) there's no way of knowing what my future holds, and it has a tendency to drive me completely insane. Priya knows that, so Priya knows just what to say.

'Remind me why you didn't audition again?'

'Because this is fun for me,' she says with a shrug. 'It's a hobby – I just so happen to be good at it. If I try to monetize my recreation, it might become less fun, and I don't want to risk losing it.'

'It never has for me.'

'Which, my love, is why you're going to be a star and I'm going to ride your coat-tails all the way to the top so I can get an actor husband and undermine him by being way more successful.'

'A much nobler dream.'

'Can't have these theatrical types getting too big for their boots,' she says with a wink. She pulls her phone out of her bra and her eyes widen a touch as she looks. 'Mum's outside – see you next week?'

'Sure.'

'And if you hear *anything*, you'd better—'

'I'll message you,' I say. She pulls me into a hug before she vanishes out of the door and into the night. The breeze is so welcome on my skin I can't help but let out a sigh. The more I think about the possibility of drama school, the more I feel like I am losing my mind. It's all I've wanted for as long as I can remember, so the fact that I am within touching distance is almost too much to bear.

'Watch your back, daydreamer.' Miss Emily appears at the studio door, dragging a ballet barre behind her. 'Get the other end of this, would you?'

I drop my water bottle and rush to help. 'Where are we going?'

'Studio Three,' she says.

We shuffle through the lilac corridor to the smallest of the four studios that make up Fox's Theatre School, putting the barre next to the mirrors.

'So, how was the callback?' Miss Emily has fixed her stare on me, that stare she uses when she's asked you the definition of a *coupé* and all your ballet terminology has left your brain.

'Was the ballet barre a ploy to get me here to talk about it?'

She leans on the barre and a smile tugs at the corner of her mouth. 'I didn't think you'd want me calling you out in front of the whole class. Though if you'd rather, some of them are still in there—'

'No, no, no, point taken,' I say. 'It was fine.'

'Fine?'

'Good!'

'Good or fine? They're two different things, Robin. I'm going to need a little more.' She laughs.

'They asked me to change my song for the callback,

which I did,' I say. 'Went for something a little less done. And the dancing was . . . hard.'

'But you managed it?'

'Every time,' I say. 'They saw it three or four times and I think I got it.' And it almost hurts me to say it out loud because it feels too much like tempting fate, but I say it anyway. 'I couldn't have done anything else. Like, I gave it everything I had. I took on the notes I was given in the first round and . . . I don't know . . .'

'Have you heard?'

I scoff. 'No, not yet,' I say. 'They said it will be within a week so naturally the last few days have felt like eighty-four years.'

'You'll be fine,' she says. 'You can stop worrying.'

'I can't stop worrying,' I say. 'It's too important.' It sounds dramatic, but that is how it feels. I have a lot riding on LAPA. My auditions at The Arts Centre and Hillview were fine, but not perfect. At The Arts Centre, I psyched myself out in the singing round. I didn't connect; I didn't put the songs across in the way I knew I could. Didn't get a callback. At Hillview, the dance was so freaking hard that I couldn't get it into my exhausted brain. Rejection. But LAPA was different. It couldn't have gone better. The dance was hard, but I got it. The singing round was tough, but I got through that too and they gave me notes. To even get a callback makes me feel like it's going to be the one. This is what I'm meant to be doing come September – I know it is. Anything else just wouldn't feel right. It just *has* to work out.

'Well, you did a great job tonight,' Miss Emily says, ushering me out of the studio. 'How did you find it?'

'As soon as I was at the front, it left my head.'

'Which is why I moved you to the front,' she teases, a smile creeping across her face. 'I'm not about to let you off easy, hiding at the back because you're tall.'

'I want everyone else to be able to see!'

'You want everyone else to learn the combination, to your detriment,' she groans. 'You need to be seen. Take up some room for once, Robin. Especially when you're at LAPA in September.'

We've made our way back to outside the changing rooms. The rest of my class have vanished, replaced by the adults taking Miss Emily's next torture session. It's a totally different vibe.

'Miss Emily, what if—'

'Uh-uh – no, we're not doing that again,' she says, holding up a hand. 'If you go down this road, you're going to make yourself more anxious . . . and I've got a class to teach.' She winks at me and calls for her students to follow her into Studio 2 while I slip into the boys' changing room.

I quickly get changed out of my shorts, vest and jock into

clean clothes and pull on my jacket before hurrying out of the building to my bike.

I've barely switched my phone back on when it rings. I jump and nearly drop it.

'Hello?'

'She lives! SHE LIVES!' Natalie crows down the phone. 'Honestly, babes, I've been trying to get hold of you for the last half an hour. I need your notes from English today — Mrs Finch wouldn't stop going on and I missed most of the class. I thought dancing finished at eight?'

Natalie is a British Grenadian pocket rocket who I have known for most of my life. Her mum's an English teacher, hence the essay panic, and her dad's a lawyer, so her aspirations are as sky-high as my own, but with added parental pressure for good measure. She was also the first person I told I was gay and her reaction was to hug me and tell me, 'When you wanted to do an Angela Lansbury marathon for your thirteenth birthday, I kinda knew.' So she's kind of the best.

'It did, but I was chatting to Priya and then to Miss Emily and then—'

'Honey,' she interrupts, 'I'm going to stop you right there, because all I'm hearing is excuses and what I want is your dulcet tones in my ear and your English notes in my inbox. Are you home yet?'

9

'No.'

'You're *still* at dancing? Why are you never around when I need you?'

'I'd be home a lot quicker if my hands weren't tied up with this phone call,' I reply. 'Hang on.' I plug in my headphones and unlock my bike. It's only as I push down on the pedals that I realize just how much my legs are burning. Miss Emily really went in on us tonight, that much is clear. 'OK, you can keep talking.'

'Oh, don't let me interrupt your ride home,' she says.

'But you want to.'

'I *totally* want to,' she says, and I can hear her shuffling about on her bed. 'So you'll send me your notes?'

'They're probably not nearly as detailed as you would have done, but at this stage I'm pretty sure you know more about *Hamlet* than Shakespeare did, so . . .'

'Thank you,' Natalie says. 'Honestly, applying for university is so stressful.'

'Really?'

'Pressure from all sides, Robin,' she says. 'Parents in one ear, Mrs Finch in the other, my law teacher chiming in—'

'How many ears do you have?'

'Missing the point!' she exclaims. 'At least the applications are done now. I've made my choices and everyone can stop asking me.' There is noise in the background.

'What are you watching?'

'*Drag Race.*'

'Season?

'Six, duh, best one.'

'Tea,' I say. 'Although arguably Season Four is . . . Wait, I thought you were working?'

She groans. 'Girl, I need your notes!'

'Sorry, I'll send them when I get in, I swear.'

'Good,' she says. 'So, have you heard from lover boy?'

'Christ, that's a subject change. Where did that come from?'

'Your *secret boyfriend*,' she stage whispers.

'Nat!'

'Wait, come on, I had one more,' she begs.

I sigh. 'Fine.'

'You're jacked up, jocked up—'

'You can just call him Connor, you know,' I say, though even I can't help shifting my gaze around as if someone might be listening. Connor is a complicated thing in my life. We go to the same school and have known *of* each other for years, but never hung out. Then we wound up chatting in detention late one night last term and one thing led to another and now we're sneaking around and seeing each other whenever we can. Natalie even changed his name to SB (Secret Boyfriend) in my phone, partly to protect his identity, partly so she could make jokes.

'Oh please, you know how obsessed with you my mum is – if she hears me talking about him she'll want to know all about it, and this is meant to be a sexy secret,' she says. 'So, what's new with him?'

'Nothing since the weekend,' I say. 'But I don't know if he's messaged because I'm on the phone to you.'

'You trying to get rid of me?' she says.

'I don't think you'd let me even if I wanted to,' I say. Natalie is my best friend in the whole entire universe and we tell each other basically everything. We plan on living together from September when I'm at LAPA and she's off being a fancy-pants lawyer-in-training. 'But he seemed fine at school today. A bit distant, but that's sort of the game.'

'Not my kind of game, babes,' she says.

'And what *is* your kind of game?'

'Ignoring advances from all genders until I'm all lawyerly and stunning,' she says. 'Though, knowing my luck, the second I decide I can take my eye off the ball, everybody will be taking their eyes off me. That's the thing, isn't it? They want you when they can't have you and as soon as you're available, *poof*, away they go.'

'What did you call me?'

'Oh, she's a funny girl now!' Natalie snarks. 'Greg

wanted me to tell you that he missed you today.'

'What?'

'He was being all studious and good over lunch so didn't see you in the common room, and when we were walking home I was telling him we had birthday chats and he was sad he missed out.'

'Natalie—'

'You have to do something for your birthday, Robin. I swear, if you try and go to a dance class—'

'We'll do something – I told you at lunch. I just don't know what.'

'Well, we're going out on Friday whether you like it or not and, frankly, I need an excuse to let my hair down now that the uni application madness is over,' she says. 'You, my love, are my excuse. Congratulations.'

'What privilege!'

'You're welcome,' she says. 'Anyway, Greg missed out and felt bad.'

'And you made him feel worse?'

'I may or may not have rubbed it in,' she says, and I can hear her grinning from ear to ear. She knows she can get away with it with Greg. They have a lot of history. They used to be together but then realized they were better as friends. Now it means she rips into him at any given opportunity and he sort of rolls over and takes it . . . most of the time.

But Greg is sweet. He's our token straight white boy. Every group needs one. He's ours. And he's better than yours, trust and believe.

'I'll give him a hug tomorrow morning,' I say.

'Bless the hetties, so simple,' Natalie says. 'Anything else to report?'

And I know what she's getting at.

'I've not been home yet, so I don't know,' I say. 'But Mum would have messaged if something had shown up while I was at school.' I sigh. 'The waiting game continues.'

'Wait all you like, hun, but this time in nine months we'll be exhausted and praying for death to release us from our workloads in London, *instead* of Essex, in our very own freaking flat and it's going to be blissful,' she says. 'OK, I'm ditching now – you should focus on riding your bike. I don't want to be the cause of death of a future superstar.'

'Why? Who am I crashing into?'

'Oh, the comedy, oh, my sides,' she deadpans. 'Love you, queen, see you tomorrow.'

'See you tomorrow.'

I hang up the phone and keep riding, ignoring the buzzing in my pocket that could be Connor trying to reach me. My heart thrills at the thought.

I ride the old country lanes into my town, the same route I've taken for six years, until I spot our little house on the corner. The unkempt front garden that Mum says she'll fix every summer is overgrowing on to the path, the ivy-covered fence that runs along the side of the pavement starting to look more like a barrier than a border.

The house is pitch dark. Mum's car isn't parked out the front, so she must be working later than she thought. I ride my bike to the gate and wheel it into the garden, leaning it against the fence before heading in through the back door.

'Mum?' Nothing comes back, not even an echo. The house isn't big enough for an echo.

The light on the answering machine is flashing, so I press the button to listen as I kick off my shoes and rummage through the post on the table. Still nothing.

'ROBIN!' It's Natalie's voice and I look up. Why the hell is she leaving me a message? 'You might wonder why I'm leaving you a message on a freaking answering machine like it's the middle ages. Reason one, you actually have one, which makes me question your mum's usually impeccable taste.'

Truth be told, Mum bought it as a gag because her mum used to have one and she always liked the idea of people leaving messages. The reality of the situation was that not many people did. Natalie certainly didn't. Ever.

'Reason two, you never bloody text back. Turn your phone on! I need your notes. P.S.: feel free to ignore this if I actually managed to reach you. No doubt you will have about seven thousand frantic messages from me when you take your phone off I-Have-Dance-Class-So-I'm-Dead-To-The-World mode. SEND ME YOUR DAMN NOTES! See you tomorrow.'

I love her in all of her weirdness. The machine beeps and moves onto the next message.

'My angel-faced boy.' Mum's voice comes through the machine. This can't be good. 'It's eight thirty here and I'm nowhere close to being done. They offered me the overtime and I took it. I could use the extra hours anyway. Don't wait up. I love you lots. There are leftovers from last night in the fridge. If you're still up when I get in, I'll be annoyed. Go to bed. Hope you had a good class. Text me so I know you've got home safe. Please. Do it now so you don't forget. I'll see you in the morning. Bright and early!'

I grab my phone and swipe past the slew of notifications, most of which are from Connor, so I can quickly text Mum. This happens a lot. There are days that go by where I just won't see her because she's working and I'm at a class and all we'll have are texts and answering-machine messages. But it's been like that for so long I don't know any different.

I don't really feel all that hungry, so I skip the leftovers and am about to get ready for bed when I notice the post by the front door. As I pick it up, I see, nestled amongst a stack of leaflets, a giant white envelope.

Shit.

It must have come after Mum left for work.

And it's the big envelope. Everyone says the big envelope means good news – holy shit, *holy absolute shit.*

I take a breath and open the seal, trying not to cause damage, trying not to wreck whatever is inside, and, holding my breath, I pull it out.

My heart sinks.

School report.

Winter term school report.

'Absolutely NOT!' I say to the dark, putting it back in the envelope and on the dining table.

I grab a Post-it from the little table where Mum keeps the phone.

School report is here. I'll see you in the morning for the debrief. Hope work wasn't too hellish. Leftovers are still in the fridge. Xx

I chuck my dance gear in the washing machine then bound upstairs and throw myself on to my bed. I turn on my bedside lamp, the orange glow lighting up my little room and illuminating the clothes strewn over the floor, the papers on my desk, the unopened textbooks and, most importantly, my phone.

I do my duty as a good friend and send my notes to Natalie, then flick through my apps to read the messages from Connor, the goofiest smile spreading across my face as

I scroll. It's the kind of smile that Natalie teases me about, but she's happy I'm happy, and there's something about Connor that makes everything a little bit brighter, like when Dorothy steps into Oz for the first time.

> Are you about tonight? x

> Shit. Forgot you had dancing, never mind.

> I missed you. The weekend was fun, we should do that again. I'll find out when my parents are next away, and you can come over.

> If you want to.

I mean, of course I want to. If he asked me to come over now, I'd be there like a shot. Christ, he has such a hold on me.

> I guess I'll see you tomorrow.

The next thing I see is a picture of him with his shirt off in front of the mirror in his bedroom. The lighting is great, his body is perfection, from his broad shoulders to his big chest that is so damn good for cuddling – I honestly can't cope with it. He's pouting a little, midway through running a hand across his dark, close-cropped hair. Stupidly handsome boy.

Are you still up?

I wait a few seconds for those magical three dots that make my heart skip in my chest, but they don't come. So I start to scroll back, through weeks upon weeks of messages, from one-word answers that were enough to give me heart palpitations to paragraphs that I could probably quote word for word at this point.

It's not lost on me how sad it is to do this. But I spend so much time struggling to believe that it's real that if I didn't have these I'd swear I was imagining the whole thing. But I'm not. It's real and I can see it because it's right here in my hands.

I know he deletes the messages afterwards. He's protecting himself in a way that I don't really have to. Natalie and Greg know all about it. Mum doesn't know I have a boyfriend, if I can even call it that, but I don't think she'd mind all that much. I told her three years ago that I like boys and it might be nice to get specific. But if Mum knows she'll want to meet him and . . . she can't meet him.

I try not to overthink it. No matter how much I care about Connor and no matter how much he cares about me (or seems to, I mean, I have the receipts), September is going to change everything. And it's exciting and new, but we've not even talked about what will happen next. I'm just trying to enjoy the moments we have, because each one is a little touch of sparkle in my life.

By the time I've scrolled to the top of our message chain, the first 'Hey' that I can hear in his gruff voice, it's way past midnight and my body is crying out for me to lie down and let the world slip away.

So I do.

TWO

'Robin, if you don't come down here in ten minutes, I'll start reading it without you!'

I practically jump awake. My phone is clutched to my chest where I must have fallen asleep holding it. Gross.

'I don't hear movement!' Mum calls.

'That's because I've not moved.'

'Sweetie, I love you, but I'm not above dragging you out of bed.'

I quickly shower, ignoring the aches that seem to accompany my every movement.

'Five minutes!' Mum screams as I turn off the shower. She shouldn't even be awake. I didn't hear her come in last night, so she must be shattered.

When I reach the kitchen, she's already at the table, the big white envelope in her hand, a selection of cereal and two bowls before her.

I have no idea where my mum gets her energy from, but even after a late-night shift she looks wide awake, her dark brown hair a little pouffey around her head, her blouse semi-ironed, a smile on her face, her hazel eyes somehow sparkling. She looks like she's had a full night's sleep. I look like I've been hit by a truck.

I check the time on my phone and grimace. 'Why did you let me sleep so long?'

She shrugs. 'You didn't even touch the leftovers of my *world-famous* lasagna!'

It's not world-famous, it's not even street famous.

'I assumed you could do with the extra time in bed. If anyone at school asks, I'll write you a note.'

'I don't know if they'd take it.'

'You need to stop talking – you're seriously cutting into my mocking time.' She flicks her hair out of her face. 'You know how much I love my mocking time.'

'I don't think there is a man, woman or child alive that could stop you,' I reply, kissing her on the cheek. 'Good morning, Mum.'

'Good morning, Robin.'

I take my seat at the table and pour myself some off-brand Cheerios, bracing myself for the onslaught. I'm definitely going to be late; I might as well lean into it. 'OK, let me have it. How bad is it?'

'I've not looked yet.'

'You've not looked yet?!'

'Of course not, Robin – it's tradition! And you said

debrief – I can't pre-brief before the debrief, then I would be briefed, and that would be wrong!' I've fully lost track of what she's saying as she sighs, smoothing out her blouse and mentally preparing herself for the moment. I'm supposed to be the actor in the family yet here she is with a ritual for opening my school report. She's ridiculous and I love her.

'I thought it was going to be an acceptance letter,' I grumble.

'Oh dear, did you collapse ont o your bed like a dramatic heroine?'

'Mum—'

'Did you wail to the sky, "When, oh, when will my acceptance letter arrive?"' She throws the report to her forehead, and I try not to laugh when the corner of it jabs her in the cheek. 'Ow.'

'Karma's a bitch.'

'And so are you,' she says with a wink. 'Sweetie, it's coming, you know it's coming. You slayed that audition—'

'Don't say slayed.'

'You left them jaw-on-the-floor speechless,' she barrels on, beaming. 'You've got this. I know you've got this. Half the street knows you've got this.'

'Half the street?'

'You think I'm going to miss an opportunity to tell them

how my son is going to be a star?' she says.

We've been talking in certainties since I got back from the audition and Mum's confidence in me is infectious. As much as Natalie would like to fight her for the spot of biggest fan, she doesn't have a patch on Mum. Mum's never missed a show. She's worked her fingers to the bone so I can do this. And now we're just waiting for the pay-off.

'If the letter comes, you have to call me,' I say. 'You can't not call me.'

'Same to you.'

'Deal.'

She holds out her little finger. I grip it with my own. Pinky swear.

'Now, back to the mockery?' She takes her glasses from the kitchen table and places them on the end of her nose as if she's about to read me to filth. The library has apparently opened early this morning.

Slowly, she opens the envelope. She doesn't turn the first page, holding it close to her chest and eyeing me carefully instead. 'Here I have in my hands, the penultimate report.'

'Mum—'

'Robin Cooper's winter-term school report.' She wipes an imaginary tear from her eye. 'I'm so proud of my boy.'

I scoff. 'Wait until you read it.'

She opens the report and begins her performance.

'English,' she announces, like she's just taken the stage at the Globe. '"While Robin shows a great understanding for the subject, and an apparent interest, he could stand to be a little less distracted in class."' She looks up. 'Ouch.'

'Wow.'

'Thanks a lot, Mr Goldberg. That's the last time I flirt with you at parents' evening.'

I choke on my Cheerios. 'Mum!'

'I'm just doing what I can to get you a good mark.'

'He doesn't decide the final mark, just predictions. I have to do a written exam in a couple of months – you know that,' I say.

'Well, who's the examiner? I'll flirt with them.'

'Or I could work harder.'

'But where's the fun in that?'

'You're terrible.'

'It's like you want me to stay single forever.' She sighs dramatically and flips over the page. 'Same from psychology. I wonder if they write their reports together so they give similar feedback. What do you think?'

'I think I probably stare out the window and daydream a little too much,' I say.

'Aha!' she exclaims. 'They've got in your head, see? Sick little game players, every last one of them.'

I can't help but laugh. Mum is always like this. She knows I work hard when I'm not off dancing, but she also knows that, at the end of all this, English and psychology don't matter all that much to me. Not really.

'Read drama next,' I say, walking over to the sink with my empty bowl. I need to wrap this up if I'm going to make first period. I don't want to rush her, but once she gets going she could go on for *days*.

'No way,' she says. 'That's far too easy and your head still looks a little big after the winter musical.' She follows me over to the sink, putting her hands around my head. 'Look, I can barely fit my hands around . . . oh no.'

Panic. 'What?'

'It's . . . it's getting bigger!'

'Mum!'

'It's swelling, it's growing, it's taking over the whole kitchen!'

'You're impossible.'

She laughs and sits back down. 'OK, drama,' she says, picking up the report again. She opens her mouth to speak but stops herself, just letting a smile spread across her face.

'What? That bad? Or did she talk about when I fell off the car during "Greased Lightnin'"? Not my finest hour and pretty damn rude for her to bring it up again. I mean, the car was slippery – what kind of sadistic stagehand decides to wax a car I have to climb on, I could have—'

'Shut up, Robin,' she says, looking up at me, her eyes a little misty. 'It's glowing.'

'Really?'

'God, this woman loves you.' She shakes her head. 'If I die, she'd adopt you in a heartbeat!'

'Mum—'

'I'm serious. Don't even worry about me,' she says. 'I'll ask her on my deathbed, really draw it out and croak to her, *Mrs Hepburn, if that is your real name, take care of my son.*' She starts violently coughing, really leaning into the role.

'What did she say?'

She clears her throat. '"No one else in my class shows the aptitude and joy that Robin has. From the start of Year Twelve, I have coached him both in classes and privately. I feel it in my bones that this boy is going to go far."'

'She really said that?'

Mum nods. 'She loves you, kid.'

Mrs Hepburn, which definitely isn't her real name – I mean *come on* – has always been on my side. She was handing me brochures and leaflets for drama college before I'd even thought about it. She's a melodramatic guardian angel sent down from the gaudiest heaven imaginable, where statement necklaces are uniform and giving prancing little gayboys a safe place to play is your job.

'She's going to lose her mind when you get in,' Mum says.

'Don't—'

'She's going to cry, she's going to scream, she's going to be living off your success for the rest of her life!'

I hope Mum's right. She has to be right. She prides herself on being right about everything – why would this be any different?

'OK, subject change, we've gotta talk about Friday,' she says.

'Friday?'

'Robin! You're turning eighteen – you're becoming a MAN.'

'Mum!'

'You're just so grown up, that's all.'

'Shut up.'

'I will not,' she says. 'You're my son – it is my god-given right to embarrass you at every opportunity.' She smiles. 'So what shall we do for your birthday?' She strokes her chin. 'Maybe I should just come out with you and your friends. Wouldn't that be fun! Where are you going?'

I shrug. 'Don't know yet,' I say. 'Natalie will be hounding me about it today because I can't make decisions. And I'm sorry, but, as much as I am totally loving this, I need to get to school.'

'Cutting my performance short.' She tuts, shaking her head. 'After all I've done for you. Do I need to tell your birthing story again?'

'I've already booked myself a few years on the couch from that one,' I say, grabbing my bag. 'You want to carry on your performance later?'

She walks towards me and puts her hands on my shoulders. 'That letter is coming,' she says. 'It's in the post as we speak. The world is waiting for you, Robin Cooper. I promise.'

I can't keep the smile off my face.

She kisses me on the forehead. 'I've picked up an extra shift tonight,' she says. 'I know we were meant to have dinner, but—'

'It's OK,' I say. 'I can fix something up myself. I mean, it won't be *world-famous*, but . . .'

'Tomorrow, then,' she says. 'I'll keep you something for after dancing.'

'Ooh, I wonder what it will be!'

She waves a hand dismissively. 'I don't know, something world-famous, probably. I'm *immensely* talented.'

I roll my eyes and laugh. 'Bye, Mum.'

THREE

I arrive at school, definitely late, definitely out of breath, and definitely surprised to see Natalie and Greg waiting for me at the bike sheds. Their height difference is so stark it's comical, and while you'd expect Natalie to have this tiny voice to go with her tiny self it's the exact opposite. You're more likely to hear her before you see her. Greg has this kind of gentle-giant vibe, softly spoken and sweet as anything while he towers over practically everyone. I mean, I'm six foot and Greg makes me feel small and weedy.

'Why are you two waiting for me?'

Natalie shrugs. 'We're not that late.'

'You're both mad.' I lock up my bike and look at Greg, who is trying to stop himself from smiling. I practically skip over to him and hug him tightly. 'Natalie told me you missed me yesterday.'

'She's lying,' he says into my shoulder.

Natalie scoffs. 'The only lies being told are the lies you tell yourself.'

'Did you literally wait for me for a hug?' I ask as Greg

31

lets me go. The boy really can hug.

'I won't be commenting on that,' Greg says as he turns and starts walking towards school. Natalie links her arm in mine and we follow. 'When are we talking about your birthday?' Greg asks. 'I need to tell Mum my plans so she can get childcare for Archie.' Archie is Greg's little brother, literally a miniature version of him and adorable.

'As soon as princess here decides what she wants to do.' Natalie squeezes my arm. 'Honestly, honey, blood out of a stone. How hard is it to make a plan?'

'Would you believe me if I said I was looking into places we could go?'

'No,' they both reply.

'Wow, your faith in me is utterly astounding.'

'That's not it,' Nat says. 'I just know you too damn well.'

We walk through the school and, like any other day, I find myself smiling at people as we pass them. The winter musical wasn't all that long ago and the cast was chosen from every year at school, so I met a huge range of people. We spent three months rehearsing this show and nothing bonds people together like a shared trauma. *Grease*, it turns out, can be pretty traumatic.

'Morning, Robin.' Katy – the Sandy to my Danny – wanders by, the rest of the drama crowd in tow. 'You hear anything?'

'Not yet,' I say.

She shrugs. It's not just me and Mum who talk in certainties. It's the drama crowd, it's Mrs Hepburn, it's me and Natalie when we're planning how good things are going to be come September. It makes me nervous. But more than that it makes me excited. It's Schrödinger's Drama School Place right now.

Natalie hits me on the arm.

'What?'

'I have goss.'

'Hot goss?'

'Piping, babes,' she says.

'Honestly, it's like you're speaking another language sometimes,' Greg says.

'New boy at school, Seth Harris, started yesterday, lasted two hours, *two*, before he walked out.'

'Like, literally lasted one lesson?' Greg says. 'Is the school really that bad?'

'No, but apparently *he* is,' Natalie says. 'It's all Holly and Eric could talk about in law yesterday. He just showed up out of nowhere, nobody has any idea who he is, where he came from, anything.'

'Christ, poor guy,' Greg says.

'What?' Natalie snaps.

'What? I feel bad for him.'

'Why?'

'Come on, you said it yourself, *everyone* is talking about him. He's just started here and suddenly he's the centre of attention. No wonder he walked out. I would have. Robin?'

'Yeah, me too,' I say. I know what it's like to have people talking about you, whispering about you. It sucks.

'Oh my God, I came here to share scalding hot dish, not feel sorry for the new boy,' Natalie groans. 'Robin, come on, is it not piping?'

'It is,' I say. 'But I'm with Greg – I feel bad for him.' It's one thing to be centre of attention onstage, but to have everybody talking about your business? I'd rather not.

'God, it's like you two morphed into the same person during Greg and Robin's Summer of Fun.'

'Stop that!' Greg groans. 'You were in Grenada for a month – it was hardly fun-free.'

'I was with my family! I missed out on everything!'

'For the last time, you didn't miss out on anything,' I say. 'It was just a lot of us hanging around complaining about how hot it was.'

'And you getting injured in a dance class,' Natalie says, trying not to laugh. 'Remind me how you fell into a ballet barre again?'

'Oh,' I say. 'Attempted triple pirouette, foot went out from under me, bang, smacked my face on it.'

Natalie cracks up laughing. Greg doesn't. Greg shakes

34

his head at me because he knows that it couldn't be further from the truth. But he promised not to tell how I really got hurt. Natalie doesn't seem to notice.

'This summer will be better,' I say. 'Summer of Fun, the sequel, featuring Natalie.'

'Honey, I'm not a feature – I'm a headline act!'

As we walk out into the courtyard, I see Connor and I can't keep the smile off my face.

It's like my body is tuned to whatever frequency his is giving off, even if it is a little bit awkward between us at school. I could be lost in a crowd and, somehow, I would find him.

He's with his friends, a cloud of smoke practically obscuring them as they pass round a joint. I've had enough homophobic bullshit in my time here to know I shouldn't stare for too long, but I want Connor to see me.

Good morning, friend.

He clocks me. And his eyes smile for the briefest moment before they resolutely ask me to stay away. I smile at him and keep walking. I'm not saying it's perfect. I'm just saying it's the way it is. I know he cares about me. He just can't say it too loudly.

'Ooh, should I leave you two alone?' Natalie whispers next to me.

'Bite me,' I say with a laugh.

'What?' Greg says. 'What have I missed?'

'SB,' Natalie replies without missing a beat.

'Still lost.'

'Shocking!' Natalie says. 'Secret Boyfriend.'

'Right,' Greg says, and that's the end of Greg's contribution to that particular conversation. Greg doesn't like Connor. I mean, really doesn't. He has his reasons.

My phone buzzes in my pocket.

> You free after school?

'What?' Natalie says. 'What is it?'

I show her and she practically screams when she sees it's Connor. Greg . . . not so much.

> Yeah. Free house too.

> ☺ See you there. x

I find myself praying for the end of the day. I practically race home so I have a chance to shower and change before Connor arrives. It's also an opportunity to double-check that Mum isn't in. There's an alternate universe where Connor isn't hiding in the closet and he can just come back to my house whenever because he and my mum are pals. It's probably an easier universe to live in.

It's not my place to decide when somebody wants to come out. Would it be easier for me if he was out? Yes. Would it be easier for him? Given what's happened in the past, I'd say not so much.

Nearly there. Free house?

Free house.

I head downstairs and open the door. Connor is swiftly walking up the path, hood up, checking over his shoulder every now and again before he gets inside. I've barely closed the door before the hood is down and he is kissing me. I'm caught a little off guard.

'Wow, someone's eager,' I say.

He shrugs. 'Just checking now—'

'No, she's not here,' I say. 'Do you really think I'd let you make out with me in the hallway if she was?'

He shrugs again before kissing me hard on the mouth. It's a pretty good answer, to be fair.

I take his hand and we stumble up the stairs, the two of us giddy, giggling. This is the good part. When we're together, alone, it's like the secretive bit doesn't even matter. It's fun, it's exciting, it's the two of us just enjoying ourselves.

We tumble into my room and on to the bed. He kisses me again. I reciprocate, our tongues dancing across each other, his fingers tracing a path across my stomach and round to my back, pressing our bodies close together. At this point, clothes just seem to be totally in the way.

We stop for a minute to take a breath.

He chuckles, looking down at me with those dark eyes. At school, he hangs out with a dickhead crowd, truly, but when he's with me he's like a totally different guy. I don't think there's a single person in that group that knows him like I do. They don't know that he cried when we went to see *Waitress*. They don't know that he's a damn good cuddler, and I mean *damn* good.

'What are you smiling at?' he growls.

'Just you,' I say.

He leans down again and I breathe him in. I could just do this forever, but the way his hands are all over me I know he's hoping for something more today. And I'd be lying if I wasn't thinking the same.

The door opens and closes downstairs. Connor stops kissing me immediately and lifts himself up. I'm suddenly very aware that we are in a rather incriminating position.

'Robin?' Mum calls.

'Your mum?' Connor asks from on top of me. The colour has drained from his face and the hope of *anything* happening between us tonight has vanished. 'I thought she was—'

'So did I,' I say. 'I wouldn't have invited you over if—'

'Shhh!'

'Don't shhh me!' I hiss.

'Robin?'

'Upstairs, Mum!'

'What the hell are you doing?' Connor hisses.

'I can't just ignore her.'

He's looking around the room like there is an alternative exit that isn't my bedroom door. I'm scrabbling around trying to think of something to do.

'Closet?' I offer.

'Excuse me?'

'You can hide in the closet.'

'That's not funny.'

'I'm only half joking!' I protest. It's a little bit on the nose, but he could totally fit in there, at least until I found a way to get rid of Mum.

'Window?' he says hopefully.

'What?'

'I can climb out of your window.'

'Yes, that's true, climb out the window, grab hold of a flying pig and let *that* take you home.'

'OK, sarcasm isn't helping – sarcasm is wasting time,' he says, but even I can see the smile twitching at the corners of his mouth. 'Can I climb out of your window?' He pauses. 'Please?'

And it's the please that tips me over the edge. He's scared of people finding out about us and, I mean, I don't blame him. I can't make jokes right now; I just need to get him out of that window without him falling to the ground and dying on my doorstep.

I hear footsteps on the stairs. Ah shit.

'Yes, yes, of course, come on,' I say, hurrying him over to the window ledge and opening it as wide as it will go. He peeks outside. I do the same. The kitchen is right underneath us, jutting out a little way from the house, so it's not like he's having to Spider-Man down the entire building. 'Can you jump that?'

He shrugs. 'Probably.'

'You're giving me probably?'

He leans forward and kisses me and I'll take probably if it means I get a kiss. God, I wish he didn't have to go right now.

He pulls away and clambers out of the window.

'You might want to do something with your hair before your mum gets up here,' he says, half in and half out.

'What? Why?'

'It looks a little . . . I don't know . . . messy?'

I check the mirror, and when I turn back he has vanished

from my window, already on the roof of the kitchen. I watch him go and try not to look too startled when the door opens behind me.

'Hey,' Mum says from the doorway. 'Is everything OK?' I turn to look at her and her expression twists to one of confusion. 'What's going on with your hair?'

'I was . . . taking a nap,' I say. 'You coming in woke me up. Didn't sleep too well last night.' Come through, improv skills! 'Sorry.'

'And you're flushed. Are you OK?'

'It was hot in here,' I say. Not a lie. But not the truth either. 'Needed to get some air. What are you doing home? I thought you picked up an extra shift.'

'I was going to, but they double booked,' she says, irritated enough by her day that her scrutiny of me seems to be over. 'So we're having dinner. You're so lucky!'

'And what world-famous delicacy is it tonight?'

'Tonight,' she says in an announcer voice, 'we will be having my world-famous Chinese food from the place down the road that I know you love!'

I whoop, I cheer, I play my part.

'I'm going to order,' she says. 'Hey, we could watch a trashy film while we eat, if you like. You don't have work to do tonight, do you?'

'Trashy film sounds perfect; I'll be right down!'

Mum heads back downstairs and I throw myself on my bed. That couldn't have been closer.

My phone buzzes on my bedside table and I practically leap for it.

> Sorry I had to run. This afternoon was fun though. Again soon? But without the interruption?

> Name the time and place.

I delete the heart emoji so I don't sound too keen and hit send.

> 8 a.m. tomorrow? Hampton Road?

> Wait! That wasn't a suggestion for a place to do THAT. I was suggesting walking in together.

> If you want.

> I'll see you tomorrow morning.

I send it with the heart emoji. Fuck it. Life's too short to not send heart emojis to the boys who have your heart. Facts.

FOUR

'ROBIN! ROBIN! ROBIN!'

The screaming is accompanied by a hammering on my door that has me so disorientated that I think the house might be burning down. I grab the duvet and wrap it round myself, shuffling to the door, ready to commit matricide if I don't see flames because, Jesus Christ, my alarm wasn't going to go off for another blissful thirty minutes.

My face is fixed in the most murderous stare I can muster as I open the door to Mum, who is grinning. No flames. She's grinning so broadly it's like she's off her absolute face on something.

'What? Ungodly hour, Mum, what's so important that—'

'Shut up and pay attention to what I am waving in front of your face!'

I look at her hand and I see it. It's an envelope, a stamp on the front with the logo of the London Academy of Performing Arts emblazoned across the top of it. It looks opulent. It looks official. For something the size of an A4 sheet of paper, it carries a hell of a lot of weight in it. The weight of my entire future.

'When did it get here?' I say, my voice barely above a whisper.

'Literally a few minutes ago,' she says.

'Holy shit.'

'Why are you whispering?'

'I don't know, reverence.'

'Fuck reverence, you need to open this!'

'Mum, language.'

'OK, weird role reversal, please, just open it before I explode. I can't take it.'

I take it from her and feel the weight of it in my hand. It doesn't feel like there's a lot in there. I don't know what I expected. People talk about the 'big envelope' like it's an indication of a 'yes' over a 'no' and my heart is pounding so hard I can feel it in my throat, in my head, in my fingertips. I am shaking.

I open it slowly, like I'm trying to preserve it, like it's going to be an artefact in a museum one day. It's taking every bit of composure I have to not tear it open and I can feel Mum's eyes on me, willing me to do just that.

Dear Mr Cooper,

Thank you so much for your attendance at the London
Academy of Performing Arts auditions on January 14th.
The standard was incredibly high this year and, as I'm sure
you're aware, we cannot accept everyone.

I am very sorry to say we will not be taking your
application any further at this stage.

I do a double take at the page.

I read it again.

'Come on,' Mum says. 'What does it say?'

She sounds far away all of a sudden. And I just feel like
I'm not really here. This wasn't the way this was supposed
to go. I've seen it in my head and in every scenario I'm
standing here celebrating with Mum; I'm out buying new
dancewear; I'm downloading new sheet music; I'm getting
excited about classes, about who I'm going to meet, about
how I'm going to fit in, about moving to London and living
with Natalie next year. Within the space of a few words,
that's all been taken away.

'Robin?' Concern is prevalent in Mum's voice. She
knows something is up. There is a part of me that wants to
lie because I feel embarrassed. I was so sure.

'I didn't get in,' I say flatly. And vocalizing it makes it suddenly real and I start to cry. Not sobbing, not breaking down, just tears rolling down my face that I can't seem to stop.

'What?' she says. 'No, that's not . . . can I . . . ?' She takes the letter from my hand and reads it herself; I watch the words hit her too. 'Oh, Robin—'

'It's fine,' I say, forcing a smile on to my face. 'I'll . . . uh . . . I'll try again next year.'

'But, Robin—'

'It's honestly fine,' I say, even though I'm crying, even though my chest hurts, even though my body aches from the sheer effort of staying upright. I'm still trying to smile, because that's what I do. 'This wasn't my year. Next year will be the one.'

But I can't believe that's it. All the work, all the rehearsal, all the singing lessons, dance classes, monologue tuition, gone. It was my last shot. And I was so sure that it was going to work out. With the other auditions I could pinpoint where I'd gone wrong. I'd not picked up the choreography quickly enough, the song choice wasn't quite right, I'd been a bit flat at the start of the song, but this . . . As far as I knew, I'd done everything right. After the first round they wanted a different song, so I changed it for the recall. I walked out of that audition happier than I'd walked out of any of the others and it still wasn't enough.

'I should get ready for school,' I say, grabbing my towel off the back of the door. I slide past Mum and into the bathroom. I catch sight of myself in the mirror, stare at my red eyes and the tears still running down my face. How could I have been so stupid?

I switch to autopilot as best I can. I shower, I dress, I take my bag downstairs, all the while my brain playing what happened on the audition day on a giant IMAX screen. I analyse every foot placement, every line, every note, every action that I took. Maybe the song change wasn't right. Maybe it was a test. I was almost right for a place, but that song just confirmed that I wasn't.

'Maybe I'm just not good enough,' I say as I get downstairs.

Mum looks up from the table. There's a cup of tea where I usually sit, a couple of biscuits next to it. Biscuits for breakfast – these really are dark times. 'Robin, it's a setback—'

'No, come on, Mum, maybe I'm not,' I say. 'I might be, like, school good, but not professional good. Maybe I just don't have it. Not everyone can do it, you know. There are so many people that—'

'Stop it,' she says, banging a hand on the table. 'Robin, this is a minor setback. The knockbacks are there to make you stronger. At least give it a chance to settle before jacking it all in to become a hairdresser.'

'What's wrong with being a hairdresser?'

'Nothing's wrong with being a hairdresser, Robin, but it's not your dream,' she says. 'Don't let them take that away from you.'

I take a seat at the table, staring down at the tea, at the biscuits. I just want to crawl into bed and sob this day away. But, given Mum's little pep talk, which she one hundred per cent prepared, she's not about to let me do that. Maybe she didn't think I was getting in either. Have I just been kidding myself this entire time?

'So, it's not happening,' she says. 'But you can try again next year. Keep taking classes. Keep working.'

I stand up. I don't want to talk about it. I don't want to think about dance classes right now. Just acknowledging the fact that I'm not going to LAPA in September breaks me, the thought that I have to keep working is too much. I want to collapse.

'I should go to school,' I say, unable to keep the gloom out of my voice. I've barely moved an inch before Mum has her arms wrapped round me, squeezing me tight as if she can force all the sads out of me. 'I'm OK.'

'No, you're not.'

'No, I'm not.' I take a deep breath, but I can't stop the tears from coming again.

'Something will come up,' she says into the top of my head. 'It will work out.'

'How do you know that?'

'Because I'm your mother.' She shrugs. 'I know things.'

She holds me a little longer. I don't want her to let go. It feels safe here. Like nothing can hurt. And I know I'm being a baby, but I don't care because this situation is killing me.

'You're going to be OK,' she says. 'It's not the end of the world.'

'Then why does it feel like it is?'

'Because you've just had all of your hopes and dreams dashed.' She says it so casually, like I've not just had my heart ripped out of my chest.

'Wow.'

'But you need to pick yourself up and carry on.' Mum releases me and puts her hand on my cheek. 'It just means that when you get there it will taste all the sweeter.' Her attempts at making me feel better are sort of working. I just wish I had some kind of guarantee that she is right because suddenly everything seems so uncertain. It's like I was following a map, and now someone has taken this giant eraser and scrubbed out the road.

'You're determined, you're focused, you'll figure something out,' she says. 'Say that back to me.'

'What?'

'Say it.'

'I'm not saying that – I'll sound like a twat.'

'My love, I've seen you playing Danny Zuko,' she says. 'And, look, I love *Grease* as much as the next person but it's not exactly Shakespeare.'

'Wow, you want me to make positive affirmations, *and* you're coming for *Grease* when I've just had all of my hopes and dreams shattered?' I shake my head. 'Are you trying to get me to cry harder?'

'Shut up and say it,' she says.

I groan and mutter, 'I'mdeterminedI'mfocusedI'llfig-uresomethingout.'

She smacks me lightly across the side of the head. 'That was terrible. You're supposed to be an actor – perform the words.'

'I'll perform Shakespeare. I will not perform a random affirmation in the middle of our dining room.'

She tuts. 'So much for all the world's a stage.'

I sigh. 'I'm determined. I'm focused. I'll figure something out,' I say half-heartedly.

'And I'm going to make you say it every day until you believe it.'

'And I'm going to pray that you forget by tomorrow morning.'

'See? You're already being catty – it's working!' She hugs

me again. 'Don't feel like you need to tell everybody today.'

'Fuck.'

'Language.'

'Do I not get a free pass today?' I reply. 'I mean, today of *all* days.'

'What are you freaking out about?'

'I have to tell people,' I say. And that feeling of embarrassment washes over me again. How many people knew I was auditioning? Natalie, Greg, Priya, Mrs Hepburn, everybody in my drama class, so many teachers, Miss Emily . . . 'God, I'm going to look like such an idiot.'

'Robin—'

'Sorry, I'll get over it, I will, just not now,' I say. 'I'll see you later?'

'Yeah,' she says. 'When you're back from class, we can do something before my shift. Bad TV, bad food, whatever.'

'I don't even think a trashy film can save me right now, Mum,' I say. 'And the last thing I want to do is take a class. I just . . . I don't know what I want to do.'

'See? Brooding and dramatic, you're already on the mend.'

I give her a smile. It takes way more effort than I thought it would.

'Go to your class,' she says. 'It might be good for you.'

'I'll . . . I'll see how I feel.'

She snorts. 'That's the spirit.'

'Love you.'

'Love you too, sweetie.'

FIVE

Riding my bike to school this morning feels like something of a godsend. I switch myself to autopilot and ride the same old route I've ridden for the past six years. Through the nearest town to ours, a rival school, my dance school, up and down hills, and crossing roads I could cross with my eyes closed (but won't, obviously, because duh), embracing the time with music pounding so hard in my ears I couldn't possibly think of anything else.

I'm about to pull out on to the main road when I see a familiar face at the crossing just by Hampton Road. The green man is beeping obnoxiously, urging him to move, but Connor stays put, leaning on the traffic light, his eyes fixed on me. He's waiting for me, just like he said he would. And I feel like a dick for forgetting. It's the tiniest bright spot that makes me feel a little less tragic, even just for a second.

I hop off my bike and push it over to where he is.

'Morning,' he says.

'Morning,' I say, fixing the smile back on my face. 'Fancy seeing you here.'

'I was about to say the same thing.' He grins, his teeth a little crooked, his smile lifting his whole face. He goes from lad to soft boy in a snap. 'Walk you to school?'

'Well, we're both heading that way,' I say. 'Be weird not to, wouldn't it?'

He smiles at this and we start along the high street, my bike between us like a barrier, like a little beacon to show anyone who is watching that we're not gay, we're just two guys walking to school together. My heart is pounding so hard I can't really cope with it.

I want to tell him. If he was really my boyfriend, I would have texted him straight away. He'd want to know.

'What's up?' he says, reaching out a hand and touching my arm. The contact makes me want to cry. God I'm needy. 'You seem . . .'

'What?'

'I don't know, like you're not at full wattage,' he says. 'You feeling OK?'

'I didn't get into LAPA,' I say, trying to keep my voice even. 'The letter came through this morning.'

'Oh.' Connor shifts his gaze from me, to our direction of travel, then back to me again. 'I'm really sorry.'

I want him to do something. I want him to take my hand and squeeze it and tell me it will be OK. I want him to wrap me up in those big arms of his so that, even for just a second, the world falls away. But he doesn't because we're in public, and today I let it affect me a lot more than it usually would.

'What are you going to do?' he asks.

I take a shaky breath. I feel like I'm made of glass, like I might shatter at any second. 'I don't know,' I say. 'I'm still processing it.'

'Well, I'm sorry,' he says again. 'If there's anything I can do . . .' He trails off. There's plenty he could do right now. All I want is to be close to him, and he must know that. Keeping the secret is just more important to him.

'Sunday?' he adds.

'What?'

'We can do something on Sunday?' he says. 'My parents aren't home, or we can go somewhere. I'll do whatever I can to take your mind off it.'

I smile. It's something to look forward to, at least.

'You don't have to—'

'But I want to,' he says. 'It will be fun.'

'Is that a threat?'

He laughs. 'A promise.'

He stops abruptly as we reach the underpass, the bit that takes us into the last stretch up towards school, where there are people who will likely recognize us and wonder why we are walking together in the first place.

'See you later?' he says.

I nod. 'Yeah,' I say. 'Message me.'

He nods, and I climb on my bike and ride away, pulling on to the main road and speeding off towards school, trying to leave my sadness in the dust. I don't think there's a bike fast enough.

Hot, sweaty, trying to catch my breath, I take a hard right so I can pull up outside Natalie's house, which is pretty much on the way. I hope she hasn't left yet. Her house is giant in comparison to mine. It's detached with a big garden, and her bedroom could fit three of mine into it with space left over for a jacuzzi tub. And, in that moment, it seems weird to me that something so huge can happen and the world is just the same. It feels like it should be on fire or something.

> Nat, I'm actually on time today. Have you left yet?

Ooh, look at her.

Coming!

Natalie hurries out the door with a smile on her face, a smile that I return as best I can. She opens her mouth to call to me when the door opens again behind her. Her dad, fully suited and booted, hurries out, dangling a set of keys in his hand. He's talking to her in French Creole. He does this a lot and she responds in kind, the words tripping off her tongue like she doesn't even have to think about it. I'm always in awe. I can barely speak one language, let alone two.

He's teasing her with the keys, snatches of words that don't translate drifting through. *Durham. Robin.* I shouldn't be listening to this.

I avert my gaze and turn my music up until Natalie manages to snatch her keys back and heads over to me.

'Good morning,' she says, her smile perhaps a little less bright than before.

'Hey,' I reply. 'You OK? Did something happen?'

She rolls her eyes. 'Just Dad being Dad,' she replies. 'But, in better news, my sister is coming back for a couple of weeks, *and* she is bringing Liz with her. Oh, I can't wait!'

'So your parents are meeting Amber's girlfriend?'

'Finally!' she says. 'She's literally the coolest person I've ever met in my life.'

'How do you think they're going to take it?'

'They'll be fine. When she came out, they were fine, when I came out, they were fine, even if they thought pansexual had something to do with cookware.' She shrugs. 'I can't see them having a problem. Both of their kids are queer, so they've clearly done *everything* right. Such blessings.'

'Huge blessings,' I say. Natalie's presence is calming.

Just to be talking about something else, thinking about something else. Maybe I don't even need to tell her. I could just move to London and find a job. How hard could it be?

'So what's going on? You're . . . off.'

No use delaying the inevitable.

'I didn't get into LAPA,' I say.

She stops walking.

'Come on, Nat, no theatrics, please!'

She doesn't say anything, throwing her arms round me and wrapping me up in the tightest hug possible instead. I reach my arms round her and hug her back, letting the tears fall because, well, I don't have a choice.

'I'm so sorry.'

'Not your fault.'

'Shut up,' she says into my shoulder. 'I know it isn't my fault – I'm just sorry that this hasn't happened for you.' She pulls away and looks at me. 'And you let me go on about my sister coming home?'

'I don't want sympathy,' I say. 'Sympathy makes it worse; I want to be the kind of person that can brush this off and carry on, but . . .'

'It meant a lot to you, Robin. You're allowed to be sad.'

I shrug. 'I don't do sad,' I say. 'I do happy-go-lucky, I do campy – I don't do sad.'

'You're allowed to do sad – you're a person,' she says.

'A real human person.' We start walking again. 'Are you telling people today?'

'I guess I have to,' I say.

'You don't *have* to.'

'I sort of do,' I say. 'I told everybody about it. My entire drama class knows, Mrs Hepburn, Mrs Finch . . .' I trail off. Mrs Finch is the one who was on everybody's case about university applications. She's going to lose her mind when she finds out I only applied to drama schools. I really thought that LAPA was the one. Now I'm left with nothing. 'Today's going to suck.'

'But it will pass,' Nat says. She takes a breath. 'Next year's looking a hell of a lot different now, huh?'

'Yeah,' I say. 'Sorry.'

'For what?'

'We had plans, Nat,' I say. 'And now they're ruined and it's all my fault.'

'It's stuff that's out of your control,' Nat says quietly. 'You can't blame yourself for that. Promise me you're not.'

'I'll do no such thing.'

She laughs. 'Gosh, you're impossible.'

We join the crowd on the road walking up to school: a sea of people, most of whom look utterly miserable. What a freaking mood.

'Morning, lads.' A big pair of hands land on my shoulders.

They squeeze tight. I turn to see Greg, who has a broad grin on his face.

'You're almost late,' Natalie says.

'Archie forgot his lunch, so I had to run back and get it, hence the sweat,' he says. He looks at Nat and me. 'Christ, we look glum this morning.'

'Greg, don't—' Natalie starts.

'I didn't get into LAPA.'

'Oh shit,' Greg says, his face falling. 'I'm sorry, Robin.'

Suddenly Greg has wrapped me up in his big arms, holding me close to him, smooshing my face into his chest. There are people around us tutting and complaining about us stopping in the middle of the street, but I'm not sure I care. This is what I wanted from Connor. This is the right reaction. I shake that feeling off.

'I didn't think,' he says. 'I just opened my big mouth and—'

'Don't worry,' I say, smiling. 'You didn't know. It's all right.'

And we keep walking to school, but there is an awkwardness now that wasn't there before. No one knows what they can say to make it better. I certainly don't.

'So what happens now?' Greg asks. 'What's the plan?'

And for the first time, in as long as I can remember, I have no idea.

SIX

After I've registered, I head down to my first class, which is drama. The closer I get, the more it feels like a walk of shame.

I take a few deep breaths as I go, trying to push the sadness out, trying to be the kind of person who can get knocked back and just let it go. I turn on the smile that everyone is expecting.

'Morning, Robin,' Katy chirps. 'Any news yet?'

I keep smiling. *Just keep freaking smiling.* 'Yeah,' I say. 'It was a no.' I shrug. 'But, you know, these things happen. There's always next year.'

She looks at Marcus, who looks a little confused. Maybe it's the disconnect between the news and my attitude.

'You're OK?' he asks, running a hand through his hair. 'Like, seriously?'

I nod and smile. 'Yeah,' I say. I can see people listening in. Lani, DL, other classmates, ears tuned in to hear gossip. Shit. 'It sucks, of course it does, but the standard was high and they can't take everybody. That's what it said in the letter, anyhow.'

Katy walks over and pats me on the shoulder just as Mrs Hepburn sweeps in. Her hair is golden blonde with black roots, her eye make-up *extra as hell* for a Wednesday morning at school, and she's wearing this red, flowy cardigan that trails behind her like a cape. She's every stereotype of a drama teacher rolled up into one. I wouldn't be surprised if in a few years' time we find out that her entire life as a schoolteacher has been a performance art piece. Today I'm grateful for her presence because she sets us off working before I can obsess over my failures any longer.

'Robin Cooper, can you stay behind, please?' she asks at the end of the class as everyone else is leaving. I wave Katy and Marcus away, turning to her.

'Is something wrong?'

She narrows her eyes at me. 'There's a murkiness in your aura.'

I sigh. 'I didn't get in.'

She cocks her head to one side. 'What?'

'I got a rejection letter this morning,' I say. 'They thanked me for coming and said I hadn't been successful this time round.'

Mrs Hepburn takes this information in. She inhales

deeply and breathes out. 'Meditate with me?'

'I'm meant to have a study period,' I reply.

'That doesn't sound like a no,' Mrs Hepburn says, grabbing two yoga mats and placing them on the floor. She sits down on her own and crosses her legs, her hands resting on her thighs, her eyes closed. 'Are you joining me, or are you going to go and "study"?'

'Um . . .'

'Sit.'

She's not asking any more. I kick my shoes off and position myself across from her.

'Mrs Hepburn—'

'Deep breath in,' she interrupts. I oblige. 'And out.'

'Mrs Hepburn—'

'Deep breath in,' she interrupts again. I oblige again. 'And out.'

I don't see how this is helping. Mrs Hepburn is one of the wisest people I know, but sometimes she can be a little kooky. Today seems to be one of her kookier days.

She sighs and I open my eyes. She's leaning back on her hands. 'Tell me what happened,' she says.

'I got the rejection letter and—'

'No, no,' she says. 'After that, what did you do after that?'

I sigh. 'I cried,' I say. 'I cried and took a shower and then talked to my mum and cried some more, told some friends, cried. I've done a lot of crying.'

She smiles. 'Good.'

'Good?'

'Yes,' she says. 'Good. Crying is good.'

'How—'

'It means you care, Robin,' she says. 'Does it hurt?'

'It hurts like hell,' I say.

She shrugs. 'It happens,' she says. 'Rejection isn't a walk in the park, but it's just part of the path you've chosen for yourself.'

'But I don't feel like I even have a path right now,' I say. 'I've been focusing on LAPA for so long and—'

'And now you have to recalibrate, figure out what your next move is and execute it,' she says.

I lie back on the yoga mat, staring up at the ceiling. 'But I don't know what that is.'

Mrs Hepburn laughs. 'Of course you don't, silly boy,' she says. 'You found out this morning! You can't expect to just bounce back immediately on to the next thing. You're allowed to be sad.'

'Why does everyone keep telling me to be sad? I don't want to be sad,' I say, sitting back up.

'Well, I'm giving you permission to be,' she says, smiling. 'Be sad, be angry, but don't let it knock you so far back that you stop. Never stop.'

'I'm sorry I've let you down, Mrs Hepburn,' I say, my voice small.

'No,' she says flatly. 'You've only let me down if you give up.'

'So, what are we doing for your birthday Friday?' Natalie asks as we get to the common room, the January weather keeping us inside. 'This is your birthday and it must be celebrated and I need to plan an outfit so . . . '

I had every intention of celebrating. I had wanted it to be my last hurrah before I spent the rest of the summer obsessively stretching to hit the splits and getting myself to a fitness level that would mean classes wouldn't be too much of a shock to my system. But now . . .

'Earth to Robin,' Greg says, poking me on the forehead. We sit down, Greg on one sofa, Nat on the other, me on the floor. I'm not being dramatic this time, it's just more comfortable. I lean against Greg's legs.

'I don't want to.'

'Robin—'

'Come on, Nat, I'm just super not in the mood,' I say. 'I've literally had my entire life ripped away from me. The thought of going out and—'

'This is exactly the reason why!' Natalie protests. 'Come on, Robin, you can't just sit around on your birthday moping. What good would that do?'

Greg tousles my hair. It feels kind of nice. 'It might be good for you to get out,' he says. 'I mean, we don't even have to go anywhere – we can just stay in and mope with you.'

'No!' Natalie cries out. 'No moping!'

'But I'm hurting.'

'No. Moping.' She's dead serious.

'Fine,' I sigh.

'Oh, the commitment,' Natalie snarks. 'At least pretend like you mean it, Robin, Jesus.'

'Well, I don't want to commit too hard. I might break something.'

'Put that in your Grindr profile. You'll be turning them away at the door,' Greg says.

'He doesn't need Grindr when he has Secret Boyfriend,' Natalie teases. 'How is he, by the way? I messaged you last night and you took a while to reply so I assume—'

'You know what they say about people who assume.'

'They're usually right?'

'He was over . . . for a bit.'

Natalie groans. 'Wow, Robin, you're walking clickbait,' she says. 'Please, oh please tell us what that means!'

'Mum came home earlier than she was supposed to,' I say.

'So, you got caught?' Greg asks.

'No . . .' I trail off. 'He climbed out of the window.'

'He climbed out of the WINDOW?!'

'Wow, Natalie, say it louder – the rest of the common room might not have heard you.'

Natalie scoffs. 'Stop changing the subject. The opportunity presented itself for you to tell your mum about it,' she says. 'It was organic, it was a sign, it was—'

'Embarrassing!' I interrupt. 'I didn't want to, OK?' I look over at Greg who raises an eyebrow at me. Greg knows things. 'Now please can we change the subject? I'm in mourning.'

'Then let's talk about a way to pull you out of mourning,' Natalie says gleefully. 'Further hot goss about the new boy?'

'Pass,' I say.

'Come on, this is a good one,' she says. 'Holly was saying he got into a shouting match with Mrs Finch and—'

'Subject change,' I say.

'He's meant to be in our English class, you know,' Natalie says. 'But he's just not been showing up.'

'You're kidding!' Greg says. 'That's ridiculous.'

'We're making it worse,' I say. 'Subject change.'

'Fine!' Natalie says. 'Back to birthday festivities. Where do you want to go?'

'I don't know,' I say. 'Somewhere . . . gay.' I swallow,

not really knowing why saying this makes me feel nervous. I sort of hate that it does – why should it?

Natalie sits up so sharply I'm surprised she doesn't give herself whiplash. 'Really?'

'Yeah,' I say. 'I don't know where. I just—'

'Want to go somewhere gay, yeah, OK, got it. I'm on it, I'm on it so freaking hard, Robin.' She is buzzing, pulling her phone out of her pocket. 'We can head up into London, but that's a bit of a mission. And on a Friday night it just feels like we're asking for trouble.'

'Last train back will mean we'll be leaving as the night gets going,' Greg chimes in. 'The pains of living in a suburb!'

'Is there anywhere closer?' I ask.

'Entity!' Natalie announces, not looking up from her phone.

'What?'

'Queer club in Southford,' she says. 'I've not been, but Amber used to go back in the day, and Anthony went a few weeks ago and said it was really cool, super chill. A safe place, you know?'

'Anthony went?' I ask. Anthony is a bi guy who takes all the sciences plus maths, so is ridiculously smart. He's Oxbridge through and through, and I honestly can't believe that someone like him would be found in a club at any point in his life, let alone while school is still in session. 'Can't imagine that.'

'Don't want to imagine that,' Greg says. 'It's too weird.'

'Let's stop imagining Anthony trying to cop off with someone and return to the matter at hand,' Natalie says, turning to me sharply. 'Entity would be good, right?'

'I—'

'Come *on*, Robin, it will be fun, and let me go somewhere queer, please?' she says. 'My crops would be in full bloom, my skin would be clear, grades high, wig snatched. I want to make out with somebody, Robin.'

It's hard for Natalie sometimes. Our school is a pretty safe place, but not massively queer. I mean, Connor's the only guy I've been with and that's a secret. And it would be fun to go somewhere we can be ourselves a bit more.

'Entity could be fun,' I say. 'Southford?'

The mention of the town makes my blood run a little cold, but I shake it off.

'It's on the high street,' she says, glancing down at her phone. 'It looks super unassuming, like you don't know that it's there unless you know that it's there.' She looks a little closer. 'Though there are rainbow flags everywhere, so you'd either think it's queer or that the owners *really* like rainbows.'

'The Room of Requirement meets gay bars,' Greg says. 'There's a leaky-cauldron joke in there somewhere.'

'And if you make it, I'll tear your nuts off,' Natalie says. 'So, you want to go?'

She hands me her phone, Entity's website up on the screen. It's pretty basic: topless guys dancing, rainbow flags all over the place, a drag queen or two bellowing into a microphone. There are certainly worse places to spend my birthday. And if I don't go here, what will I do? Mope about at home by myself? At least this way I'll be with friends, and it will keep my mind off . . . well . . . everything.

'Wait,' I say, clicking through a couple of links, finding myself on their events page. 'Wait.'

'What? Change of heart? Is it a place for creepers?'

'No wonder Anthony went,' Greg says with a chuckle.

A word floats on the screen in front of me in glittery letters, a drag queen below it dressed in a magnificent gown, her neon-pink hair stretching out of the confines of the screen.

'Dragcellence,' I whisper. The word in my mouth sounds reverent. It's like a spell. Natalie's eyes widen.

'What is that?' she says. I show her the phone. 'Holy shit. Yes!'

'What?' Greg asks, suddenly sitting up straight.

'Dragcellence!' Natalie practically screams.

'I don't know what that means!' Greg says. 'I'm not quite as deep into the world of drag as you two are.'

'And you're a poorer soul because of it,' I say.

'This is perfect,' Natalie hisses. 'Dragcellence.'

'Will you stop saying that?' Greg groans. 'Just tell me what it is. I hate being out of the loop.'

'There is a drag show on my actual birthday,' I say, the excitement strutting through my veins. 'At Entity. We have to buy tickets, but still – it will be fun!'

'Fun?' Natalie echoes. 'It's going to be more than fun; it's going to be freaking fabulous. I can't believe this! How long has this been going on for? Why haven't I been going to this since the dawn of time?'

'You don't have to come, Greg,' I say, ignoring Natalie who is going into some kind of mental breakdown about who is performing, squeaking out names like Pristine Gleaming, Julie Mandrews, Dawn Raid and Ay Tee Em like she's heard of them before now. 'I get that it might be weird.'

'No,' he says. 'I want to come out for your birthday.'

'Oh, Greg, I'm so proud of you!' says Natalie.

'Not like that!' he exclaims. 'Not that there's anything wrong with that, but—'

'Do we need to get a new straight white guy for our group to, you know, diversify?'

'And you'll be all right going to a gay bar?' I say, ignoring Natalie. 'Because we don't have to. We can go somewhere else—'

'Robin,' Greg says, putting a hand on my arm. 'I am more than fine going to a gay club for your birthday. I want to go wherever you want to go.' He pauses, puts a little bit of thought into it. 'The music is probably going to be better anyway.'

'Facts are facts,' Natalie says.

He smiles and I pat his hand, which he takes hold of and gives a quick squeeze. Greg is honestly the best. Everybody needs a Greg. And I'm happy that he will be there as well as Natalie. In an ideal world, Connor would come along and ingratiate himself with my friends, but if he's not going to hold my hand in public I highly doubt he would even consider stepping foot in a gay bar.

'Oh my God, invite Priya!' Natalie squeaks. 'I love her!'

'I don't know if I can face people from dance right now,' I say. 'I'm meant to go to class tonight and I just . . . I don't know. Drama this morning was a slog and I—'

'You're not going to a class, Robin, you're having a night out,' Natalie says. 'We're taking your mind off all that, and Priya would love it.'

'True. I mean, if you guys don't mind.'

'The more the merrier,' Greg says.

I pull my phone out and send Priya a quick message, trying to keep it as chirpy as possible.

'What about Connor?' says Natalie. I look up sharply.

'Natalie, don't be ridiculous,' Greg says.

'What? He might want to come and spend time with his secret boyfriend on his birthday,' she teases.

'He wouldn't be caught dead there,' I say.

Natalie stops short, realizing she's struck a nerve. Greg averts his gaze.

'Robin—' Natalie starts.

'I'm fine, honestly, sorry, just being dramatic,' I say, trying to brush the situation off.

'OK.' She shrugs. 'But if anything is going on—'

'I'm fine,' I say. 'We're great, honestly, I just know him enough to know that asking him would be awkward.'

I look at Greg, who is staring off a little into the distance. He looks almost disappointed in me before he rearranges his face into a smile.

'OK,' Natalie says, pulling my focus back to her. 'I need to find something to wear. Maybe I should wear something new.' Her face brightens. 'Shopping? I need something that won't make me look like a walking dustbin.'

'You know you always look gorgeous,' I say. 'You could show up tomorrow night in a paper bag and, one, you'd look brown cow stunning and, two, the gays would worship you. And I'll be in the corner having spent all day picking out a shirt that I don't look terrible in, waiting for you to have five minutes for the birthday boy.'

She shrugs. 'And what would you do with that kind of attention, hmm?'

'Crawl up into a ball and die, most probably.'

'You're an actor!'

'People would approach and you'd just see my soul leave my eyes. Nothing medically wrong, just death by attention.'

'You're impossible,' she says. 'God knows why you want to be on the stage.'

'Yes, she probably does,' I reply. 'And maybe at some point she'll give me a sign that it's all going to work out OK.'

Natalie opens her mouth to answer, but the bell sounds, quickly followed by groans as people start to make their way out of the common room. I pick myself up, stretching, actually feeling a little bit of lightness inside. I like birthdays. There's something inherently good about them. The world is wishing you well, like there's good karma in the air and it's all for you.

'Look at you smiling,' Natalie says. 'If I'd have known all it would take was a couple of drag queens to lift your spirits, I wouldn't have bothered being sympathetic. I would have sat you in a room, turned *Drag Race* on and thrown glitter at you until you stopped moping.'

'I'm sorry, you've been sympathetic?' Greg snorts. 'I'd hate to see you being harsh.'

'Ooh, a read from Greg!' I exclaim. 'You got read by *Greg*! You've been spending too much time with us,' I tell him.

'Sorry, "a read"? What's "a read"?'

'It's fun-da-mental!' Natalie replies. I roll my eyes so hard I practically pull a muscle.

'Throwing shade, darling,' I say, linking my arm in his as we walk. 'An insult or exposing someone's flaws, but in a way that's sassy and not being a dick.'

'Right,' Greg says, a smile creeping across his face.

'Just think,' Natalie says. 'If this night is as amazing as it looks, it can be a *staple* in the Summer of Fun remix.'

'You need to stop,' I say.

We start towards our next class, my arm still linked in Greg's, Natalie still cackling over Greg learning how to 'read', and I am smiling. Friday night will be a welcome distraction from today's news or, at the very least, a sunny spot in what looks like an endless sea of gloom.

SEVEN

I spend a little time in the library after school, killing time before my dance class is meant to start. I'm still not sure I want to go. I've spent the day painting a smile on to my face and, frankly, I'm exhausted.

I spend a bit of time reading through my notes from English, not that any of them are sinking in, then I browse through the LAPA website, torturing myself as I look at studios I won't be dancing in, stages I won't be performing on. The smiling faces of the current students just make me feel worse.

Christ, I have to get out of here. I'm going to drive myself nuts.

As I pack up my things and head out of the library, I hear a voice booming loudly down the empty corridor.

'I'm not starting anything — you're the one starting this!' The voice catches a little as it drifts towards me from a boy pacing back and forth, his jeans ripped, his blond hair covering his eyes. 'Is that all?'

He listens to the person on the phone a little longer and

I turn and walk the other way. 'I just didn't want to hear everyone talking about me, OK?' he says. And I realize this must be the new kid. Seth? Is that what Natalie said his name was? Then he growls down the phone, 'Well, I think you just called to inform me, yet again, that I'm a disappointment, so if you're done—'

I pick up the pace, keeping my head down so that he doesn't think I've overheard. I don't even know the guy, haven't even seen him around yet, but to have him feeling bad about people talking about him sucks. When I came out, I knew people were talking about me, heard them whispering, and I hated it. Whenever we had P.E. the other guys would make comments, but Greg was there to put a stop to that. Seth doesn't even have anybody to do that right now.

My head spinning a little, I walk the tree line that surrounds the school, past the languages block, round the courtyard, down the stretch that runs alongside the geography block, my feet taking me on a route I know so well I could walk it with my eyes shut.

'Robin?' a voice hisses nearby. I stop so sharply I almost trip over my own feet. 'Robin!' The same hiss, the same intonation. I turn my head and see Connor, hanging out of a window on the ground floor. He's smiling, his face bright, his eyes twinkling at me, even at this distance. He beckons me closer.

I abandon any sense of cool and rush over to the window, trying to ignore the fact that he's looking left and right to see if there's anyone else around.

'What are you still doing here?' I say quietly, conspiratorially, playing the game he's set up for us over the past few months. 'I thought you'd be long gone by now.'

'I had work to do,' he says. 'Revision, work I didn't finish in class.' He sighs. 'I'm trying to keep up and failing miserably.'

I look behind him into the classroom and there's no one else there. 'Do you want me to come in?'

Suddenly I'm pulled back to when we first met in early September, the two of us in an abandoned classroom. If I'd known it was going to turn into something so significant, I would probably have tried to remember it better.

He laughs. 'I can't imagine that will help me get any work done,' he says, winking at me. My legs turn to jelly, my heart to mush. 'What are *you* still doing here?'

I put my jacket down on the grass and sit on it. 'I had time to kill before a dance class,' I say. 'But I'm not sure I want to go.'

'Right.'

'I just can't face it.'

'I get that,' he says. 'You don't have to, you know. I know I wouldn't want to.'

'It's just hard,' I say. 'I literally have no idea what I'm going to do.'

'You could talk to Mrs Finch?'

'Ah, well, she'll just end up saying "I told you so" and make me apply to the first uni that pops into her head.'

'You know what she's like,' he grunts. 'She wants everyone at university because it's the only option as far as she's concerned.'

I shrug again. 'I guess.'

'It might be an idea, you know,' he says, looking me in the eye. 'There will be a drama course somewhere—'

'Did she put you up to this?' I say, trying to keep it light but probably failing.

'No, I'm just saying it would be sad for you to stay here when everyone else is going.'

I open my mouth to speak, but I don't know what to say. Doesn't he get it? It's not about a drama course — it's about a dream and . . . is it sad to not want to throw that away so fast? *Sad?*

'My life only fell apart this morning. I've not really had a lot of time to think about it,' I say, lying back on my jacket so I'm sort of looking up at him. 'But I'm about to lose Natalie to London, Greg to Edinburgh . . .' I hesitate. 'You to Portsmouth. I hate it.'

'Then do something about it.'

I shake my head. 'But I don't . . .' I trail off.

'Well, you're running out of time,' he says quietly. I didn't come here for a lecture, but I don't want to walk away from him. His presence is exciting, even with the vague risk of being found out all around us. I only care about getting found out because he does. And if we get found out then I'll lose him for good. 'You need to—'

There's a noise inside and he pulls himself back in through the window so sharply it's like someone has dragged him inside. I resist the urge to sit up and see what's happened. I can guess.

'You staying much longer?' I hear a yell from across the room, a voice I know belongs to his friend Ryan. Just hearing his voice makes my heart pound a little harder. My palms go sweaty. Ryan's a prick. 'I want to go.'

'Ten more minutes?' Connor calls back, his voice a little strained. 'I'm almost done, I swear.'

'Whatever,' Ryan calls back.

I hear the door slam and can practically hear Connor counting down the seconds before he pokes his head out of the window again to see me lying in the grass, staring back up at him.

'Sorry,' he says.

'Don't worry about it,' I say. 'So Sunday?'

He grins. 'Definitely.'

'But if you fancied doing something sooner, we're going out for my birthday on Friday,' I say. 'Do you . . . do you want to come?'

'What?'

'It's just casual.'

'Who's "we"?'

'Me, Nat, Greg, my friend Priya from dancing,' I say. 'We're going to Entity and—'

'Entity?!' he echoes, sounding a few shades short of absolutely disgusted. 'Why?'

'Because it's my birthday. It might be fun.'

'I'm not going there, Robin,' he says. 'I can't go there. If anyone saw me at a gay bar, I'd be crucified – you know that.'

'All right.'

'You know what my friends are like, what my parents are like. I just can't—'

'All right,' I say again, trying to say it with a sense of finality that will stop us going round in circles. 'It's honestly fine. I just thought I'd ask because . . .' I trail off. *Because I like you. Because I want to spend time with you.*

I don't want him to feel like I'm pushing him into doing something he's not ready for. I don't want him getting hurt because of who he is afraid to be. That's the last thing I want. I know what that's like.

'I just thought I'd ask,' I say quietly.

'OK. It's a no.'

I sigh. 'Yeah, I got that.'

I pull myself up and put on my jacket. I force a smile on to my face, the same smile I've been forcing all day. Everything's fine. It's always fine. He smiles back like everything's OK, but nothing is and it sucks.

'I'll see you tomorrow?' I say, hopeful.

'Sure,' he replies, non-committal, the one word that could probably sum up our entire relationship, if you can even call it that. Though that doesn't seem fair.

I don't say anything else, walking away from the window and away from him, trying to imagine what it would feel like to let him go.

But I know that at some point he'll message me and my heart will skip, or he'll come over in the middle of the night and if Mum's not home I'll sneak him in and stuff will happen. We only have until September. Why stop it now?

EIGHT

When I make it to the studio, I don't feel any better. I stare at the converted warehouse that has been a home away from home for the past six years and I can't bring myself to go any further. And I hate that.

This should have been an amazing day. This should have been the day where I went in and got to celebrate with Priya and Miss Emily, where we got to talk about what I needed to prepare for September . . . and now September is just this big empty space and . . .

I take a breath.

I can't do it.

I take my phone out and text Priya.

> I'm not really feeling all that well. Can you let Miss Emily know? I'll see you Friday?

I'm about to pedal off into the distance when the door to the studio opens and Priya appears in fluorescent pink dancewear.

'You are a LIAR, Robin Cooper!' she calls over, but the smile slips from her face so fast it's like she's read my mind. She knows something is up. 'Get over here.'

'Hey, babes,' I say, trying to smile at her, but, as the day has gone on, it's become harder to keep up the facade.

'Oh shit,' Priya says. 'You've heard, haven't you?'

I nod.

'And you're not faking me out, are you?' she says. 'This is real Robin Cooper sadness right now.'

I nod again.

She pulls me into a hug. I resist at first, but then allow myself to melt into her and let out a little cry.

'I feel so shit,' I say between sobs.

'I'm sorry for going on about it,' she says.

I pull back from the hug. 'What are you talking about?'

'Every time we mentioned it, I would say how you were guaranteed to get in or whatever,' Priya says, looking away from me. 'I didn't mean to do that. I just didn't think for a second that you wouldn't. Maybe next year.'

I shrug. 'Yeah, me neither. And yeah. Maybe. We'll see.'

I wipe my tears away on the back of my hands. Need to stop crying all the freaking time. This isn't how I do things. Shit.

'So you're not coming in?' she says. 'It might be good for you, babe, endorphins and all that. Or you can go full Billy

Elliot and Angry Dance it out. It's a little dramatic, but fits with your aesthetic.'

'I think it's too early to be ripping me about this.'

She snorts. 'Oh, babes, no it isn't.' A pause. 'So, are you coming?'

I shake my head. 'I don't think I can. Not today.'

She nods and takes a breath. 'OK, cool, well, I'll tell Miss Emily you're sick, won't let a single thing slip, and you'll come back tomorrow.'

'Maybe.'

'Or next week?'

'Sure.'

She eyes me carefully, pushing a few strands of dark hair out of her face and behind her ear. 'Robin Cooper, you'd better not be quitting on me.'

'I'm not.'

'Famous husband, Cooper,' she says. 'My future is in your hands.'

I laugh, or do my best to. It feels sort of hollow. 'I won't let you down.'

She smiles and hugs me again. 'I'm being serious, Cooper,' she says. 'Don't quit on this. You're too good to quit, OK? No matter what they say.'

'Thanks Pri,' I mumble into her shoulder. She squeezes a little tighter and then lets go, and I cycle off towards home.

I've hardly missed a dance class in the past six years. It feels weird.

I'm surprised when I make it back home to see that there is movement in the house. Mum's car is parked outside, the kitchen window is open and, if I'm not mistaken, I can hear Celine Dion playing. Either I'm high or Mum is.

I throw my bike through the gate and into the garden, hurrying through the back door and into the house. It *is* Celine Dion playing, and it's coming from the kitchen, where there is also the sound of someone singing off-key.

'Mum?' I say as I drop my bag on the floor. If it's not her, we're being burgled by a Celine Dion-loving criminal.

'You're home!' she calls out from the kitchen, turning down the music and, thankfully, stopping singing. 'Is everything OK?'

I try not to break down. 'I couldn't do it.'

'What?'

'I couldn't go to the class. I just . . .' I trail off. 'I'm not ready.'

She smiles sadly at me. 'How are you?'

'Confused.'

'Why?'

'Well . . .' I gesture to her, to the house. She's wearing an apron, which is bizarre in itself, and has her hair pulled into a messy bun on top of her head. There is a sheen of sweat over her forehead and, as she opens the door to the oven, a wave of beautiful smells tumbles towards me. 'Oh my God, and you're baking!' I cry. 'What is happening?'

'You've got to have a birthday cake,' she says. 'And my world-famous Devil's Food Cake—'

'It's not world-famous.'

'Well, famous or not, it's your favourite so you get to have it for your birthday.' She walks towards me and pulls me into her arms. I hug her a little tighter than I would normally because I need it. I let out a heavy breath.

'So you couldn't go to your class tonight,' she says, her voice a little muffled against my shoulder. 'What happened?'

'Nothing,' I reply.

'Lies and fairytales,' she says. 'No one sighs that heavily because nothing is wrong.'

'Ooh, she's a detective,' I tease.

'No, I'm a mother,' she says, pulling away and looking me in the eyes. 'How was school?'

I sigh. 'I pretty much told everybody.'

'Oh, Robin.'

'It wasn't totally intentional, but Natalie knew something was off and then I told Mrs Hepburn—' I break off as Mum winces. 'What?'

'Well, I can imagine the reaction, throwing herself all over the drama studio, wailing from the staff room, performing some dramatic monologue . . .'

'The opposite, actually,' I say. 'We meditated and she gave me a pep talk.'

'You *meditated?!*' she repeats. 'Christ, just when I think that woman is going to zig, she zags.'

'Ever the unexpected,' I say.

'Eugh.' She rolls her eyes. 'Then you're not going to like this.'

'What?'

'That old crow Mrs Finch emailed me.'

'Oh God, what did she want?'

'She wants to talk about your future,' she says. 'Why she couldn't have this conversation with you, I don't know.'

'Because the last conversation I had with her was when she told me I wasn't allowed to go to the callback and I told her to bite me,' I say, heading out of the kitchen and sitting at the dining table.

Mum stifles a giggle. 'Well, that wasn't very nice.'

'Me or her?'

She thinks on it. 'Both,' she says. 'That seems the most diplomatic.'

I sigh. 'She's going to want me to go to uni in September.'

'You can't!' Mum says. 'You've not applied.'

'There are ways,' I say. 'If you go through Clearing, you can basically go anywhere that will take you.'

'But you don't want to, do you?'

'No,' I say. 'I don't. Actually, I don't know what I want to do right now.'

'You have to at least try again next year,' she says. 'More experience, more time, it will be good for you.'

I look over at her and smile. She got an A in 'Supportive Parenting 101' at Mum School. She's backing me when, right now, I'm not even backing myself. I don't know if I have it in me to go through all that again: the stress, the panic, the gruelling audition process. But she does know.

'Thanks, Mum,' I say.

'So you'll work for the next year, earn some money, get some experience at auditions if you can and go again,' she says. 'Talk to Miss Emily – maybe she can get you some teaching work at the studio.'

I shrug. 'Maybe. I want my brain to stop feeling so fuzzy – that's what I want.'

'I'll go and talk to Mrs Finch, because that's what she wants, but what I have to say about it doesn't even really matter. This is about your future, so it's about what you want. And if you want to not go to uni in September and try out for drama school again next year, then fine. If you don't want to do the uni or college thing at all, that's your decision too. It's your life.

'And I know you can't face the studio right now, but at

91

least if you're teaching it's something you love, somewhere that you love spending your time,' she says.

She goes back to pottering around the kitchen and I head to the sink and start to clear up the mess she's made.

'Don't do that,' she says, trying to get me to move out of the way. 'You don't have to wash up – it's your freaking birthday cake.'

'I'm trying to make myself useful,' I say. 'Other mothers would kill to have sons who help them clean up. Don't take it for granted.'

'OK, fine, but tomorrow don't do anything,' she says. 'And on Friday don't either. Go out, see your friends, enjoy yourself. Please don't clean. Be young. I don't want you washing dishes on your birthday – it's weird.' She takes a beat. 'Have you decided where you're going yet?'

'Yes. Today, actually,' I say. 'There's this gay bar called Entity and it just so happens that Friday night is their drag night, Dragcellence, so we're going to that.'

The silence that follows throws me off balance, a tension creeping into the air that wasn't there before. I take my hands out of the soapy water and look at her, busying herself by the oven.

'Mum, what?' I say.

'Nothing.'

'Mum?'

She sighs. She can't even look at me. Why won't she look at me?

'Where is it?' she asks.

'Southford.'

She tenses again.

'Mum, what? Come on.'

'You really want to go back there?' she says quietly. 'Robin—'

'Mum, we're going to a drag night, at a gay bar. I'm not dressing up myself,' I say, trying to laugh it off, trying to make this less awkward, trying to ignore the worried look on her face. 'I mean Natalie's been on at me to do drag for years but—'

'I don't think you should go,' she blurts before she can stop herself. 'After everything that's happened, Robin, you really want to go back there? You really want to go to a gay bar in Southford? I just don't want anything to happen to you. Not again.'

The memory of it hits me like a truck.

I was waiting for Greg in Southford one afternoon last summer. Natalie was away, in Grenada with her family until pretty much the day before we went back to school. Greg was running late because he was looking after his little brother. A crowd of people approached me. I didn't notice them at first because my headphones were in, and my feet were tippy-tapping on the pavement while I waited. I didn't notice they were there until one of them yanked my headphones out of my ears and started yelling in my face.

I recognized some of them. There were faces of boys and girls from my school, some of them I could name, many I couldn't. I pleaded with them to leave me alone, but they wouldn't.

Then the first punch came.

It came out of nowhere and I couldn't even say which one of them it was, but when I stumbled one of them caught me and held me so they could do it again.

When Greg got there, he had to pull a guy off me. He punched him, and it wasn't long before they were all running scared because Greg was making enough of a scene that people came over to see what was going on.

He picked me up.

He dusted me off.

He bundled me into his car and he got me home.

I had a black eye, cuts across my face, blood pouring down, bruises blooming across my stomach where they'd kicked and kicked and kicked, more blood pouring from a split lip. I looked like I'd been through hell. And I had.

'You're so effervescent, Robin. I don't want you to make yourself a target.'

I shake myself from the memory, trying to find my resolve. 'Mum, do you have any idea how homophobic you sound right now?'

'Robin—'

'I know I'm camp – it happens to be something I like about myself. Sure, if there's a bigot out there looking for a target, then there I am, but I can't dim myself, Mum. You taught me better than that. I can't be afraid all the time.'

'And I don't want you to be, Robin. I just want you to be careful,' she says. 'If Greg hadn't been there, you could have been . . .' She can't finish the sentence because she's trying to stop herself from crying.

And she's not wrong. Greg showed up at just the right moment like a big, hulking saviour in shining armour and kicked the shit out of one of my attackers, enough that they all went running. Mum was in pieces. She's used to dealing with blood, with people who have been hurt, but seeing it happen to her own son was too much. She was so grateful to Greg. I was too.

And as much as I didn't want to, I sort of did become a little more afraid. After it happened, I shrank. I didn't leave the house for the rest of the summer. Greg came round to keep me company because Natalie was away. My shoulders rounded a little more, I'd walk with my head down, I didn't look at anybody in case it provoked them. And I knew it was stupid, and I knew it wasn't anything that I had done that made it happen to me, that made me into a target. All I'd done was exist, but I thought that maybe if I made myself smaller they wouldn't see me next time.

When Natalie got back, she noticed straight away. She thought I was more downbeat than usual. I told her I was just distracted, that auditions were pulling my focus. I felt too embarrassed to tell her. I wanted it all to be over, and dredging it up again just felt like too much. I'd healed by the time she got home and I just didn't want to have to go through it again.

'I don't want you to get hurt,' Mum says when she's regained her composure. And I suddenly wish I could take back saying she sounded homophobic. Because, sure, she totally did, but she's just a mum trying to do what is best for her gay son. I know she worries every time I leave the house, every time I get on a train to go to an audition, every time I even get on my bike. She'd probably wrap me in cotton wool if she could, but she knows it's not practical to hold me back. She wants me to thrive. When I got beaten up, it compounded all her fears.

'Greg will be there,' I say softly. 'He saved me once . . .'

'Honestly, that boy is so wonderful,' she says.

'I know, Mum — it's why we keep him around,' I say. 'I'll be careful, I promise.'

'I know, I know, I just want to protect my baby,' she says. 'And, you know, go full murderous bear on anyone who tries to hurt you.'

She takes a deep breath and rearranges her face into a smile. 'You're going to have so much fun!' she says. 'You'll have to tell me all about it when I see you on Saturday.'

'I'll be careful, Mum, I promise,' I say again.

'Oh, I know, I know,' she says. 'Greg and Natalie will be there. They'll look after you – I know they will. Just make sure you text me when you get home, OK? I need to know you're OK when I'm not here.' It's the only deal we really have. She works late, but I make sure she knows I'm safe.

'I will,' I say. 'Promise.'

Mum finishes decorating the cake and we have a slice before she heads upstairs for a power nap. I'm left in the dining room, my head spinning a little out of control. I try not to think about the attack if I can, but every now and then something will happen that pushes it to the front of my mind. Like when Natalie quizzes us about what happened over the summer.

I felt bad keeping it a secret, but as time went by it got harder to tell her. And then Connor happened. Which made it all the more complicated.

The people who were kicking the shit out of me weren't just a bunch of assholes with a flouncy gay boy vendetta, they were people at my school. Connor's friends. He was there and he saw the whole thing happening. He didn't say anything. He didn't do anything. Probably because he didn't know me. Not yet. We didn't start seeing each other until a month or so later, when he apologized for what had happened, apologized for not stepping in, for not doing something. If Greg hadn't been there to stop it, who knows what would have happened.

But when I asked Greg not to tell what happened, or that Connor was there, he promised that he wouldn't. When he found out I was dating Connor, he thought I was out of my mind, but he hadn't been there when Connor had talked to me. He'd not heard about his homophobic family, about his asshole friends that he couldn't really get away from.

We'd not been together when it happened, so why would he step in?

Greg hated the excuse but kept it to himself. So now I feel tense whenever Connor comes up in conversation. If Natalie knew, she would make me break it off and probably break Connor's face in the process. I hate secrets, I do, but I need Connor. And I think he needs me too. At least that's what I tell myself.

NINE

Thursday goes by without incident. I have breakfast with Mum in the morning, before leaving her to go to sleep in the afternoon before her night shift. When I get to school, I pass the day with my bravest face on. Mrs Hepburn and the rest of my drama class are tiptoeing around me, I can feel it, and whenever I look round I swear someone is whispering about me. That lovely feeling of knowing lots of people was great when it was about *Grease*, but now it's about my failure I'm not so keen.

After school, I ride home and Natalie comes over. We watch a lot of *Drag Race* to make me feel better. It cheers me up when I'm feeling even the tiniest bit low. There's something oddly comforting about it, even when the queens are being horrible to each other.

'It's self-care, but with lip syncs and bitchiness!' Natalie says.

It's almost like we're preparing for Dragcellence tomorrow as we watch, speculating about what it's going to be like and eating a hell of a lot of cake. It's nice to be thinking about something else.

Hun, are you not coming tonight?

Miss Emily is worried.

'Who's that?' Nat asks through a mouthful.

'Priya.'

Natalie sits up sharply. 'Is she coming tomorrow? Tell me she's coming tomorrow.'

'Yeah, yeah, she's coming – she's just wondering where I am.'

Natalie raises an eyebrow. 'Were you meant to have class tonight?'

I hesitate. 'Maybe.'

'Girl—'

'Nat, don't, I just can't right now.'

'So you're giving up on everything because of one failed audition?'

'Natalie, don't do this right now. I don't want to, OK? Please?'

She opens her mouth to speak, but quickly stops herself. I don't think I'm ready for whatever it was she was about to say. 'Fine.' She turns back to the TV. 'One more runway?'

'One more runway.'

> I'm really not feeling it right now.

> Still on for tomorrow?

> Oh, I wouldn't miss it! See you tomorrow!

Natalie and I keep watching *Drag Race* until it's way too late and, by the time she leaves, I can barely move.

But I stay downstairs and keep watching.

I stretch as I watch, sitting on the floor, legs out in second, eating my third slice of cake and killing time, letting the evening slip by runway by runway until it's nearly midnight. That's when I start staring at the clock on my phone.

I forget how many years I have done this for, but I enjoy the moment when 11:59 turns into 00:00, when the previous day turns into my birthday. I watch and wait, the minute seeming like the longest of my life.

At 00:00 my phone buzzes in my hand and I flinch and drop it.

'Skittish!'

I scream and turn to see Mum standing in the doorway.

'Mum!'

'What?'

'You scared the shit out of me!'

'Language!'

'No,' I say. 'I feel like it's warranted. I nearly had a heart attack.'

'Stop being so dramatic,' she groans, leaning on the doorframe.

I take a few deep breaths, trying to locate my composure, but it has vanished into the night.

'I thought you were sleeping,' I say.

'I was. And you should be,' she says. 'I got up to get ready for work, heard you down here and wanted to be the first one to wish you a happy birthday.'

I roll my eyes. 'Well, you could have killed me.'

'The phrase you're looking for is thank you,' she replies. She clasps her hands together and puts them in front of her chest, looking a little misty-eyed. 'Oh, my boy.'

'Mum—'

'Let me feel emotional,' she interrupts. 'Eighteen years old. I have a son who is eighteen years old. It's a wonder really. I look so young—'

'Focus, Mum, *my* birthday!'

'Of course, of course!' she says, taking a seat on the sofa behind me, her hand tousling my hair while I keep stretching on the floor. 'I know you're having a rough time—'

'Mum, please—'

'No, no, let me do this.' She sighs. 'I know you're having

a rough time figuring out what you're going to do next and that's fine, that's totally allowed, but please remember how young you are, how talented you are, and how much you have going for you. You're the most determined person I know, so I know you're going to make it, one way or another.' She reaches out her hand and extends her pinky finger. 'OK?'

I take her finger in mine. 'Thanks, Mum.' It's all I can really manage without bursting into tears because it's late and I'm tired and the last thing I want to do is talk about my most recent failure, but her words mean a lot. She wouldn't say them if she didn't mean them. I'm sure of it.

'Right, I'm going to go and start getting ready for work,' she says. 'And you should go to bed – you have school in the morning.'

'One more episode?' I say. 'It is my birthday, after all.'

She sighs in mock annoyance. 'Fine, but, after that, bed. I should see you when you come in from school later, but if I don't I'll leave some cash on the table—'

'Mum, you don't have to—'

'I'll leave some cash on the table for your night out.' She bends down and kisses the top of my head. 'Happy birthday, my darling boy. Sleep tight.'

She walks back upstairs and I hear her go into the bathroom and turn on the shower. My phone buzzes again. I

103

look and see two texts from Connor. The first reads 'Happy birthday', sent dead on midnight, the second 'I'm outside'.

I sit bolt upright.

I guess Mum wasn't the first person to wish me a happy birthday. How about that?

> What are you doing here?

Three dots. Three dots that make my heart thump a little harder in my chest.

> It's your birthday. Why else would I be here?

Three dots again. He's a confident double texter.

> Is your mum here?

I go to write back immediately, wanting to see him, wanting to kiss his face off even for a second. But Mum is upstairs. And there are no closets down here to throw him in or windows to throw him out of.

But, suddenly, I don't care.

> No, hang on.

I leave the TV running and walk out of the living room, past the stairs and to the door. When I open it, he is standing there in a T-shirt and jeans, the light from the hallway illuminating his handsome face. When he sees me, he smiles and I all but melt on the spot.

'Happy birthday,' he says.

'You already told me that.'

'By text,' he says. 'Now I get to tell you in person.'

He reaches out and takes my hand, starting to trace little patterns on it, his fingers calloused. Every little bit of contact with him is stolen, so it feels electric.

He steps inside, kissing me hard on the lips out of sight of the watching street, the twitching curtains of people who probably care less than he does.

But I don't overthink it. I just kiss him back. I just let myself have this one moment.

When we stop, his forehead is resting on mine, my hand on the back of his neck, and we're breathing on each other like it's a scene from a film.

Happy birthday to me.

'Robin?'

Shit.

'Robin, is the front door open?'

Holy shit.

'You said she wasn't here!' Connor hisses.

The moment is gone, shattered into a million pieces. He looks so panicked, all the colour draining from his face, and I'm reminded just how freaking fragile this entire non-relationship is.

'She was in the shower,' I whisper back. 'She's got work, so I thought—'

'Robin?' I hear her footsteps on the landing, on the stairs. 'Robin, would you just answer me?'

'Robin, you can't do that to me!' He seems genuinely angry. Upset.

'I know, I didn't think, just go,' I hiss. 'I'll make something up.'

'Don't tell her.'

'I won't, just go.'

He runs. He actually runs down the garden path and makes a sharp left, nearly falling over his own feet as he scuttles off into the night, out of sight.

'Why are you standing there with the door open?' Mum asks, arriving at the bottom of the stairs, a little out of breath in her dressing gown. 'You could have answered.'

'Sorry,' I say. I feel flushed. I wonder if I look flushed. 'I thought there was someone at the door. Wondered if it was Natalie or something.'

'OK,' Mum says, staring at me, then at the door. 'Are you waiting for someone or can we close the door now?'

'Oh, yeah, sorry.' I close the door and switch off the hall light, hoping the darkness hides the fact that my cheeks are burning.

'OK,' she says again, eyeing me suspiciously. 'Well. I'm going to carry on getting ready.'

She disappears back upstairs and I finally breathe again. I make my way back to the living room and sink to the floor to watch RuPaul do the walkaround in the Werkroom but I'm not taking it in.

My phone buzzes. It's Connor.

> Don't do that again.

> If I didn't know any better, I'd say you got a thrill out of it.

>> I'm sorry.

>> It was sweet of you to come over.

>> I just wanted to see you.

> It's fine.

> Happy birthday, Robin. ♥

I sit up straight.

He sent a heart emoji.

I hate how much I know I'm going to analyse that later.
Wow.

> See you Sunday. ♥

Friday at school is better. Determined to stop me from
feeling gloomy, Natalie and Greg bring snacks and treats so
that while we're sitting in the common room during lunch
we have a little birthday party. Some people I do drama
with come along too: Crystal, Katy, Marcus, Vicky, Lani,
DL, Reid, Chuck – all of them happy to spend their lunch
break laughing and eating cake with us. It takes my mind off
things a little. Even when I have to happy-face when drama
college stuff comes up, I can brush it aside a little easier
when I have Entity to look forward to, Natalie at my side
counting down the hours, minutes and seconds until the
day ends.

'It's going to be great,' she says as we leave school. 'I'll
see you at mine later.'

There is a knock at the door at around six and Mum answers
it before I can even get out of my bedroom. I think I look
nice. I've picked out a new shirt and I'm trying to leave

the college stuff at the back of my head. Tonight is meant to be fun. And it will be. I'm sure of it.

'Robin, Greg is here!' Mum calls up the stairs. I could leave her happily talking to Greg for the next few hours if I really wanted to, but Greg would probably be standing there sweating and dying a little on my doorstep.

I pull on my boots, grab a jacket and head down the stairs to see Greg in a polo shirt and chinos, looking incredibly handsome. He's even put a little bit of product in his hair so it looks sort of messy, but in that carefully placed way.

'Bye, Mum,' I say, kissing her on the cheek.

'Be careful,' she says. 'And have fun.' She turns to Greg. 'You'll look after him, won't you, Greg?'

'Mum, come on, embarrassing,' I say.

'It is my right as a mother to embarrass you,' she says, ruffling my hair. I immediately smooth it down. 'Have a lovely night. I'll see you tomorrow.'

'Have a fun shift!'

'I imagine it will be the most thrilling twelve hours of my life!'

She closes the door and we head to the car. 'Sorry about her,' I say. 'She's nervous.'

'About you going to a club?' Greg asks.

'A gay club, a drag night, in Southford of all places,' I say. 'After what happened, she . . .' I trail off. I don't really want to bring it up again. It hardly seems like the moment. 'Anyway, I don't think she'd have let me come if you weren't going to be here.'

Greg starts to drive us to Natalie's house. 'Do you blame her? Imagine her reaction if she knew you were going out with one of them.'

'If she knew Connor was there, she'd probably kill him.'

'He's lucky I didn't,' Greg says, a little laugh telling me he's half joking. 'Sorry.'

'For what?'

'I know you're seeing him and I don't mean to be so . . . spiky,' he says. 'I just don't want you to get hurt.'

'I know.'

'Because you're my friend.'

'I know,' I say again. 'But we weren't going out at the time. If we had been, I'm sure he would have—'

'Yeah, I hope so,' he says. 'I just hate keeping it from Nat. It's hard that she likes you two together and I'm there looking all grumpy about it.'

'Let's not do this now,' I say as we pull up outside Nat's.

'Yeah, yeah,' he says. 'It's meant to be your birthday! Are you buzzing?'

'I'm nervous,' I say.

'For a night out?'

'For a drag night,' I say. 'I think Mum's got in my head

about it. She thinks I'm in mortal danger by association.'

'Well, if the gay mafia show up and see you in those shoes, *then* you might be in trouble!' He is grinning broadly, so obviously pleased with himself.

'Oh my gosh, you've been practising your reads. I've never been so proud!'

'Robin!' Mrs Josephs, Natalie's mum, has appeared at the door with the biggest grin on her face. 'Happy birthday!' She wraps her arms round me and kisses me on both cheeks.

'Thank you, Mrs Josephs,' I reply.

She's wearing a pink, flowing dress that floats as she walks, her hair a little darker than it was last time I saw her.

'You look fantastic,' I say. 'New hair?'

'How did you know?'

'It looks really good on you,' I say with a smile.

'Hello, Greg,' she says, kissing him on both cheeks and ushering us inside. 'Welcome, welcome, welcome, Natalie is upstairs and, of course, not ready yet.'

'I heard that!' Natalie shouts down the stairs.

'When is she ever ready on time?' Another voice, this one deep and booming, comes from the living room. I see Mr Josephs coming towards us, ducking down a little to get through the doorframe. 'Nice to see you, Robin, Greg.' He shakes our hands. 'Happy birthday.'

'Thank you,' I say.

The way Natalie talks about her parents sometimes, you'd think they were monstrous, but they're just pushing her to be her best. Greg and I head upstairs to see Natalie in front of her mirror, doing her eye make-up.

'Sorry about them,' Natalie says. 'I told you, Robin, my mum is obsessed with you.'

'She is not.'

'Oh come on, she has never been that excited on one of my birthdays,' she says.

'I find that almost impossible to believe,' I say.

Natalie goes back to doing her face in the mirror, Greg and I taking seats on the bed and on the floor respectively. I watch her add highlight to her cheekbones that makes them pop like you wouldn't believe. She glances at me in the mirror, a mischievous look in her eyes.

'Greg,' she says, waving an eyeliner pencil at him. 'Can I tempt you?'

Greg snorts. 'No, I'm good.'

'Come on, Greg, you're going to a drag night and you're wearing chinos and a polo shirt. Live a little.'

'Robin is wearing a shirt and jeans – why aren't you bothering him?'

'Thanks, buddy,' I say. 'Thanks for having my back.'

'Come on, Robin,' she says, coming towards me with

a fan brush packed with highlighter.

'No,' I say, pushing it away, the powder puffing up into a glittery cloud.

'What? You look good in it,' she pleads. 'When you do your shows, you're always wearing make-up. How is this different?'

'In practically every way!' I reply. Stage make-up is one thing, a little bit of base and some eyeliner so I don't get washed out on-stage, but wearing it out? I might as well have a neon sign over my head saying, 'Please kick the shit out of me.' And I don't want Mum to worry more than she already is. She might be overreacting, but I sort of see her point. 'I don't want to. It's too much,' I add.

'We're going to a gay bar – no one is going to judge you,' Nat exclaims, applying so much highlighter it's like she's wearing a hi-vis jacket on her face. Annoyingly, it actually works for her. She's stunning.

'That's not why I'm not doing it.'

'Glitter?'

'I'll blind you with it,' I snap.

'Wow, OK, let's take the crazy down a few notches, huh?' Greg intercepts. 'I'd like to make it to this bar at some point before closing, so if you could speed this whole process up a little, Nat, I'd really appreciate it.'

'Don't rush me,' she growls. 'You boys take a shower and

throw on a shirt and you're good to go. This is a process. Works of art take time.' She looks at herself in the mirror. It pains me to admit it, but she really does look like a work of art. She will be worshipped . . . or people will assume she is a drag queen. 'Last chance to look like a work of art, Robin.'

'I want to watch the queens, not be one of them.'

She shrugs. 'Fine, fine, fine, it's your birthday.'

'Speaking of which,' Greg says, 'any word from Connor?'

I feel the energy fly out of the room.

'Robin?' Greg pokes my arm. 'You're looking off into the middle distance like a bad actor in a power ballad music video. What's up?'

'I invited him.'

Natalie chokes on the air. 'What?'

'Is he coming?' Greg asks.

'Of course not,' I sigh. 'I was right. He made it abundantly clear he wouldn't be caught dead there. He texted me last night, though.'

'A text, how romantic,' Greg groans. I ignore it.

'And he came over late to see me.'

Natalie drops her lipstick. 'And you kept this quiet all day?'

'I'm embarrassed!'

'Why?'

'Because Mum came running down the stairs and almost caught us together,' I reply, feeling the blood rush to my face. 'I basically told him to run and he scrambled off down the street. I've never seen him move so quickly.' Natalie and Greg stare at me for a moment, then they start laughing. They start laughing so much that Natalie is dabbing at her eyes with tissues and Greg is doubled over, holding his stomach. And it *is* funny. It's so ridiculous and so completely insane that I have to laugh or I might just have a breakdown at the sheer tragedy of my life. 'I request a subject change!' I say between giggles.

The doorbell rings and Natalie sits up dead straight, her excitement renewed. 'I'll get it!' she shouts, running downstairs to answer the door. There are screams, there is excitement, then there are footsteps on the stairs that precede Priya entering the room in a purple jumpsuit. She poses in the doorway.

'Girl!' I shout.

'I know,' she says.

'Seriously!'

'I KNOW!' she says, twirling. 'I thought it might be too much, but what's too much?' Natalie reappears behind her, dragging Priya over to the mirror and offering her the highlight that I said no to.

'Oh, God, I'm awful,' I say. 'Priya, this is Greg, Greg,

this is Priya, I don't think you two have met before.' I gesture from Greg to Priya. She waves at him in the mirror and Greg awkwardly waves back.

'You OK?' I ask.

'Yeah,' he breathes. 'Yeah, I'm fine.'

'Let's go,' Natalie says, checking herself one more time. 'I look fantastic. You're all welcome.'

We take some pictures before we leave. Natalie in her short red dress, Greg in his polo shirt and chinos, me in my new black-and-white checked shirt and jeans, Priya – freshly highlighted in her purple jumpsuit. There are no other people in the world I'd rather spend my birthday with so, even with all the other shit that has been going on, I can't keep the smile off my face as we leave the house.

TEN

Entity is about twenty minutes from Natalie's house in a cab, a tucked-away building on the corner of a high street that is bustling with shoppers during the day and drunkards at night. It would look like every other place in town were it not for the giant pride flag hanging in every window, and from a flagpole over the front door. Oh, and the music of my people – Cher, Madonna, Gaga and other single-name divas – bursting out into the street every time someone opens the door.

There is a nervous sort of energy rushing around my body as we walk up to the door to face the bald man dressed in black stood out the front. He fills the doorframe, muscular, tall, scary-looking. I guess that's the idea of being a bouncer, but it makes my steps more tentative.

'ID?' he asks as we approach. I scrabble around in my pocket, my fingers fumbling over the cards in my wallet. His face cracks into a smile as he looks at the ID, and suddenly he looks a lot less serious. Handsome, even. I don't know how it's happened, like a veil has been lifted from his face.

'Happy birthday, Robin,' he says. 'Have a good night.'

I definitely prejudged him and it makes me walk into Entity with a smile on my face.

Automatically, I feel myself breathe out a sigh. It's as if the entire building has just wrapped its arms around me and squeezed me tight, my anxiety dissipating like I've taken off my coat.

'You look happy,' Natalie says, appearing next to me. 'I've not seen you smile like that in a while.'

'Look at him – he's practically giddy,' Greg says.

'Thank you for coming here with me,' I say, finding the words strange in my mouth. They seem too formal, too forced in some way, but I really appreciate it. Normally the place I feel most comfortable at is the dance studio, but this is a whole different level. It's like I've found a little home.

'You're more than welcome,' Priya says, bumping my hip.

'It's your birthday, mate,' Greg says, pulling me into a hug. 'Of course we're going to come here with you.' He looks over to the bar, already two people deep even though it's barely eight o'clock. A couple of the men behind the bar are topless and muscular in ways that you only really see on Instagram. Greg heads over, Priya following close behind.

There are people everywhere, some sitting around little tables, looking over at a small stage in the far corner where

I assume the queens will be performing later. Behind the stage, sparkly silver streamers hang down, moving as if they have a life of their own, glittering in the lights. There are speakers on high stands at either side of the stage pumping out music that makes me feel at home and a small, hobbity man sitting behind a sound desk, shoulders hunched, glasses on, staring at a MacBook screen.

Other people are standing around high tables, all chatting conspiratorially, smiling, happy. There are men holding hands with men, women kissing women, men in crop tops and make-up, people dressed so freaking fabulously it's like I am on an entirely different planet. And I don't think I ever want to leave.

'You OK?' Natalie asks.

I nod, struggling to find words. 'I just think I like it here.'

'We've barely been here five minutes,' she says with a laugh.

'I know,' I say. 'But I really like it.'

Conversations suddenly stop all around us, replaced with the sound of a roomful of people turning to face the stage.

A queen walks through the crowd and on to the stage. Never has the royal title been so fitting: she's tall, and by tall I mean glamazonian. Her hair is bright pink and perfectly coiffed atop her head, not a hair out of place, adding to the sheer regal power of her. Her eye make-up is dramatic in neon pink and blue, with small jewels along her browbone that seem to sparkle of their own accord. Her lips are overdrawn to comical proportions but not a single person laughs or titters because she looks, for want of a better word, radiant. Faultless in every way.

'Good evening, my darlings.' Her voice is a low, Scottish rumble, sending ripples through the audience. Someone whoops somewhere behind us. 'Calm yourself, dear boy. We have a whole evening of entertainment to get through and I don't like my men to peak too soon.' She is looking over in my direction, her eyes fixed on me. A couple of people turn round, thinking I'm the one who whooped and I feel . . . fine. In any other situation, I would want the ground to swallow me up, but I don't mind. I'm safe.

Laughter follows. Raucous laughter. And I'm part of it. I can't help it.

'You OK?' Natalie whispers next to me.

'Yeah,' I say, as surprised as she is concerned. 'I am, yeah.'

'The magic starts in ten minutes,' the queen says. 'So grab your drinks now and get yourselves settled in for a wonderful evening of entertainment. Tonight, for your viewing pleasure, you have the incredible Anne Drogyny!' A cheer, a wild scream from somewhere near the front. 'Miss Pristine Gleaming!' Another cheer. 'The handsome beast from Birmingham, Cole Shower!' Another cheer. 'The incomparable queen of the people, Kaye Bye!' Another cheer, louder this time, I'm sure. 'And, of course, let's not forget your wonderful host, the immensely talented, frankly gorgeous, ME! Carrie D'Way!' The crowd lose their minds, screaming, stamping, clapping wildly.

Natalie grabs hold of my arm. The grin on her face is so wild, so crazed, she looks like she's about to cry.

'You OK?' It's my turn to ask.

'I'm just so excited!' She is shaking, actually shaking. 'I am so, so glad we're here. Watching drag queens that actually live near us! This is amazing!'

We've been to see queens at theatres before. We saw the last season of Ru Girls when some of the queens from *Drag Race* performed in London, and it was unreal, but there's something different about seeing them in your actual town. They feel like celebrities before they've even done anything.

I look over to the bar where Greg is standing with Priya, the two of them deep in conversation, pressed together by the crowd. They don't seem to be focusing on getting drinks as much as they are focusing on each other.

'I don't think we'll be getting a drink any time soon,' I say to Natalie, nodding to the bar.

She looks over and gapes. 'Go on, Greg!' she giggles.

A few minutes later, Greg and Priya appear with the

drinks and we stand there, waiting for the show to start. I find myself looking around the bar, trying to commit every little detail to memory. I notice the fireplace off to one side, the tiny nook in the furthest reaches of the club, away from the hustle and bustle, and the stage where a studious young man is reading a dusty-looking book, which seems so random and yet so perfect.

'Are you enjoying yourself?' Natalie whispers as Carrie makes her way back to the stage, her gingham-print dress tailored perfectly to her padded frame. She's dressed like the category is neon fifties housewife realness, and I am living.

'I think it's about to get better!' I say as Carrie takes the mic.

'Good evening, my darlings!' she calls to cheers and whoops. 'And welcome to Dragcellence. We've got an incredible line-up for you here tonight, starting with someone you all know and love. My darlings, please welcome to the stage, ME!'

The crowd laughs and goes wild as Carrie hands the microphone back to the beardy, bespectacled young man at the side of the stage. 'Rose's Turn' from *Gypsy* starts to play through the speakers and Carrie takes centre stage, all eyes on her, a light hitting her in a way that it hadn't before. She begins her lip sync, hitting every word, hitting every breath, and it's captivating watching her mouth move like that. It's so precise. She could be singing for all I know.

She plays with the audience. A man in the front row with glitter around his eyes is June, a woman standing at the bar wearing head to toe florals is Herbie, and Carrie's gaze falls on me once more as Imelda Staunton's voice screams 'MISS GYPSY ROSE LEE!' I could die right now and be entirely content.

The final build-up has my entire body jittering, the ending climactic, the crowd wild. If this is the opening act, I can only imagine what the rest of these queens are going to do.

Carrie curtseys, waiting for the applause to die down before demanding more, playing mock coy.

'Thank you so much, my darlings,' she coos. 'You sure know how to make a girl feel special. Now, our next performer is one of my favourite drag daughters, and every time she performs this next number she makes Mummy proud. So please welcome to the stage Anne Drogyny.'

The song is 'Anything Could Happen' by Ellie Goulding and, almost in unison, every audience member turns to see Anne Drogyny walking through the crowd, wrapped head to toe in strands of black and grey chiffon. She dances through us, the words coming from her as she dances. The slightest twitch and the material seems to breathe, like the outfit has a life of its own. She makes direct eye contact with me, then Natalie, as she lip-syncs a few lines, working her way through the crowd to hit the stage in time for a chorus. She twirls and unveils her face, beat like you wouldn't believe.

As the number continues, more of the fabric is removed, her silhouette changing. Literally anything could happen; no one has any idea where this is going.

The number ends and the crowd goes absolutely insane. Anne Drogyny, who is now wearing significantly less than she was a moment ago, bows and bundles the discarded fabric into her arms before prancing off the stage. She runs past us in the direction of a blue door to what I assume is the backstage area.

'She's so beautiful. Did you see her dancing?' Priya is beaming next to me. 'I mean, what? That was insane.'

'My darlings, our next performer is one I'm sure many of you have been waiting for.' Carrie is back on the stage, her champagne flute full once again, her make-up still somehow entirely flawless despite the heat. 'I love her like a cold sore. My darlings, please welcome to the stage, the incomparable, the insufferable, Kaye Bye!'

The music starts and I vaguely recognize the song, a techno beat that awakens something in the back of my mind, though I can't place what.

'Good evening, Sydney!'

We couldn't be further from Sydney if we tried. But the welcome isn't coming from a person that's here. It's Kylie Minogue's voice. I know the voice and I know the song. It was in the first show I did with my dance school. I can remember practically every single move. I can see it playing out in my head. It's from Kylie's live album, so there is cheering and clapping coming through the speakers as well as from the people in the room.

'How're you feeling tonight?'

My eyes find the stage as the lights change, as a new face stands in front of the sparkly streamers. She's wearing a leotard covered in so many sequins and rhinestones she looks like a walking star, with purple fringing on her chest and at her cinched waist. The leotard is practically skin-coloured and, were it not for all the rhinestones catching the light and giving me some kind of sparkle blindness, I'd swear she was nude.

Her hair is blonde, perfectly swept into a pouffey, barely shoulder-length do that is absolute unclockable. It moves with her as she twirls about the stage, hairography for days, her make-up perfection. She's hitting every lyric, matching every breath, every sound of Kylie Minogue's 'In Your Eyes' as if Kylie were standing in front of us actually singing it.

She spins and twirls, and the audience are losing their

minds and I am standing here feeling like I'm losing mine. I can't move. All I can do is stare, watching as every sequin sparkles, as she mesmerizes me, pulling me into her world.

Kaye Bye throws her feather boa into the audience and as the girls in the front row fight over it I find myself wishing we'd got here earlier to get a seat that near to the stage because I want to be close to her. She drops to her knees and I'm screaming and cheering with everyone else. Watching the way she dances across the stage, every move precise, choreographed, things I could definitely do, but not in a six-inch heel. I know I want to be like her. I want to do this. I could do this. I could be like her.

The number ends and I am a little delirious. Kaye Bye waves to us as she leaves the stage, somehow still holding my focus as she disappears through the door.

'Robin? What's up?' Greg asks, appearing at my side and snaking an arm across my lower back to give me a squeeze.

'I'm fine,' I say. 'Why?'

'You're crying, Robin,' he says.

'Yeah.' I sniff. 'That was just—'

'How freaking amazing was that?!' Natalie appears in front of me, like she's just materialized out of thin air.

'I love it here!' Priya screams. 'Babes, great birthday location.'

'It was amazing!' Greg replies.

Natalie looks at me again, suddenly noticing the tears. 'Whoa, hang on, are you all right?' she asks. 'You shouldn't be crying – it's your birthday!'

'No, no, no,' I say, wiping my face. 'I'm not sad. It's just, that was . . . shit, it was . . .' I trail off. I don't know how to describe watching her on that stage. It was almost like an out-of-body experience. 'That,' I say decisively, 'was amazing.'

'She was pretty great,' Natalie says. 'Another drink? They'll be back to start performing again in a minute.'

I nod and Natalie vanishes, but the world feels different all of a sudden. The evening rushes past in a blur of drag excellence and I cheer so hard that I know I will be paying for it by having no voice tomorrow morning, but I don't care.

Even as we leave, the four of us tumbling into a cab, my world is still spinning around, and I don't think it's the alcohol doing that. It's Kaye Bye. She performed twice more, a mix of Britney Spears songs and then a lip sync of 'Applause' by Lady Gaga peppered with quotes from *Keeping Up with the Kardashians*, every second of it executed flawlessly. Which isn't to take away anything from the other queens on that stage. Anne Drogyny, Pristine, Cole and Carrie were incredible performers, all blowing my mind, but there was something about Kaye that caught my imagination. She's in my head, she's everything that I see and somehow everything I want to be, dancing, twirling, singing, lip-syncing the mother-tucking house down. I'm floating and I don't feel like coming down.

ELEVEN

I barely stopped thinking about Kaye Bye all weekend. Natalie took some videos of her and put them on her Instagram stories and I lost track of the amount of times I watched them before they vanished. How could one person be so mesmerizing?

It sounds silly, but there was something about her up on that stage that made me feel like everything was going to be OK. Sure, my future was uncertain, but in that space none of that mattered.

When Mum got in at three o'clock on Saturday afternoon, we celebrated my birthday. We had toast and talked about what had happened to her at work and what had happened to me at Entity and, in spite of myself, I found myself leaving out details. After hearing her worries, it was like I didn't want to share too much. She had to go to bed so she could be up again at midnight to go back to work, so I spent the evening by myself.

On Sunday morning, I've not heard from Connor. I message him first thing asking what we're doing, what time

I should come over, but I don't hear anything.

I do my homework.

I check my phone with aggressive frequency.

It's not until later in the afternoon that his name pings up on my screen.

I'm sorry about today. Parents didn't go out. Haven't been able to get away . . .

That's OK.

I'll make it up to you. Promise. Xx

OK. Xx

It's not OK. And I know it's not OK. And yet . . .

TWELVE

I'm at my locker on Monday morning after a manic cycle ride to school when someone appears next to me. I look down to see battered Converse, jeans with rips at the hems, at the knees, so many rips in fact that they're barely jeans, they're just bits of denim held together by a hopeful stitch and a prayer.

We accidentally slam our lockers simultaneously and I let out a yelp as I'm suddenly face to face with him, mine no doubt covered in sweat, my hair stuck to my forehead, everything about me showing off the fact that I am late, late, late.

But I lose my breath a little more as I take him in.

And holy shit.

Holy absolute freaking shit.

He's even prettier up close.

He's about my height, his blond hair cropped close to his head on the sides but a little fluffier on top, and he's smiling at me. So it's all but confirmed that I look ridiculous and I wish I was smart enough to keep a mirror in my locker or something so I don't have to walk around school looking like I've been dragged through a hedge.

'Hi,' he says, still grinning. He honestly looks like he should be wearing a leather jacket or something right now, he's just got that vibe, a level of confidence I can only dream of. And I realize I'm literally just standing there staring at him.

Christ, Robin, say something.

'Hey.'

Inspired.

'Guess we're locker buddies,' he says, gesturing to the grey metal like I've not seen them before. He has a jawline so sharp it could cut me.

'Certainly looks that way,' I reply, the shake in my voice unmistakable. I hate myself so much right now.

'I'm Seth.'

'I know,' I say.

'What?'

'Sorry, I just—'

'You've heard about me,' he says, shuffling a little on the spot. 'All awful, I imagine.'

'Um . . . well—'

'It's not all true,' he says.

'I try not to listen when people talk about it,' I say. 'It must be hard to be new.'

He looks at me carefully.

'That's nice of you,' he says. 'Some of it's true, maybe, but not all of it. Can I introduce myself properly?'

'Clean slate,' I say.

He reaches his hand out towards me. 'I'm Seth.'

'Oh, a handshake, OK, then.' I shake his hand, laughing nervously, cursing every word I have just said. Why am I like this? Why am I allowed to be around people?

'I'm Robin.'

'I'm new here.'

I mock gasp. 'You are?'

He laughs. 'Yeah, I just moved here.'

'Did you?' My voice squeaks a little, and I cough to try to cover it up. 'From where?'

'London.'

'London?' I say like I've never heard of it before. 'Shit. From the big smoke to little old Essex – you'll be bored out of your mind.'

'I don't think so.' He shrugs. 'I'll find something to do.'

I *so* want to be the something he would find to do. Wait. Hold on. That's a bit wrong. Let me rephrase that.

'Which way is the student office?' he asks. 'They're . . . um . . . not happy with my attendance so I've been told to go there. I just don't know where it is.'

'Sure, no problem,' I say, walking him away from the

lockers and pointing down the corridor. 'Straight down there, make a right. If you bump into a bunch of stoners outside the tech block, you've gone too far.'

He laughs. I don't really want to tell him I'm being serious because his laugh sounds like music.

'Thanks, Robin,' he says. 'I'll see you around.'

'Good luck!' I say. 'Nice to meet you.'

He laughs again. 'Yeah, nice to meet you too.'

He walks away and, in spite of myself, I find myself watching him go.

I head into my English class, thankful that Mr Goldberg is buried in paperwork and letting the class chat before he starts his lesson, and slide into my usual place next to Natalie.

'Ooh, look at her all stealthy,' she teases. 'Call me, beep me, if you wanna reach me.'

'Is that a Kim Possible reference?'

She shrugs. 'It might be.'

'OK, work.' I say. 'And good morning to you too.'

'Good morning,' she says with a grin. 'How many times have you watched that video?'

It reached the point where I had to see the video of Kaye Bye again so I asked Natalie to send it over. I watched it periodically on Saturday between rounds of homework. And then before bed. And then on Sunday when I was waiting for Connor to text. And then when I woke up this morning. It's been a long time since I've been totally obsessed with something, but this feels like another freaking level.

'My homework is very half-arsed,' I say. 'I'm genuinely scared there are Kylie Minogue lyrics in my *Hamlet* essay.'

'To do or not to do the locomotion.'

'A little more than kin, and less than confide in me.'

'Friends, Romans, countrymen, your disco needs you.'

'That's not *Hamlet*,' I manage, choking on my own laughter.

'No, but picture a drag queen called Julia Sees-Her and tell me that's not perfect!'

We fall about in fits of giggles and I hear chairs scrape and jackets shuffle as people turn to look at us making a scene at the back of the room. Mr Goldberg fixes us with a withering stare and we calm down. He goes back to his paperwork, Natalie leans closer to me.

'So, you really enjoyed yourself?' she whispers.

'Oh God yes,' I groan. 'I didn't want to leave.'

'I noticed,' she says. 'You were begging for a third or fourth encore.'

'They could have kept going forever and I wouldn't have got bored,' I say. 'How did they even do all of that? I mean, the performances were one thing, but the make-up, the outfits, the wigs . . . All of it was so . . .' I sigh and rest my head on the table. 'It was so bloody perfect.'

Natalie eyes me curiously. 'Why are you looking all sad about it now? We had a great time. Don't turn back into sad Robin! Sad Robin is so . . .'

'Sad?'

'Wow, you know, it's like you're inside my head,' she deadpans.

'I just want to go again!'

'Well, we can!' she says. 'It's great there.'

'It's gay there!'

'Lucky you're massively gay and I'm massively supportive of that as a pansexual princess.' She smiles, nudging me.

'Morning, kids.' I hear Greg plant himself at the desk next to mine. 'You're quiet, Robin.'

'I have the post-birthday blues,' I say, though I can't bring myself to tell them about what happened with Connor yesterday. Or rather what didn't. 'I miss Kaye Bye.'

Natalie snorts. 'We can go again,' she says. 'You don't need to be so dramatic about it. What's really up?'

And the reason for my weird mood has been sitting in my head for basically the whole weekend. Or at least the part of it where I wasn't thinking about Connor. I've not really had the courage to say it out loud, not even to myself, because the idea seems so unbelievably ridiculous. It's on the tip of my tongue and if anyone would understand it, it would be Natalie and Greg.

'I want to be her.' The words float out of my mouth and I watch them as they drift up and smack Natalie in the face.

'Oh my gosh, hang on, wait, we need to—'

She stops dead. There's a pause all around us. I can feel it in the air. And I'm suddenly worried that I've said it too loud and the whole class now knows. I sit up to see what's going on, expecting all eyes on me, everyone with a question on their lips about the all-singing, all-dancing queen who now wants to be a different kind of queen.

But they're not.

They're all focused on the door.

Seth is standing there looking somewhere between unsure of himself and like he owns the actual room.

'That's him,' Natalie whispers. 'Don't all stare at once, but that's the new guy.'

I find myself waving at him before I can stop myself. When he notices me, his face bursts into a smile and I see him start breathing again, his entire body reanimating before he walks over to us.

'Wait, you *know* him?' Natalie hisses. 'Since when? Tell me more, tell me more, like, does he have a car?'

'You tell him about *Grease*, I will murder you,' I say just as Seth appears in front of us. 'Hey, Seth, long time no see.'

Natalie chokes on air as my voice cracks over his name.

I want the ground to swallow me up.

'This is Mr Goldberg's English class, right?' he says.

'You'd know if you'd actually shown up to one since you got here.'

'Nat!' Greg says.

'What? I'm not wrong.'

'You're in the right place,' I say, which earns me another one of his smiles. I'm so doomed. Natalie clears her throat next to me. 'This is Natalie, this is Greg.'

They greet him in turn and the silence that falls is so heavy and awkward it may just kill us. Which would be a blessing. My cheeks are so red you could see them from space.

'How did you two meet?' Natalie asks, leaning forward on the desk, eyeing Seth extremely carefully.

'In the corridor about ten minutes ago,' Seth says. He doesn't know Natalie well enough to realize this is the beginning of an interrogation and he is doomed as all heck.

'We're locker buddies,' I blurt, and immediately regret it. But Natalie either hasn't heard or is too focused on Seth to rip me apart.

'So you're new?' she says. 'Exams are in, like, five months. What's that about?'

'It's a long story,' he says, taking the empty seat at the desk in front of us.

'I like stories,' she replies.

'Leave him alone, Nat,' I say, jabbing her in the side.

'I'm sorry, do you want me to address "locker buddies"?' She smiles a smile so sinister I want to disappear.

I turn to Seth who is once again smiling at me. His teeth are a little crooked, maybe too big for his mouth, but still cute. Ah shit. Why, God, why?

'You're on your own,' I say, with what I hope is a coy smile. Whatever I manage, it's enough to make him laugh just as Mr Goldberg stands up and clears his throat to start the class.

'Saved by the bell,' Seth says, reaching into his bag and pulling out a notebook.

It's fair to say I don't get a lot done in that English class, instead choosing to memorize the back of Seth's head while weathering scathing glances and eye rolls from Natalie. Every now and then he looks like he is about to turn round and ask me something, but he doesn't. The class flies by and, when it's over, Seth asks us for directions to the science block, which Greg gives him.

I want to walk him there, purely because there is something about him that is fascinating. Maybe it's the brooding behaviour, maybe it's the no-shits-to-give attitude, but I want to know more. Before I have a chance to offer myself up as tribute, he's gone and I'm watching him go again. I need help.

'You have some explaining to do,' Natalie practically screams as she turns me round and walks me towards the common room. 'What the hell was all that?'

'Why did you have to accost him like that?' I reply.

'He was fine,' Greg says. 'If it had been you, you would have been on the floor praying for death, but he was a pro. I don't think he even blinked.'

'Yeah, he was holding his own,' Natalie says.

'You could have been a little nicer – he is new.'

'OK, I'll be nicer to him next time I see him,' she says. 'But we need to talk about *your* behaviour, sir.'

'Excuse me?'

'Come on, Robin, he looked at you and you practically melted.'

I groan. 'I request a change of subject!'

'Absolutely not,' Natalie replies. 'What's with you and new boy? What about Connor?'

'What do you mean?'

'No, you do *not* get to play dumb with me right now,' she says. 'You're staring at him like some lost puppy when you already have a perfectly fine secret love of your own happening. Do you want to finish things with Connor?'

'No.'

'Do you want to start something with Seth?'

'We don't even know Seth! Period. And he's *way* out of my league,' I say. 'Our leagues aren't even next to one another. His league is a dot to my league.'

'That is the most polluted *Friends* reference I've ever heard in my life,' Greg groans.

'But it wasn't a no,' Natalie says. 'What's going on? Come on, Robin, he's bad news.'

'What's going on is I don't want to talk about it,' I say. My brain is fuzzy with too many things. 'New subject, please?' I'm practically on my knees.

'Fine,' Natalie says, linking her arm in mine. 'Let's talk about you wanting to be Kaye Bye.'

And there's a sort of overwhelming pressure in my chest that is something like suffocating and having too much air at the same time. It's a sensation that is so familiar to me that I'm taken back to the exact time I last experienced it. When I was sitting out on the field with Natalie at the height of summer almost five years ago and I told her that I thought I was gay. I actually knew for sure that I was gay as heck, but that's how I worded it at the time. For some reason, the drag-queen thing feels like coming out all over again.

We make it to the common room and sit down around one of the tables. I can barely meet their eyes.

'Maybe it's weird, but I want to do it.'

'Drag?' Greg asks.

'Yeah,' I say as plainly as I can. 'I felt something when I was watching her.'

'Like what?' Natalie says.

'It was the same as when I went to see *Singin' in the Rain* in the West End. Like, I loved it so much, like the rest of the audience did, but then there was that extra little something that had me wanting to be up there, to be doing it,' I reply, the words tumbling out of my mouth. This was pretty much how I answered questions during the interview portion of my drama-school auditions. 'When I saw that show, I could see myself doing it and it filled me with this sort of *need*. And I got that same feeling when I was watching Kaye Bye on Friday night. There was something about her, the way she performed, that made me want to get up there and do it.'

The performance had been like a window into gays gone by: of Kylie when she did her homecoming tour after she had cancer. That was a huge moment for her and it meant a lot to a lot of people, the gay community included. It was like a little time capsule of a truly powerful and influential gay icon.

'Haven't you ever thought about doing it before?' Natalie asks, hardly able to contain herself. 'Like, didn't *Drag Race* ever do that?'

I shrug. 'Yeah,' I say. 'I mean, I've watched them lip-syncing and walking the runway and thought, "Wow, I'd love to do that," or even that I *could* do that, maybe, but seeing it happen two metres from your face is different. Like, I want to do *that*. I think.'

My face is red, my eyes feeling like they could fill up with tears at any moment. After what Mum said about making myself a target, maybe the idea of doing drag is scaring me a little more than I thought it would.

'OK,' Greg says. 'So, you want to do it, but where do you even start?'

'You think I know?' I reply with a laugh. 'I have no idea.'

'I do.'

We both turn to Natalie, who is practically bouncing in her seat at this point.

'I know exactly what we need to do.'

THIRTEEN

Natalie had a cunning plan, one that she went over for the rest of the day between classes and was determined we should put into motion straight away. So, when school let out at three thirty, she walked me over to my bike because she didn't want to waste any more time before starting my journey to becoming 'Essex's Next Drag Superstar'. Her words, not mine.

'High-street stuff should be fine,' she says as we walk out of school.

'I'm really not sure about this, you know,' I say. It suddenly feels like it's moving too fast. Wanting to be a drag queen is such a new thing in my head that I'm not even fully on board with it yet.

'The sooner you get started, the sooner you figure out if you really want to do it,' she says.

'So I've gotta jump in heels first.'

'Purse first.'

I suddenly feel like I'm going to throw up. 'Can we not talk about it until we get there?'

'Are you requesting a new subject?' she asks with a careful cock of her eyebrow.

'Yes, I'm requesting a new subject.' I stop abruptly as I see Connor walking by. He's with his friends so barely looks my way before keeping his gaze fixed forward. I feel my heart sink.

'What was that?'

'Hmm?'

'With Connor – are you two OK?'

I laugh. 'Probably, I don't know.'

'You don't know?' she says, rolling her eyes. 'Christ, Robin, come on, it's your relationship—'

'Not a relationship,' I say. 'I don't think.'

'Explain.'

'We were meant to hang out yesterday,' I say. 'And we didn't.'

'I'm going to need a little more.'

'Well, I spent the whole day waiting for him to message me and he didn't until the evening,' I say. 'But I got all my homework done, so . . .'

'Robin, that's messed up,' she says.

'I mean, his parents didn't end up going out like he thought,' I say. 'He couldn't do anything about it.'

'He could have messaged you,' she says.

And of course I freaking know that but I don't want to

talk about it. I can't have another thing in my life falling apart right now.

'I don't want to talk about it. I preferred the old subject.'

I start to push my bike, the two of us falling into step. We knock arms every now and again, needing the closeness.

'OK, then,' she says. 'But I'm going to start throwing out words like "eyeshadow palette" and "translucent setting powder" and I need you to be prepared to take that on.'

We head towards town, our conversation drifting to her sister being home, which she loves, and how great her sister's girlfriend is. She talks about uni things, how her dad is still on her back about Durham and her mum is piling on the pressure with exams coming up. When we make it into town, I lock my bike up to a nearby railing and stand with Natalie, staring at the shop. It's brightly lit inside, girls with high ponytails and full faces of make-up wandering up and down the aisles, weaving between counters, every one of them immaculate in their form-fitting black outfits.

There is a shifting in my stomach, the butterflies waking up again as Natalie moves to walk inside. I hold her steady, keeping our arms linked together. If I'm not going anywhere, she certainly isn't.

'What?' she says.

'I'm nervous,' I reply.

'Robin,' Natalie says, unable to stop herself from

chuckling. 'You honestly look like you're about to throw up.'

'I feel like I am.'

'In the words of the late, great Taylor Swift, you need to calm down.'

'You know Taylor Swift is alive, right?'

'Just trying to take your mind off your worries,' she says with a smile. But I'm not smiling. 'Come on, Robin, cheer up or you can figure out how to drag up your life by yourself.' She's being deadly serious. I know that tone. But I can't get Mum out of my head, talking about making myself a target. When I got attacked, I wasn't doing anything but tapping my feet, now I'm buying make-up. What if someone from school sees us? I must be out of my mind. It's times like this I wish Natalie knew what happened.

'Maybe I could just buy it online—'

'We need to get your shades.'

'I'll guess!'

'I'm not being funny, Robin, but how the heck are you supposed to be a drag queen if you can't even buy make-up? What's happened to you? You're the boy who played Lady Macbeth when you were fourteen! You've done drag – what's happening?'

And I almost tell her. I almost just come out with the whole thing . . . but I want to put it behind me. And putting it behind me means walking into that shop and moving on, right?

'OK,' I manage. I start towards the shop, opening the door and immediately being hit by the heady scent of several hundred different perfumes. It is obnoxiously bright and I'm so far out of my depth I'm pretty sure I'm drowning.

'Can I help you at all?' A woman with a high ponytail is looking directly at me, her eyes sparkling, glittery eyeshadow around them, false eyelashes so big every blink practically sends a gust of wind my way. But she's smiling and she seems friendly enough.

'I think we just need to take a look around,' Natalie says, pulling me off to one side.

'How did she know we were in here for me?'

'Because you look like you're about to pass out.' She takes in the shop like an expert. There is no way on this planet I would be able to do this by myself. 'OK. Let's start with base.'

'Base?'

'Foundation,' she groans. 'How can you be this clueless? You watch as many tutorials as I do.'

'I know, but they say these words and it's in one ear and out the other. I've never watched them thinking about doing it to myself.'

She guides me over to one of the fixtures on the wall,

the whole unit filled to bursting with make-up. She grabs a beige tube from the testers and opens it, holding it close to my face. I flinch. She groans. We repeat this process until she finds something that looks about right.

'OK, you need to not freak out right now,' she says. 'But I'm going to need to put this on your face.'

'What?'

'I said *not* freak out,' she repeats. 'It's a bit of foundation. If you're scared of foundation, we haven't got a hope in hell.'

And that about shuts me up. I present my cheek to her and she swipes the stick across. It's sort of wet, and she dabs it into my skin a little with her fingers. I can see a couple of girls down the aisle looking at me, watching as Natalie tests another shade on my skin. I avert my gaze.

Natalie smiles. 'What?' I ask defensively.

'It's not you,' she says, rolling her eyes. 'I'm just really good at this. This is your base.' She hands the stick foundation to me and turns back to the wall, picking out a much lighter one. 'This will do for a highlight.'

'And something darker for contour?' I offer, grabbing a rich brown shade.

She smiles at me. 'Look at you, getting into this,' she says. 'You know more than you think you do.'

'Do you need a basket?' The woman with the large

eyelashes has returned, a basket hanging from the crook of her arm.

'Yes, thank you,' I say, taking it from her and dumping the foundation sticks into it. I take a deep breath. I can do this. It doesn't need to be embarrassing or difficult, it's just make-up. It's paint.

I start looking at the station we're currently standing at, reading the labels, looking at the pictures, trying to decide where to go next. I already have an eyeliner pencil I can use, so I won't need one of those, but I grab a white one just in case. I pick out an eyeshadow palette, swatching a couple of the colours on my hand before I pick out one that is a little more vibrant-looking instead.

'Lips,' Natalie says. 'I don't think they have what we need here,' she adds, looking the station up and down. 'You'll need—'

'A lipstick and a pencil,' I interrupt. 'Right?'

She clutches at imaginary pearls round her neck. 'By RuPaul I think he's got it.'

'Shut *up*,' I groan as she drags me over to an entire bay of lipsticks and lipliners.

'So what colour?' she asks. 'Do you feel like more of a red or a black or what?'

There are so many options I feel more than a little overwhelmed. The choice is honestly ridiculous. There are at least three shades of black and probably around a hundred shades of red, all with names that don't really tell me anything about them.

'Um . . .' is all I can manage.

'I think you look like more of a red to me.' The voice comes from behind us and I jump. It's the woman again. I check her name badge to see her name – Ally – and look back up at her face. She is smiling. 'But they're buy one get one free,' she adds. 'So maybe you can try both.' She then reaches into a little pouch around her waist and pulls out a packet of make-up wipes. 'You've got swatches all over your arm and foundation on your cheek,' she says in response to my no doubt totally confused look. 'Trust me when I say you need this.'

I laugh. 'Thanks.'

I scrub at my face and then at my forearm which is currently a rainbow of different shades, all of which look brilliant, all of which I want to try out, and this is exciting. It's actually exciting. There are possibilities in every single one of those colours. I could transform into anything at all.

'Look at you,' Natalie says, nudging me.

'What? Talking to the sales girl?' I ask. 'She offered me a make-up wipe – I'm hardly in a position to say no.'

'No, not that, you complete and total fool,' she says. 'You're smiling.'

'I am?'

'Yeah.' She nods. 'You were smiling like that on Friday night and you're smiling now. And it makes me happy to see you happy.'

We pick out two lipsticks and lipliners, a setting powder, a white powder, beauty blenders, brushes, cotton pads, micellar water, a primer and contouring powders. When I look down at the basket I'm suddenly panicking about how much this is going to cost. It's definitely not what my mum thought I'd be spending my birthday money on, but there we go.

Ally is waiting for us at the main counter, eagerly beckoning us over. She takes the basket and starts putting everything through.

'Did you find everything you were looking for?' she asks.

'I think so?' I reply.

She starts going through my basket. 'You seem pretty well stocked to me,' she says. But then her face twists a little. She leans over the counter and grabs a small, rectangular box. 'You need these.'

'What is it?'

'Lashes!' Ally and Natalie say in unison, like it's the most obvious thing in the world.

'Crap, I should have thought of that,' Natalie says.

Ally looks at Natalie and smiles. 'You had everything

else covered,' she says. 'I wouldn't worry.' She doesn't scan the box, she just puts it in the bag. I open my mouth to speak, but she stops me by holding up her hands. 'Just let me know how it goes,' she says.

We pay and leave, my heart pounding hard in my chest as I walk out with the black bag, the logo emblazoned on it suddenly feeling like a neon light. I shove the bag into my rucksack. Buying the make-up was bravery enough for today.

'See?' Natalie says, squeezing my arm. 'You did it! How are you feeling?'

I take a breath. 'I'm OK.' But I'm still sort of freaking out and I wish I could just tell my body to calm down.

'In a weird way, that's the easy part,' she says.

'Huh?'

'You've got to use it now,' she says. 'Is your mum home? We can try it now if you want?'

'Really?'

Natalie shrugs. 'No time like the present. Plus I'm worried that if you don't do it now you'll lose your nerve. And it does take nerve.'

Nervous doesn't even begin to describe how I feel when I make it back to my house, Natalie in tow. Mum won't be in until later on this evening, so I have the whole place to myself. It's the perfect opportunity to try some of this out and then get it off my face before she gets home. The last thing I want is for her to see me in make-up. She panicked at the very idea of me going to a drag night, how would she react if she knew I was actually doing drag?

We grab drinks and head upstairs. I immediately boot up my laptop in the hope of finding a make-up tutorial that we can follow.

'Do you want to do it yourself, or should I do it for you?' Natalie asks. 'Like, what is the best way to do this?'

'I think I should do it myself,' I say. I want to at least try, even if it's going to be a disaster.

The video starts and I realize what an error we've made.

'We don't have any glue,' I say, pausing the video.

'What are you talking about?' Natalie asks.

'Look, she's glueing down her eyebrows with that purple glue stuff. I don't have any purple glue stuff,' I say. I'm annoyed. I shouldn't be annoyed but I'm totally annoyed.

'Do you have a Pritt Stick?'

'I am *not* putting Pritt Stick on my eyebrows!'

'But you'll put some random purple glue you've never even heard of on there?' Natalie raises an eyebrow to a perfect arch. 'Come *on*, Robin, are you kidding me?'

I sigh. 'Well, no, I don't have any Pritt Stick because, I mean, I haven't glued anything since I was, like, seven.'

'OK, OK, we don't need to panic about this. We can do without.'

'So I'll be a queen with these giant caterpillars on my face?' I don't know why I'm getting so bent out of shape about this. I think I'm looking for a way out. I feel stupid.

'We'll figure out the glue thing later – this is hardly going to be the last time you put make-up on,' she says. 'I mean, it won't be if you actually want to do this thing, so let's just calm down and focus on doing the rest of your face, OK?'

'OK.'

'And can we maybe breathe a little?' she suggests.

I nod and do as the tutorial suggests, apart from the eyebrow part. I'm still annoyed about the eyebrows. I should have thought about the eyebrows. I don't know how this queen has managed to do it but hers are lying so flat, you can*not* see them. It's like freaking magic.

I wet my make-up sponge and, just like the queen on the video, swipe the foundation on to my face before bouncing the sponge on it. I add the highlight, the contour, setting the face with powder, and it doesn't look horrible. I mean, for a first try, it isn't all that bad. Once the powder is on the contour is sort of gone, but you can see the shadow of it; there is a base there, even if it is a little rough around the edges.

'Am I allowed to be a tiny bit impressed with myself?' I say, looking in the mirror. 'It's not horrible, right?'

'No,' Natalie says with a smile. 'It's actually pretty good. I mean, you're well blended, so you have a good starting point at least.'

The tutorial continues and we start on the eyes. Suddenly everything seems a hell of a lot more complicated. I can't draw in a straight line, so my first bit of eyeliner looks like it's been put on with a Sharpie by a toddler. The powder under my eyes seems to be doing a decent job of catching fallout from the eyeshadow, but the colour isn't coming through like I want it to. What looked so vibrant on my wrist in the shop looks sort of dull on my eyelid, and I can't get the colours to blend in the same way the queen is.

When it comes to the second eye, things go from bad to worse. The eyeliner isn't as even as it should be, the eyeshadow blends better, but in a different place to where it did on the first eye, so now I'm sweating and panicking about it and—

The door opens and closes downstairs.

Natalie sits up sharply like a meerkat and I find myself staring at her, full deer in headlights realness, a deer with a half-painted mug and white powder all over the floor in front of her. And I mean a lot of powder. It looks like I'm either on coke or have a sudden obsession with sherbet and I honestly don't know which is worse.

'Oh my God,' I mutter. I look at myself in the mirror and

157

what a few moments ago had felt like a really good starting point for me suddenly looks messy, and just not at all right.

'Oh my gosh, your mum is going to love this,' Natalie says, a smile on her face. 'Maybe she can teach you to—'

'This isn't funny,' I interrupt, going into full panic stations. 'She can't see me like this.'

Natalie blinks, confused. I rummage in the bag trying to find something to clean the make-up off with. I pour way too much of the micellar water onto a cotton pad and attack my face with it like I've totally lost my mind.

'What? She already knows you're gay – what's the problem?'

'She got really weird about us going to Entity the other night,' I say. 'Like, panicky that I was going to get hurt or something. If she sees me in drag, I . . . I don't think she'll be mad, that's not her gig, but I don't want her to worry more than she already does.'

'OK, then.' Natalie takes a deep breath. 'What do you want me to do?'

'Can you clear this up?' I say, gesturing at the pile of make-up and brushes all over my carpet. 'In my drawer, just the top one.'

Natalie starts piling as much of the make-up as she can into my desk drawer. 'Oh, look! A Pritt Stick!'

'Shut UP!'

'Robin!' Mum's voice comes from downstairs. If I'd have kept quiet instead of screeching like a howler monkey, then she wouldn't have even known I was here. 'You home, sweetie?'

'We're upstairs, Mrs Cooper!' Natalie calls.

'What are you doing?' I hiss, scraping at my eye with a cotton pad, annoyed at the cinematic parallels to what happened between me and Connor. Maybe *I* should jump out of the window this time.

'It's weirder if we don't answer!' she hisses back, grabbing a cotton pad and going at my face too.

I can hear her footsteps on the stairs. I check my face in the mirror, scrubbing at the remnants of foundation in the stubble along my jawline. I didn't even shave before doing this. I was so unprepared. Christ.

Just as I throw the last cotton pad in the bin and Natalie throws herself across the mess of powder on the carpet, the door opens and Mum appears, her face smiley, open, me a little bleary-eyed, my whole face no doubt covered in a sheen of cleansing water. The smile is wiped from her face so fast I'm suddenly unsure it was even there in the first place.

'Robin, are you OK?'

'Um . . .' I can't form words. There isn't a single thing that I think I can say in this moment that would explain the current state of my face. 'I—'

'Mrs Finch has been getting on his case today,' Natalie says. 'So we came back here and started talking about it and Robin got a little upset.'

Mum offers me a sad smile. 'Well, rest assured I'm going to give that old hag a piece of my mind when I see her.' She looks to Natalie. 'You want to stay for dinner, hun? I'm making curry.'

'World-famous?' I ask, finding my voice.

She snorts. 'Of course, nothing but the best.'

'Sure,' Natalie replies. 'That would be nice.'

Mum heads downstairs and I instantly feel guilty for keeping this from her. That's not how we do things. We share basically everything, and this is probably only the third thing in my whole life that I've kept from her, the first two being 1) that I'm gay, which she now knows, and 2) Connor, which I don't know if she'll ever know.

'What are you thinking?' Natalie asks. I look over at her and she's brushing the powder from her T-shirt, the remnants falling on the floor. Surely the sign of the truest of true friends is someone who would throw themselves over a pile of setting powder for you.

I sigh and smile. 'Just that I'm lucky to have you – that's all.'

She makes a retching sound. 'You're gross,' she says. 'And you have foundation in your hairline.'

FOURTEEN

As I'm locking up my bike at school the following morning, I see Connor approaching. We've not really spoken since the Sunday incident and I don't know how ready I am to talk about it.

'Hey,' he says, looking around, double-checking and triple-checking that no one has seen him come in the bike sheds. 'You all right?'

'Yeah,' I say. 'You?'

He shrugs. 'I wanted to apologize again for Sunday,' he says. 'I swear they said they were going out.'

'It's OK,' I say. 'Couldn't be helped.'

He steps a little closer to me. 'Maybe, if you're free this weekend—'

There's a clanging sound on the fence nearby, probably just somebody rushing past, but Connor jumps back and it kills whatever moment he was trying to create. He smiles at me, trying to regain his composure. 'I'll message you.'

'OK.'

And, quicker than anything, he slips away and back

towards school. I want the ground to swallow me up right now.

'Did something scare him off?' Greg is at the entrance to the bike sheds. 'I've never seen him move so quick.'

'I think he heard someone coming so . . .' I trail off. I can't talk about this with Greg. 'How are you?'

'Don't deflect,' he says. 'How is lover boy this morning?'

'Please don't, Greg. I'm not in the mood,' I say.

'Neither is he, unless you're under cover of darkness and completely alone,' he says. 'Remind me how many times he's had to sneak out of your bedroom window?'

'It's far too early for this shit. Can we not?'

'Sorry.'

'Don't be.'

'I was only teasing. I . . . I didn't know you were . . .' And I don't know what Greg's going to say. Maybe he's getting the sense that I'm a bit sick of it. And I'd be lying if I said I wasn't. 'I'm only looking out for you, I swear. I don't want you—'

'Good morning, you two!' Natalie squeaks, bounding up to us. 'You are never going to *believe* the night I had.'

'Christ, do I want to know?' I ask. Smile on, defences up.

'I was looking up make-up tutorials for you,' she says. 'I want to see you as done up as basically everyone who has ever entered the Werkroom.' She turns to Greg. 'It turns out he's quite good at it. The boy can blend.'

Greg blinks. 'If I knew what that meant, I would applaud you, Robin.'

Nat rolls her eyes. 'God, you're clueless.'

Just a little way ahead of us, I see Seth walking towards school, his blond hair bouncing as he walks and, oh my God, is he actually wearing a leather jacket? Christ. I almost want to pinch myself or check with Natalie that I'm not dreaming this boy up in my head.

'Robin? Have I completely lost you to——' Natalie clocks where my gaze is. 'Oh, I see. Christ, is that a leather jacket?'

'Uh-huh,' I say.

'Hey, Seth!' Natalie calls out. He stops and turns round, taking off his headphones. He waves and his shirt lifts a little and be still my beating heart. 'Do you have chills?'

He blinks and looks down at the jacket. A smile crosses his face. 'Yeah, they're multiplying.'

'I like the jacket,' Natalie says.

'Do you?' he asks as we get a little closer. 'Because, if I didn't know any better, I'd say you were making fun of me.'

Natalie fake gasps. 'Me? No, I wouldn't. I'm just an innocent flower. I'd never do such a thing.'

Seth scoffs. 'Innocent flower, huh? Venus flytrap more like?'

'Ooh, did the attitude come with the jacket or did you

need to pay extra for it?' she teases, and he laughs and I'm standing here with Greg watching the two of them flirting, wishing I were dead. How the heck does she do that? I go near him and get tongue-tied, Natalie goes near him and . . . well . . . wow.

'Sorry, I've gotta run,' he says. He looks at me for what is probably the first time since he stopped. 'See you guys later.'

He walks away and I stare at Natalie. She shrugs and we carry on into the school.

I'm distracted when I get home. I try to work, but I can't concentrate. I can't sit still. All of this excess energy from not dancing is rushing through my body. There is a part of me that wants to go back, but right now I can't. It all feels too tainted. A little too close to my failure. I pick up my phone and check my messages. Among them, I find one from Priya.

> Seriously, babe, dancing isn't the same without you! Come back to me!

> Soon!

I don't know how soon, but soon is the best I can hope for.

I hop on to my bed and lose myself in some drag videos

for a while, rewatching Kaye Bye, stalking her online, following her on every platform possible. And then Seth's face pops into my head.

I google him, feeling an instant rush of nervous energy when I do it. I don't know where it's come from. It turns out he's not easy to find – there are a lot of Seth Harrises on Instagram – but thankfully I'm persistent and would rather do this than think about my trainwreck of a life. His page is mostly black and white, a lot of line drawings of skylines, a couple of people if you scroll further back, artsy photographs of himself, of landscapes. He's an artist. Of course he's an artist – why would he not be an artist?

There are a few group photos dotted around. Some with two other boys who look like they could be his brothers, another with a man and a woman who are one hundred per cent his parents. He looks exactly like his dad.

My finger hovers over the follow button. But we don't know each other. We've only just met and I don't want to scare him off. So I just scroll until I can't scroll any more.

I must be out of my mind. I message Connor.

> You around?

I wait for the three dots. And now I really know that I'm out of my mind here. My phone buzzes and I jump.

But it's Natalie sending me a video.

> Start here.

> Honestly can't wait to see you
> in full Trixie Mattel get up.

I click the link and watch Trixie doing her make-up on a budget. She makes it seem easy. Mum isn't home, so I could at least try this out.

After last time, I ordered the purple glue online, but it hasn't arrived yet so Pritt Stick will have to do.

I watch the tutorial again, finding out just how difficult it is to get my eyebrows to lie flat and, after following step by step, brush stroke by brush stroke, I have an incredibly messy desk and a totally finished face. It doesn't look half bad.

I snap a picture and send it to Natalie.

> BITCH!

> YES!

> It's OK?

> Honey, you are a WORK! OF! ART!

My phone buzzes in my hand. My heart jumps and I curse it. Connor.

> Maybe. Is your mum home?

She's not. She won't be home until later tonight and I'm sat here looking like a wigless Trixie Mattel copycat. I could remove this face and tell Connor the house is free, have him over and forget everything that's happened. But there's a niggling in the pit of my stomach and a picture of Seth in my head that is telling me not to do that.

> She's just got home. Sorry. Maybe some other time.

Natalie's encouragement gives me the painting bug. I double-check Mum's shifts and start to paint my face as often as I can. It's a long process to get things to go right, to get my eyebrows flat, to get the contour in the right place. But every time I do it I get a little better, and every time I follow a tutorial I get closer and closer to looking like the queen at the end rather than a busted mess.

The process is weirdly calming, and a pretty decent

distraction from the other things in my life. When I'm painting my face, I'm not thinking about my current chaos, I'm just thinking about the face.

You free?

Hey.

Hey????

I ignore message after message from Connor as the days go by, instead filling my group chat with Natalie and Greg with photos of the faces I've been painting. Natalie replies exuberantly to them with gratuitous emojis; Greg does the absolute best he can. But I know I need more than paint: I need to ask for help. It's Natalie who tells me where I need to go.

Priya, TELL ME you're at the studio tomorrow night.

FIFTEEN

Walking up to the studio for the first time in over a week is pretty daunting. Priya told me she would be here and was more than happy to help. I just have to convince Miss Emily that I'm not totally hopeless first.

'She's going to be fine,' Priya says. 'Honestly, she'll just be glad you're back. I've not told her, by the way.'

'She's probably worked it out?'

Priya shrugs. 'Maybe.' She checks her watch. 'You've got ten minutes – go see her now. I'll wait out here.'

I knock on the office door and Miss Emily calls to come in. She's sitting on the edge of her desk, and her eyes widen when she sees me walk in. It's a pretty big office because she shares it with all the other teachers at the school, each one of them with a desk, but somehow it feels tiny now that it's just the two of us in here, her eyes fixed on me.

'There was me thinking I was never going to see you again,' she says. 'From four classes a week to none. That was some illness.'

'Yeah,' I say. 'I wasn't sick. I . . .' I trail off. God, it still hurts to say it.

'You didn't get into LAPA,' she says.

I try not to let the disappointment appear on my face. Instead I take a breath and paint on that smile.

'No,' I say. 'How did you know?'

'Dan got an acceptance letter last week, so I just assumed,' she says. It's an absolute punch to the gut. He's another boy in our class. 'I'm sorry, Robin. How are you feeling?'

'I'm OK,' I lie. 'I'm figuring it out.'

'Honestly?'

I laugh. 'Honestly?' I repeat. 'Honestly, whenever I think about it, I feel like I'm about to shatter into a thousand pieces.' But I say it with a smile. I keep up the facade. Everything is fine, I'm laughing, I'm joking, it's all right.

She blinks a couple of times like she's trying to process the disconnect between the words I'm saying and the look on my face. Maybe she goes off my look, maybe. Somehow, I'm telepathically asking her not to talk about it any more because it might kill me.

'You'll figure it out,' she says, smiling. 'Of course you will.' She checks her watch. 'Right, to the studio then. If there's one thing you need right now, it's a dance class.'

The class is hard. Even with just a week out, I'm

170

struggling to get back into it. I'm nervous before every step, worried I can't do it, analysing every little thing that I do, like there is another me outside of my body criticizing my every move.

The girls are dancing in their New Yorkers tonight, a three-inch beige heel, and I watch them a little more intently than usual. Their balance is, by some divine miracle, the same as it is when they are dancing in bare feet or a jazz shoe, and I can't figure out why. All I know is that I want to try. That's what I'm here for.

Priya looks godlike, T-shirt flowing, leg kicking so high she could whack herself in the face if she wasn't in total control. She turns to me at the end of the class.

'How did it go?' she asks.

'She was fine,' I say. 'Just wanted to get me dancing again.'

'And are you feeling any better?'

I shrug and paint my smile back on. I know I don't need to hide in front of Priya, but I don't want to be a downer. I'm trying to keep looking forward, focus on what can be, not what hasn't been. 'Some days are better than others. Today is a good day. Dancing feels good.'

She smiles. 'Good. You'll get in next year. What do I want? A famous husband! When do I want him? ASAP!'

'You don't seem to need a famous husband just now,' I

say, raising an eyebrow. 'How is Greg?'

Her face bursts into a grin. 'Oh, he's yummy, where did you find him?'

I shrug. 'He just appeared one day. We keep him around because he's cute.'

'He certainly is that!' she says, heading towards the door. 'Are you coming?'

'I just want to talk to Miss Emily,' I say. 'I won't be long.'

Miss Emily is standing at the sound system. She looks up, surprised that I'm still here. She narrows her eyes, fixing me with that stare that tells me she knows something is going on.

'You need to stop overthinking it.'

'Huh?'

'All of this,' she says. 'It'll drive you mad.'

'It might have already,' I say.

'What's up?' she asks.

'You know how the girls were dancing in heels tonight?' I start. 'Do you think I could do that?'

She blinks. I find it hard to believe she's never had a boy want to dance in heels before, but this is Essex, after all. She seems a little unsure.

'Can I ask why?' she asks. I feel suddenly uncomfortable.

'Drag,' I say. 'I'm . . . I'm trying something new and if I'm going to do it then I need to be able to move in a heel. Plus, you know, there are so many shows around these days that need boys that can . . .' I trail off and I know I'm babbling, my nerves getting the better of me.

She looks off into the distance, towards the windows where the light of the day is fading away into glorious purples and oranges. A smile tugs at the corners of her mouth. She loves a challenge as much as I do. She managed to whip me into shape in flat shoes, she's probably wondering if she can manage it in a three-inch heel. I know I am.

'Stay here,' she says, slipping out of the room and quickly returning with a pair of tan heels that look positively giant. 'You're a ten, right?'

I nod.

'Try these on.'

I slip them on my feet and do up the buckle. I can't help but laugh a little as I look at my slightly hairy man feet in these quite dainty shoes. It's a strange image. And looking in the mirrors makes it seem stranger as my eyes travel up my hairy legs to my dance shorts. I mean, my legs have never looked so fantastic in all my life.

'First things first. Can you walk in them?' she asks, plugging in her phone and putting on some music.

If I'm totally honest, I don't know the answer to this question. Standing there, I feel this odd sense of power. I'm already six foot tall, so adding the extra inches would make me tower over anybody who walks through that studio door. Miss Emily looks tiny next to me now.

I take a step, pitching my weight into the balls of my feet.

'That's right, keep your weight forward,' Emily calls over the pounding bass. 'Use your arms, it might help.'

My arms seem to gain a life of their own, out to one side to balance me, or instinctively finding my waist as I walk back and forth in the studio. It's hard, though not entirely impossible. I stumble once or twice, but I manage to recover before I fall.

The song changes and I look up and see Miss Emily walking towards me, her heels on, her face determined.

'The routine from earlier, you remember it.' It's not a question. 'Let's go. Be careful. If you can't hack the pirouette at the end, prepare it and we'll figure it out later.'

'So you'll help me?' I ask.

She snorts and rolls her eyes. 'I'm struggling to think of a situation where I wouldn't do my absolute best to help you,' she says. 'Five, six, seven, eight.'

We dance, and I mean we dance hard. It's not easy dancing in heels. This routine was hard to begin with, let alone being pretty much on my tiptoes the entire time. But I make it through, sweaty, tired, and with some minor ankle pain.

'Oh, ho-ney!' Priya is at the door, the biggest smile on her face. 'Yes!'

I can't help but smile, a giggle coming from my mouth before I can stop it. 'Good?' I ask.

'Looked pretty good to me,' Priya says. 'Do you mind if I . . . ?' She gestures to the room and I beckon her in.

'It wasn't bad,' Miss Emily says as she goes over to her phone to stop the song. 'I mean, you need to work on it, but that's why you asked for my help.'

'So what do I do now?' I ask.

'Well, when the girls put on their heels, you can either put those on or not, it's totally up to you,' she says. 'And if you don't want to do that, you can just practise after the class is over. I always have paperwork to do so I can teach you some things and then leave you to your own devices until I have to close up.'

I can't help but smile at her. She's the best. She really is. She totally doesn't need to do all this for me, but I'm super glad that she is.

'Can we . . . um . . . can I just use the studio time rather than dancing in front of the rest of the class? It might be . . . weird.'

'Is this for your drag thing?' Priya asks.

'Greg told you?'

175

'He mentioned it,' she says. 'You need to show me these faces you've been painting.'

'You want to stay now?' Emily asks me. 'The studio is free for another hour.'

'If that's OK?'

'Can I stay too?' Priya asks.

Miss Emily turns to me. 'If Robin doesn't mind, I don't.'

'Yeah, that's fine with me,' I say, knowing just how much I can learn from Priya.

Miss Emily smiles. 'I'll leave you two to it.'

Days pass by and seem to blur into a mixture of late nights dancing in heels at the studio, even later nights painting my face and entire days struggling to give two shits about school.

'Robin?' I look up and see that Seth has turned round in his seat. I do my best not to look at him all gooey-eyed, but when he's smiling at me like that it's pretty much impossible.

'Yeah?' I say.

'Do you have a pen?'

'Sure.'

I hand him my pen.

'Do you not need this?' he says, looking at me sceptically.

'Yes,' I reply. 'Yes, I do.'

Natalie groans next to me and hands him a pen from her

pencil case. 'Here you go, Seth,' she says. 'If I don't get it back, I'm coming for you.'

'Duly noted,' he says, turning back round and carrying on with . . . well . . . with whatever it is Mr Goldberg has asked us to do.

'What are we supposed to be doing?' I whisper to Natalie.

'We have an essay due next Monday morning,' she says. 'The question is on the board. Where is your head at?'

'Not in this classroom,' I mumble, writing down the question, which is the only thing that I have written down for this entire hour of class. Christ, I really was letting myself get distracted.

The bell rings and before Mr Goldberg can stop anyone, we're all out of our seats and heading for the door.

'So, if your head isn't in the classroom, where is it?'

'I think the question is, "How's your head?"' I suggest.

'Ooh, avoiding the question,' she says. 'Come on, Boy Queen, tell me what's in that beautiful brain of yours.'

'Just drag stuff mostly,' I say. 'Dancing with Emily is going well. I mean, I've not fallen over yet and I can pretty much do it, I think. The make-up is looking better, right?'

'Right!' Natalie says. 'So how much is it going to take for you to put on your drag rags and take it to Entity?'

I almost choke on the air. 'No way. I'm not ready for that,' I splutter.

'OK,' she says. 'Then how about we just go there tomorrow then. It's not Dragcellence, but it will be fun. Might be nice to see what it's like when we're not obsessively staring at the queens. Greg said he'd come, said he'd bring Priya.'

'Really?'

'Yes,' Natalie says with a smile. 'Greg and Priya, sitting in a tree.'

'You be nice to him.'

'I will, I will, it's just adorable,' she says.

'Cool,' I say, taking a breath. 'And maybe this time I'll wear a little bit of make-up.'

She grips my arm tighter. 'Are you serious?'

'Yes,' I say. 'But just a bit. Boy brows, a little eyeshadow maybe and some highlight, nothing more.'

'If you go out without a lip on you might as well just stop breathing here and now,' she snarks.

'I will not stand for this abuse,' I retort. 'I said what I said.'

'Hey, Natalie.' Seth appears behind us, his blond hair perfect, his smooth skin perfect, his perfectly crooked teeth perfectly crooked. I realize I'm smiling at him like a lovesick puppy, but I don't really care because wow, pretty boy. He hands Natalie the pen. 'I didn't want you coming for me,' he says as she takes it.

'A wise boy,' she says, putting the pen in her jeans pocket.

'Where are you off to?' I ask him.

'Science block,' he says. 'But I had to give the pen back, so . . .' He trails off and we're just standing in the corridor staring at each other. But he's smiling, at least he's smiling. I want to say something clever, something that will make him laugh. But no words are forthcoming, and the longer we stay like this, the more uncomfortable I'm feeling.

'Well, I've got the pen now,' Natalie says, and we both snap to look at her.

'Uh, how are you settling in?' I ask, not wanting him to go yet. I can feel Natalie's eyes on me.

'Oh, it's all right,' he says. 'It's the same work I was doing before, just somewhere different. The school is still a maze, though.'

'I know, I swear the staircases move,' I say.

'What?' he says.

'Right, I have to go. Mrs Finch wants to talk to me about uni offers,' Natalie says. 'So, Entity tomorrow night, yes?'

'Entity?' Seth says. 'What's Entity?'

Natalie looks at him, almost like she's surprised he's still here. 'It's a gay club one town over, in Southford. Google it or whatever.'

He looks a little taken aback, but quickly shifts his face to a smile, a smile that is directed squarely at Natalie.

I literally may as well not be here.

'I'll . . . uh . . . see if I'm free,' he says, with a wink.

'Wow, never wink at me again,' Natalie says, but she laughs so he knows that she's kidding. 'Hang on, what did you say?'

'Right, got to get to class,' he says abruptly, raising a hand and waving goodbye to us before practically sprinting down the corridor. We both stare after him.

'What just happened?' she asks.

'I think you just asked Seth out tomorrow night,' I say. 'And I think he just said yes.'

SIXTEEN

I'm not painted by any means – far from it, in fact. But I'm wearing the matte foundation powder I normally reserve for dance shows, the smallest amount of eyeliner and a little bit of colour on my eyelids. It's the lightest drag make-up I have done so far.

'You look *really* nice,' Greg says with a sort of gormless smile on his face. It's like he's never seen make-up before. Honestly, straight boys can be so adorable sometimes. 'Like, the colour really brings out your eyes.'

'Careful, Greg,' Natalie says, a warning tone in her voice. 'There are going to be a lot of boys at Entity tonight – you're going to have competition.'

'Leave him alone,' I say, unable to stop the fizzing in my stomach. 'He's just rehearsing his compliments for Priya.'

'Oh *please*, I'm nicer than that!' Greg says. 'She does have really nice eyes, though.'

'Is she coming?' I ask.

'She's going to try to make it after class,' Greg says. 'But she isn't sure. She might have work to do.'

'Well, I hope she comes,' I say. 'You two are sweet.'

Greg grins, like properly cheesy-grins. He does a lot of that when Priya gets mentioned.

'What about Seth?' Greg asks. 'Is he coming?'

I look at Natalie. 'What are you looking at me for?' she asks. 'How would I know?'

'You invited him,' I say.

'Hardly,' she says. 'I mentioned that we were going and he basically invited himself. Besides, he's not going to come. He's barely showing up to school – why would he meet us at a gay club?'

When we get out of the cab in Southford, I feel suddenly exposed. I'm nervous about going outside like this. The fizzing in the pit of my stomach won't go away.

Natalie links her arm in mine, as if she can sense the nerves crashing over me like waves threatening to drag me under. She squeezes tightly, supportive little thing that she is.

'You got this, Travis,' she whispers. 'Make 'em wait for it.'

I laugh. 'Boom?'

She nods. 'Boom.'

Greg tuts. 'You two are gross.'

Priya meets us just outside Entity, kissing Greg on the cheek and linking her arm in his as we approach, two by two.

Entity looks like some kind of holy ground from this distance. I can't believe people just walk past it, managing to ignore the music coming from inside, the sounds that scream SANCTUARY to any rainbow sibling wandering by. I can't keep the smile off my face as we approach, the same bouncer from a couple of weeks ago checking our IDs and letting us inside with a warm smile and a polite nod of his head.

I am taken slightly aback when I see a heavyset man onstage in a navy shirt, chest hair poking out from the collar, a microphone in his hand as he wails his way through a Queen song. It's not the kind of voice you'd expect to come out of him at all, but it's freaking gorgeous.

'Wow,' I breathe.

'He's amazing!' Greg's face is lit up like a Christmas tree. 'I didn't know people sang here.'

'You a singer, Greg?' Priya asks.

Greg snorts. 'No. Professional watcher of singers, is more like it.'

'It's open mic – I think they do it every week,' Natalie says with a shrug. 'Who wants a drink?' She doesn't wait for us to answer, heading over to the bar and leaning across it to make her order.

There is a tap on my shoulder and I turn round.

'Hello!'

I stop dead. Seth is here and Seth is talking to me. It takes my brain a second to process.

'Fancy seeing you here!' he says, smiling. I've never seen someone so happy to see me. It throws me off balance. I replay the conversation we had yesterday, the one where he winked at Natalie and acted all coy about his schedule.

'What are you doing here?' I shout over the music, having to lean in a little closer to him. I can smell his cologne. I don't know what it is, but it's musky and breathing it in makes me feel a little weak.

'Natalie invited me, remember?' he says.

'Right,' I say. 'Of course.' I feel like the physical embodiment of the noise a balloon makes when you let go of it.

He must notice my disappointment because he looks really confused now. 'I thought you might be glad to see me here.'

Now it's my turn to look confused and I wonder if I should just ask him if he likes boys or not. A question every queer person gets asked at one point or another for the rest of their lives; whether it's clarifying your partner's gender or having to watch someone realign everything they think about you in a split second when they realize you're not hetty AF. But I've got to know.

'Seth, I need to ask you something—'

'Hey, buy a girl a drink first,' he interrupts with a laugh.

'So you're . . . I mean . . . you like . . .' I gesture around. It's a roundabout way of asking him without actually asking him because, if his pre-out teenager years were anything like mine, he would have been asked this question a lot, by a lot of shitty people.

He laughs. 'Yeah.'

Be still my big, glittery heart.

'Cool,' I manage. 'That's cool.'

He grins. God he's cute when he grins. 'I'm really glad you think so. I was hoping you'd approve.' He sighs. 'One less thing to worry about when you're the new guy trying to fit in.'

'So, what's the deal with you being new?' I ask. 'I know Natalie tried to get it out of you when you first got here, but I'm definitely a little curious.'

'Like I said,' he says with a smile, though it seems a little more forced than the last one. 'It's a long story. And I don't want to monopolize you.'

'You wouldn't be.'

He sighs. 'Robin—'

'If you don't want to talk about it, that's fine,' I say.

'Tonight isn't really the night for it.' He smiles at me and I smile at him and maybe I'm drunk off the moment, but there is an energy between us that I swear I can see sparking on the air. It makes me want to get closer to him, to take up a little more of the space between us.

Someone knocks into him on their way to the bar or the bathroom and I see that veneer of cool slip from his face as he tries not to spill his drink on me. And we're so close now that I can feel the heat radiating off him and fucking hell did it just get warm in here?

Our eyes lock and he seems as aware of the lack of space between us as I am. A smile twitches at the corner of his mouth and it brightens my actual soul. Don't ask me how. I smile back. I can't help it.

The guy onstage finishes singing behind us, wondering if anybody can find him somebody to love. The crowd goes a tiny bit wild, which knocks us out of whatever magnetic force was holding us together.

We step apart and turn our attention back to the stage, our arms touching, and it's the tiniest bit of contact, but apparently I'm needy enough that it sends my stomach absolutely wild. I look over at him and he's looking at me. We both quickly look away and I feel so alive that I want to die.

'You ready?' Natalie says, handing me a drink. There is a mysterious grin on her face. 'Oh, Seth,' she says, drawing out the name, making it all sing-songy. 'You here to see Robin perform?'

I turn my head so sharply I swear I give myself whiplash. I look from her to the stage and back again.

'What are you talking about?' I hiss.

'The open mic?' she says. 'Yes. You are getting up there and performing. I couldn't let you and your boy drags go to waste.'

'Nat, I don't know. I—'

'Come on, if I'd have asked, you would have said no!'

'So you've decided to just throw me to the lions? Thanks a million, Nat,' I grumble. 'What am I supposed to do up there?'

'Hmmm,' Natalie says, putting a finger to her chin and looking skyward. 'I wonder what the actor-dancer-SINGER could do at an open mic.' She punches me in the arm. 'Sing out, Louise!'

'I didn't know you were a singer,' Seth says, reminding me he is there and I look like a total dick right now.

'Can you be called a singer if you don't sing?' Natalie postures.

'Stop it.'

'Come on,' she groans. 'It's just a suggestion. You go up there, you sing a song – what's the worst that could happen?'

'The worst that could happen?' I repeat. 'The worst that could happen is that I could burst into flames and die. I'm unprepared, I'm not warmed up, I'm—'

'Making excuses,' Natalie says. 'Look, you can go and get your name taken off the list if you want but someone needs to get you to bounce back, OK? So bounce the fuck back, or bounce.'

She stares me down. I love singing, I really do, but if I'd known I was doing this I would have prepared something, rather than just going up there, plugging my phone in and hoping for the best.

I take a breath. I can totally do this. I'm frantically searching for the Robin I was before and coming up with nothing, so it looks like I'll just have to fake it.

'OK,' I say, pulling my phone out of my pocket, scrolling through the instrumentals I have. 'But I'm still a little bit mad at you for doing this,' I add.

'Understandable,' Natalie says. 'But you can thank me later.' She walks away, heading in the direction of Greg and Priya, making eyes at Seth and I as she goes.

'You're looking a little green,' Seth says, which pulls my attention back to him. He is smiling at me, trying his best to be supportive in the face of my breakdown. 'Maybe you should get some air before they call your name,' he adds. 'The last thing you want to do is go up there and vom.'

I blink. 'Is this you giving me a pep talk?'

'It was meant to be.' He chuckles. 'Definitely not my finest. Can I try again?'

'Shoot.'

'You've totally got this,' he says.

'You've never even heard me sing before.' And something about this is calming me down, something about the way he is looking at me, the way his eyes twinkle a little bit in the limited light.

'I know,' he says with a shrug. 'But Natalie wouldn't put you up for this if she thought you were going to be shit. She's your friend – she wouldn't want to embarrass you.'

'True.'

'And I'm excited to hear you sing,' he says, flashing me that smile again. 'It's not what I was expecting for my night out, but sometimes unexpected is better, right?'

That is quite possibly the dorkiest thing I have ever heard, but I kind of want to write it into a journal over and over and over again until it's imprinted on my soul.

'Thanks, Seth,' I say. 'I'm going to step outside. Do you . . . want to join me? You can keep working on your pep-talk skills.'

He smiles. 'Sure,' he says. 'I'll meet you out there.'

'OK.'

I work my way through the crowd, glad to be out in the night air when it hits me with the slightest chill. I keep my head down, trying not to let anyone see my face. It's one thing to be in Entity wearing make-up, but out on the

189

street alone I feel exposed. I start to hum quietly to myself, a desperate attempt at a warm-up.

I decide on a song, 'Feeling Good' by Michael Bublé in a pretty high key. If I'm going to sing in front of Seth, I might as well try something impressive.

The streets are a little more crowded than they were earlier. Sure, it's not as bad as it would be if we'd come down here for Dragcellence, but this town has a thriving nightlife during the week because of the nearby universities and colleges. I'm nervous, Mum's words echoing in my head, but I keep my head down, keep on pacing, keep on humming.

'Robin?'

I look up and am suddenly face to face with Connor. Connor who I've not spoken to in days. Connor who has stopped trying to catch my eye at school. And now he's saying my name like nothing has changed. And I can feel myself getting sucked back in.

He is smiling at first, but then his face twists into a look of absolute disgust. I look around him, looking for his friends. Is he out here alone?

'What are you doing?' Connor hisses.

'What do you—?'

'What are you doing here? What's . . . ?' He trails off and looks at my face. He can't find the words and I suddenly realize what I must look like to him. A boy standing in the middle of town, a face covered in bright colours, a war paint that is supposed to make me fearless, but which right now makes me want to curl up into a ball and die. 'Why are you wearing *that*?'

'The make-up?' I ask dumbly. Of course the make-up.

'What do you think I'm talking about?' he hisses. 'You look weird . . . like a . . . What are you doing, Robin? It's disgusting.'

The word is like a dagger in my chest. It punctures my heart and I bleed out any bit of confidence the make-up had given me when I'd first put it on.

'Disgusting?!' I echo. It comes out like a squeak. I expect him to say something else, to correct himself, to apologize, but he's just staring at me.

'What the fuck are you doing here?' A new voice comes from nearby. Connor is still staring at me, his mouth a little open. He doesn't know what to say. 'Oi, queerbait, I'm talking to you.'

I turn my head, ever so slightly, and see that Connor isn't alone. I was so focused on him, so fixated, I didn't even think to check my surroundings, to be careful like we usually are.

Ryan appears at Connor's side, his eyes locked on me, wide, angry. He was there when it happened the first time.

Oh shit, what was I thinking coming outside? Connor's other friends are around him too. Thomas, Sean, Will, Zach, every one of them staring at me.

'I was just—'

'Speak up!' Zach shouts.

'I'm here,' I say, pointing behind me at Entity. 'I'm here with my friends.'

'Faggot boy at the little faggot club with his faggot friends?' Ryan spits. The other lads laugh, backing him up. Every time he says that word it's like a thousand cuts.

'Ryan . . .' Connor starts.

'What? This little faggot trying it on with you?' he grunts. Another thousand.

Connor looks past Ryan to me. 'Yeah,' he says. 'Little faggot.' Another thousand. Though coming from Connor, more like a million.

It's a word I can't stand. I hate giving power to words, but that one gets me something rotten. And I can feel my eyes filling up because I don't know what to do, and I don't know what to say, and I'm thrown back to what happened over the summer and have no idea how to defend myself right now because all I can think is how it shouldn't be happening *here*.

This is supposed to be a sanctuary. How can it be that I'm only a metre away from the doors and I'm already having this kind of shit thrown at me, just because I've got a bit of make-up on my face. Is this what the world is like? We get these little pockets of queerness to thrive in, but the rest of it is a straight man's playground and they can call me that word if they want. Why are there people walking by on the street, watching this happen? Watching as Ryan steps closer to me, getting right up in my face now while I cower away, desperate to go back to Entity, back to the safety of those four walls.

'Hey!' I turn to see Seth hurrying down the steps of the club and pushing himself between me and Ryan. 'Leave him alone.'

'Or what?'

'Just leave him alone,' Seth growls.

'Something going on here, fellas?' I turn my head and it's the bouncer. He's bigger than Ryan, taller, broader, built like a brick shithouse, with the most perfect poreless skin you've ever seen on any human being. He puts a hand on my shoulder. 'You all right?'

'No,' I squeak.

'On your way, lads, come on,' he says, ushering them away, stepping in front of Seth. Ryan and his friends start to disperse, heading off down the street into the night, but Connor is still standing there, squaring up to Seth. 'Back inside, fella,' the bouncer says to Seth. 'It's not worth it — trust me.'

I look at Connor, watching him blur and ripple through the tears in my eyes. He is still looking at me like my very existence is disgusting to him. Like a giant beacon asking me what the hell I was thinking. He opens his mouth. He closes it. He walks away.

'You OK?' Seth puts a solid hand on my shoulder and it grounds me somehow, but it doesn't make me feel any better. I must still look like I'm about to shatter into a million pieces because he cautiously pulls me into a hug. 'It's all right.'

'It's not all right,' I sniff. 'It's really not.'

'Who was that? Do you know him?'

'Robin?' a voice calls from Entity, and I pull myself away from Seth to see Natalie poking her head out of the door. She sees me and I catch the smile before it vanishes. She looks confused. I can hardly blame her – I was hugging Seth when she stepped outside. She quickly rights herself. 'They're calling your name. It's time to show them what you've got.'

SEVENTEEN

What I've got.

Show them what I've got.

All I've got right now are nerves that are rattled and a whole lot of issues that no audience or therapist has enough time to work out, at least not tonight.

'Robin?' Natalie says again, because I've not moved. She hurries over to me, grabbing my hand.

'I don't know if this is such a good idea,' Seth says as she starts to lead me back towards Entity, but I shoot him a warning glance, willing him to keep quiet about what's just happened.

'What?' Natalie snaps.

'Look at him – he's shaking,' Seth says.

'He's just nervous.' Natalie is looking at me with hopeful eyes and I don't want to disappoint her. 'Come on, they're waiting for you.'

I nod. I turn my smile back on, try to make everything look fine because I don't want to worry anybody, but behind the smile I'm scrambling. My brain runs through a million and one scenarios, every single one of them giving me a way out. But I stay quiet and let Natalie lead me back inside and up on to the stage. She heads back over to where Greg and Priya are standing.

I hand my phone to the little techie, who nods and plugs it in, getting the song going before I have a chance to say anything.

Natalie is smiling, so are Greg and Priya, both of them sending all the good vibes they possibly can from over at the bar. Seth is with them and he's forcing a grin on to his face, but he looks worried, like he knows this isn't going to end well.

It's disgusting.

I open my mouth to sing and . . . well . . . something comes out. It's not the sound I'm used to, not the usual power behind it, the usual confidence that I have when I perform this song. Where has that Robin gone? It's Michael Bublé. He's cocky when he performs, he's a badass (you know . . . sort of). The way to do it is big and bold, but I'm up here like a mouse, barely whispering the words.

Natalie knows something is wrong. The encouraging look has vanished from her face and been replaced by big, concerned eyes. The bridge comes and the notes aren't there and I am butchering this song in front of the entire room.

People start talking, whispering to one another, maybe

wondering what the hell I'm doing, what I'm playing at, why I even bothered to get up here, and I want to explain to them what happened outside.

It's disgusting.

I want to wipe the make-up off my face, wipe this entire night from existence. Is there a make-up wipe big enough?

It's disgusting.

I wipe a tear from my eye because now I'm crying apparently, unable to stop the tears from falling down my face because this is horrible. I'm hot and embarrassed and wishing the song away, but it is the longest four minutes of my life.

I push into the last chorus, battling my way towards the final note, which I reach for and miss by a mile. Natalie can't hide the disappointment on her face, Greg winces, Seth is still trying to look supportive, still trying to smile, but it's a struggle.

The song ends and the applause is modest to say the least. And I rush from the stage before they can even call another name, before anything else can happen to make this night worse. But I don't go to my friends, I don't go to Seth, I hurry back outside because this doesn't feel like a sanctuary right now. It feels like a nightmare.

I push through the doors and into the night, turning down the alleyway down the side of the pub and leaning against the wall. Tears roll down my face, but I try not to make a sound. I don't want anybody's attention right now; I just want to disappear. I should have just said no when Natalie told me it was happening.

'You forgot your phone.' There is a voice to my left. I look up and see a man holding it out to me. It's the techie. He's taken his glasses off and is smiling at me sadly. 'Come on, hun, I haven't got all night.'

'Sorry,' I say, taking it from him. And I'm not sure if I'm apologizing for the shitshow of a performance I just did or for keeping him waiting. 'I forgot it . . .'

The man chuckles. 'No,' he says. 'And there was me thinking it was a parting gift or something.' He's still there. What does he want, a tip? 'Are you OK?'

'Oh me?' I say, sniffing. 'Yeah, I'm fine, perfect, never better.'

'Ooh, she's a feisty one, huh?' he says, stepping a little closer.

'I messed it up,' I say. 'It happens, right? Everybody has bad performances.'

'Well, sure, but usually they just shrug them off and carry on, not have a full diva breakdown in an alleyway outside the klerb,' he says, folding his arms and pouting. 'Seriously, hun, you don't seem OK. You seem like you're on the verge.' He looks around. 'Where the hell are your friends?'

I sigh. 'Probably waiting for me to be less dramatic,' I say. 'Or waiting until I come out of hiding. I mean, I did just come down this alleyway to hide.'

'You're shit at hiding. If they do an Olympics hide-and-seek, give it a miss, m'kay?' he says.

He's still waiting, his eyes still fixed on me. Is he waiting for me to calm down? Does he want me to come back inside?

'I'm honestly fine,' I say. 'You don't have to wait for me. Don't you have to get the next act on?'

'We're taking a break,' he says. 'That performance was a lot to process.'

'Tell me about it.'

'You were there,' he says. 'Some of it wasn't horrible.'

'Great.'

'I mean, your make-up looked good when you started.'

I snort. 'What do you know?'

The man laughs. 'Oh, more than you'd think,' he says. He lifts my chin and looks into my face. 'What you need sweetheart, apart from a make-up wipe because *wow* she's a messy girl right now, is a little bit of eyeshadow primer on that lid,' he says. 'It works a treat. Those colours will really pop if you do that.' He claps his hands together, a smile stretching across his face. 'I have some upstairs in my dressing room, hang on.'

He rushes back inside, reappearing moments later with a

pack of make-up wipes and a small mirror. I take the make-up off, my face looking a little shiny and a lot red when I manage to get it all off.

'Thank you,' I whisper, my voice finally steadier. 'Why are you helping me?'

He shrugs. 'I don't know, sweetheart,' he says. 'You looked a little wounded and sometimes a girl has to do a good deed for a sister in need. Don't think for one second I do this for everyone. And maybe don't tell anybody that I helped you. I like to keep the idea that Kaye Bye is an almighty bitch as part of the persona.'

'What?'

'A persona, dear. It's like a personal brand but better because it just sounds more posh and less like a wannabe influencer.'

I blink. Hold on. What did he say?

'*You're* Kaye Bye?' I say, incredibly slowly, more slowly than is entirely necessary. I can hardly keep my breathing steady, so much for me calming down. 'Kaye Bye the drag queen who performs at Dragcellence?'

The man steps away from me and lifts his arm in a flourish, popping his leg and flashing his perfect teeth. 'The very same,' he coos. 'I see you've heard of me, all bad, I hope.'

I don't know what I expected Kaye Bye to look like out of

drag. As a boy he looks, well, unremarkable. He's wearing dark blue jeans and a plaid shirt, a little stubble across his chin. If I passed him on the street, I would have no idea. The only thing that really gives him away is that when he lifts his arm and smiles, I can actually see her, a glimpse of her at least, like she's absolutely busting to get out.

'I saw you a couple of weeks ago at Dragcellence,' I say, in a hurry. 'It was my birthday, and the absolute best thing I've ever seen. My friend took a video and I have watched it far too many times. You're incredible.'

'Oh well, darling, you're awful kind,' he says. 'And I do my best.'

'You made me want to do it,' I say. 'You're the reason I was here in a little bit of make-up. I've been painting my face, following tutorials, all sorts. I'm a theatre kid.'

He raises an eyebrow. 'You are?'

My face goes red hot. 'OK, tonight was not a good example,' I say. 'But usually I am.'

'And *I* made you want to do drag?' he says, placing a hand on his chest. 'Well, oh my stars, I am quite flattered, young man, thank you.' He checks his phone and sighs. 'OK, I need to head back inside, and you should too. Your friends are probably looking for you. Apparently this *is* a good hiding place.'

'OK,' I say. 'Thank you for bringing my phone back,'

I add. 'And it was a pleasure to meet you. You really are incredible. Like, I've never seen anything like what you do. It was amazing.'

He smiles and there she is again, bubbling up towards the surface. 'Well, thank you.' He curtseys and starts back towards Entity. He stops as he reaches the end of the alleyway, turning back to look at me carefully. 'Look, I don't normally do this because, like I said, Kaye isn't exactly the nicest of ladies.'

'Right.'

'But do you want to come back here tomorrow night?' he says. 'Come by early and we can talk about drag, talk make-up, wigs, heels, the whole shebang. I'll get you a ticket for the show too.'

'Really?' My heart flutters a little in my chest. He can't be serious. 'You're sure?'

'Absolutely,' he says. 'We need to look out for each other and if I can stop one baby drag queen from going out into the streets like a busted mess, then I'm doing a good deed.' He pauses. 'Not that you looked like a busted mess,' he says. 'You just cried your make-up all down your face and *then* looked like a busted mess. That we can fix.'

I don't know what to say.

'Sweetheart, you can speak. I won't bite,' he says.

'I'll be there,' I say. 'What time?'

'Well, the show starts at around eight thirty, so if you can get yourself here for four thirty we'll have time to chat and I might even let you watch me paint,' he says, winking and walking away. 'If you're looking for your boy, he's down there.'

Natalie appears at the end of the alleyway, Greg, Priya and Seth in tow. She runs towards me and wraps me in a hug, her grip so fierce it almost knocks the breath right out of me.

'I was so worried,' she says. 'I followed you outside, but you freaking vanished. The bouncer didn't even see you go – we were looking in town.'

'Sorry,' I mumble into her neck.

'I don't think you're the one who needs to be apologizing right now,' she says, pulling away and looking at my face. 'You've taken your make-up off.'

'Kaye had a wipe.'

She blinks. 'Kaye? Kaye as in Kaye Bye?'

I nod.

'Holy shit' she says. 'Well, I'm glad we didn't come outside and interrupt you getting to know Kaye Bye. Are you OK?' she adds. 'That performance was . . .' She trails off. We both know what it was. It's just whether or not I want her to know why it was the way it was.

'It wasn't my best moment,' I say, taking a deep,

shuddering breath. I look past Natalie's shoulder to Seth. 'I swear I'm better than that.'

He nods. 'Greg's been telling me.' Greg goes a little bit pink. 'We'll have to try again sometime.'

I nod. 'Let's go back inside.'

We go back inside and I'm fizzing. The knowledge that I'll be seeing Kaye Bye tomorrow night stops me from caring so much about the people eyeing me as I walk back in, people who probably think I'm shit and wonder why I even got up there. I can't hear them. I shift my focus. It will get me through.

EIGHTEEN

'OK,' Natalie says as she walks out of her front door the following morning. 'I feel freaking awful. Please don't tell me these auditions have ruined you forever because that would be *beyond* tragic.' She looks at me, eyes wide, waiting for me to fill in the blanks. I refused to talk about it last night, but now she's looking at me expectantly and either I tell her now and get it all out, or I hold it all in and feel like shit.

And while the words are on the tip of my tongue to tell her exactly what happened with Connor last night, I swallow each and every one of them. They taste like acid on the way down. The words have been running around my head all night, despite everything that happened with Kaye. *Disgusting. Faggot.* A constant loop of torment from a boy who is supposed to care about me.

'My nerves got the better of me, I think,' I say, blinking back tears, averting my gaze from Natalie. 'I saw Connor outside and realized what I was doing and got so, *so* nervous. It's honestly nothing. Stage fright.'

'You saw Connor?'

'He was with his friends,' I say. 'But that's nothing. It was the nerves. I just could have done with a little bit of warning that it was going to happen.' I add a laugh so she knows I'm OK, so she knows that I'm not annoyed about it, not really.

'And that's why you were hugging Seth?'

'Yeah,' I say. 'He was really good, actually. Pep talks and everything.'

Natalie shrugs.

'What?'

'Sorry,' she says. 'I just don't trust him with you – that's all.'

'Why not?'

'I don't know . . . He just seems like bad news, Robin, don't you think?' she says. 'Not showing up for classes, getting into shouting matches with Mrs Finch—'

'You're always so flirty with him.'

'That's just fun,' she says. 'I'm being nice, but being nice doesn't mean I want him all up in your business.'

'Well, he was nice to me last night,' I say.

Natalie sighs. 'I'm sorry I did it, Robin. It was shitty of me to throw you in at the deep end like that,' she says. 'I thought it would be good for you, thought it would get you out of this funk that you're in right now. I thought I could help and instead I've ruined your confidence.'

'No, no, don't say that,' I say. 'I wouldn't have done it by myself – you know what I'm like. And, sure, it's knocked me a bit, but that's not because of the singing.'

'Hey, if nothing else, at least you got to talk to Kaye Bye,' she says. 'What is she like out of drag? Like, is she any different?'

'Oh my God, completely,' I say, the subject change welcome. 'I mean, once I realized who he was, you could totally see it. And I'll know more tonight, I guess.'

Natalie screams. 'I am so excited for you! Look at you! You're going to be a real drag queen!'

'I dunno,' I say. 'Maybe she just feels sorry for me. I was kind of a mess last night.'

'You stop this!' she says. 'Find happy Robin again! This is going to be great for you! I'm so jealous!'

'You can come with me if you want. I'm sure she won't mind.'

'I can't.'

'Why not? I thought you'd jump at the chance!'

'Amber is home,' she says. 'Mum wanted to do a family dinner, just us, but Dad invited *everybody*. It's a full extended family extravaganza. It's going to be a lot. And by a lot I mean a lot of food, a lot of people and just . . . a lot!'

'How did your mum take that?'

'She's had to go out and pretty much quadruple everything she bought,' Nat says with a laugh. 'But I'm going to help her cook, which means I can earmark leftovers.'

'Ah, good daughter, but with a motive.'

'An original Natalie Josephs move!' She bows and then sighs. 'Promise me you'll be careful if you're going by yourself.'

'I'll even leave my phone on loud and text you when I get home.'

She smiles and squeezes my hand. 'Great, and take videos because I'm really freaking gutted I'm not coming with you,' she says. 'Maybe next time. What did your mum say about two nights out in a row?'

'Well, she wasn't home last night and she thought I was singing, which technically I was, so I messaged her when I got home as normal. What she doesn't know won't hurt her,' I say. 'And tonight she thinks I'm at a class again so . . .'

Natalie takes a sharp breath.

'What?' I ask.

'Come on, Robin, lying to your mum is a little much,' she says. 'If you'd explained to her, she might have been all right about it.'

I shake my head. 'I told you she was funny about us going

to a drag night in the first place,' I say. 'So if she found out we were at Entity last night or that I was going to learn about how to drag with Kaye Bye, she'd lose her mind.'

'Robin—'

'I don't want her to worry,' I say. 'I know it's not good, but one little lie can't hurt, right?'

'What about Connor?'

'That's not a lie – that's a lie of omission,' I say.

'It still has the word "lie" in it,' Natalie says. 'Be careful, OK?'

'Yes, yes, I'll text you when I get home—'

'I don't mean that, Robin,' she says. 'I just mean—'

'Yeah, I know,' I say. I hate lying to Mum more than anything. I try to shake that feeling of awfulness from my head as we make our way into school.

When the bell rings at three thirty I want to hurry home and put on some decent clothes before I head out again to meet Kaye. I'm still a little bit in shock that it's even happening, half expecting to show up at Entity and be turned away.

It's as I'm coming down towards the bike sheds that I see Seth. He's leaning against the technology block, his phone in his hand, his eyes fixed on the screen. He's wearing his leather jacket, all blond Danny Zuko in a faded Pokémon tee and Converse that are so beat up I'm surprised they're still on his feet. It suits him, though. You can't deny that the boy wears it well.

He hears me coming and looks up, a smile tugging at the corners of his mouth. My heart thrills to think that someone as gorgeous and sweet as Seth is that pleased to see me.

'Hey, you,' he says. 'I've not seen you all day.'

I raise an eyebrow. 'Were you looking for me?' I ask.

'Uh, well . . . not looking exactly, but I kept an eye out,' he says. 'I wanted to check in and see if you were OK after last night. And I saw your bike was still here when I was leaving so thought I'd wait and ask you in person.'

I'm a little lost for words. A silence pushes its way between us, him looking at me, me looking at him and taking in every inch of his face: the sharp jawline, the crooked teeth (still smiling – gosh, this boy loves to smile), the sparkly blue eyes, the swoopy blond hair. He flicks it out of his face with a twitch of his head. I'm doomed.

'So are you going to ask me?' I whisper.

'Huh?'

'If I'm OK?'

'Sure,' he says. He clears his throat and waits a beat, like he's thinking of a way to do it that isn't so obvious. 'Are you OK?'

'Profound, did you come up with that yourself?' I say, which makes him laugh and oh God yes I love it when he laughs. 'I'm fine,' I say. 'I wish you didn't have to see me, one, make an ass of myself last night and, two, cry.'

'Well, I didn't run away screaming.'

'You flatter me,' I say.

'And last night was fun,' he says. 'We should do it again sometime.'

'Yeah, the five of us should—'

'Robin, you can't honestly be that innocent,' he says flatly. And it floors me. I really don't know what to say. 'I like Priya, Natalie and Greg, but I meant that we, you and I, should do it again sometime.'

I take a deep breath. 'I'd like that.'

He smiles. 'Me too.'

'I gathered.'

'And I need to hear you sing properly,' he says. 'So next time Natalie decides to throw you up onstage at a moment's notice you let me know.'

'I'll be waiting for your pep talk,' I reply.

'I'll start working on it now, shall I?'

I'm just looking at how perfect his face is again when I realize that I need to go. There are so many bits of me that want to spend more time talking to him because I want to get to know him so badly, but opportunity awaits and it is in the form of a drag queen.

'I'm so sorry to do this to you, like you have no idea how

sorry, but I have to go. I have a thing tonight.'

'OK,' he says, shrugging. 'But how will I know?'

'If he really loves me?' I reply.

'What?'

'Whitney.'

'Yes,' he says. 'I just meant how will I know if you're performing again.'

'Wow,' I say. 'I really want to die right now.' And he laughs again and holy shit this is such a score. 'Well, you could always give me your number?'

His eyes widen. 'I could?'

'Is that horrifyingly forward?'

He puts out his hand and I give him my phone. I watch his fingers as they tap the screen, and I'm aware of how close to him I am, of how, as he's typing, his tongue is sticking out of the corner of his mouth while he concentrates. He suddenly looks up, catches me staring. He laughs.

'Here,' he says, handing me the phone. 'Message me.'

I smile. 'Sure.'

Seth leans in. 'We've got company,' he says.

I turn sharply and see Connor standing behind me. Seth is looking directly at him, confused, challenging. The events of last night suddenly come crashing over me as I see Connor's face. I don't want to have to go through this right now.

'Isn't that the guy from last night?' Seth says to me.

'Yeah . . .' I trail off.

'Are you OK?' he says. 'Do you need me to—?'

'No, no, no, I'm fine,' I say. 'Um . . . I'll message you.'

Seth eyes me curiously. 'Okaaaaay. See you tomorrow?'

'Sure,' I say, watching as he walks away. I'm singing Whitney Houston in my head. He's got me good.

'Robin?' Connor says, and I turn to face him, fixing him with the harshest stare I can manage.

'No,' I reply, walking past him and to the bike sheds. I can hear him following me. I know what he wants, I know what he is expecting, but I do not want to deal with it right now.

'Robin—'

'Please don't,' I say, checking my phone and feeling my heart jump at the fact that it is already getting close to half past three. I still have to get home and then actually get to Southford. At this rate I'm not going to make it.

'I just wanted to talk to you.'

'I think you said enough yesterday,' I say, and I see the words stab him. He looks hurt and I do my absolute best not to feel the slightest bit of sympathy towards him.

'It's complicated.'

'I know it's complicated — it's always complicated,' I snap. 'But last night you stood there and you let that happen to me. You didn't stand up for me *again*, Connor. What the hell?'

'Robin . . .' He trails off. None of it sounds like an apology and it's making me angry. I like him. I like him a lot. But then there is Seth, sweet and lovely Seth, who just gave me his number and wants to spend time with me. It's not complicated, it's not making me upset, it's just light. All of this Connor stuff feels too dark right now.

'Will you move so I can get to my bike, please?'

'No.'

'Connor.'

'Robin.'

'I have places I need to be,' I say.

'You have to let me explain,' he says. 'When I saw you, I didn't know what to say.'

'That's funny, because you seemed to know exactly what to say,' I reply, and I can feel myself getting upset, and I don't want to get upset in front of him, nor do I want to show up at Entity with tears in my eyes. 'The word you chose was *disgusting*, Connor.'

'I'm sorry.'

I open my mouth to speak then stop. I don't know what to say to that.

I steel myself and move towards him, and there is the briefest moment where I can tell that he thinks I'm going to kiss him and it scares him. He flinches backwards and moves out of my way. I take a deep breath, keep telling myself not to cry, and unlock my bike.

'Robin, please—'

'I don't have time for this, Connor,' I say. 'I have to go.' And I don't know if I'm talking about right at this very second or us as a thing entirely, and I can see he's thinking the same thing.

I ride off, trying to push thoughts of Connor out of my head, trying not to think about Seth and his perfect face, the fact that I lied to Natalie, to my mum. None of that matters right now; all that matters is that I make it to this freaking club and that Kaye actually lets me in.

I swing home and get changed, before heading off again, pedalling like my life depends on it, because it feels like it does. I lock my bike up over the road from Entity and walk in. The bouncer from last night isn't there to check my ID or anything, and no one behind the bar seems to care, so I wander inside.

'What can I get you, babes?' A gorgeous black man is standing behind the bar. He's wearing a waistcoat in place of a shirt, which is more than a little unnerving, and has enough tattoos over his body that he can only truly be described as a walking work of art.

'I'm here to see Kaye,' I say. 'Kaye Bye.'

'Oh yes, I know Kaye,' he says with a little laugh. 'She's not performing until later, but you're more than welcome to wait.'

'No,' I say. He looks taken aback and I realize just how short I sound. 'Sorry. I'm meant to be meeting her here. My name is Robin, and I'm late. Would you mind getting her?'

'I said four thirty,' a voice says from a door near the back of the bar. Kaye, in her male form, is standing in the doorframe wearing a T-shirt bearing a picture of Kaye in full drag, make-up stains all over it. 'What time do you call this?'

I check my phone. 'Quarter to five,' I say, still a little out of breath. 'But I cycled here, and I swear I got here as fast as I could, and I'm not normally late and—'

'If you know *anything* about the theatre, it's that to be early is to be on time, to be on time is to be late and to be late is unacceptable,' he says, looking unimpressed. 'Let this be your first lesson about drag: to be on time is to be early, to be half an hour late is to be top of the bill.' He giggles. 'Don't be the kind of queen that's late – I will not have it. Not in my house, do you hear?' He sighs and pinches the brim of his nose. 'Come on up. The girls are waiting.'

'The girls?'

He smiles. 'You didn't think it would just be me, did you?' He chuckles. It's girlish, a little high-pitched. 'No, my dear, you're going to have to get acquainted with the whole Dragcellence family. Follow me.'

NINETEEN

Kaye leads me through a blue painted door and up a creaky set of stairs. Along the wall, written in whatever the writers could get their hands on, are tiny messages, signatures and lipstick marks.

'Elly Phant was here' is written next to a giant purple lipstick mark. 'Dawn Raid is a fugly slut and PROUD!' is written just below that.

'Come on, sweetheart, we don't have all day,' Kaye says from the top of the stairs.

I vault the last few steps and walk into the room. It's not what I was expecting, not by a long way. When Kaye had mentioned a dressing room, the first thing that came to mind was something close to one in a theatre with the mirrors surrounded by yellowish white bulbs and vanity mirrors. This is an out-of-use function room.

The paint on the wall is peeling and was blue once upon a time but is now more of an off-green colour. Dotted around the room are tables with mirrors, some with lights in them, some without, all of them covered in make-up. There are people already in here, most of them in daywear, almost all of them fixated on their own reflections.

'Ladies.' Kaye claps his hands. 'I'd like to introduce a friend of mine. This is Robin, he is a musical-theatre boy—'

'Gross.' My eyes flick to the far side of the room where Pristine Gleaming is wandering around half in drag, half out, in a corset, a wig cap and some tights. She's big, she's black, she's cinched like you wouldn't believe and is already fully painted.

'Pristine, don't start,' Kaye says. 'Pristine hates musical theatre,' he whispers to me. 'If someone dares to do a musical-theatre number and Pristine is here, she will boo and she will heckle.'

'Wow.'

'She made Julie Mandrews cry once, Julie freaking Mandrews.'

And he says it like I should really know who Julia Mandrews is. But, beyond a name, I don't. So I just nod, trying to look surprised.

'Anyway, Robin has come here to learn a little something about drag,' Kaye says, clapping his hands together. 'Please be kind to him, nothing too vulgar. He's still at school, after all.'

'Us? Vulgar? Never, darling.' Someone with no eyebrows is currently in the process of drawing them on with a vibrant blue neon pigment, particles of it floating in the air, a lot of it on the table.

'Are you . . .' I hesitate. 'Are you Carrie D'Way?'

'All the time, dear boy.' He reaches out a hand. 'Pleasure to meet you. Welcome to Entity.'

'I've actually been here before,' I say. 'I was here a couple of weeks ago for my birthday. You were amazing, by the way.'

Carrie shrugs and pouts. 'Well, what can I say? You have very good taste.' He looks at Kaye. 'Though you're spending your time with this one, so perhaps not.'

'Carrie has been hosting these nights for . . .' Kaye turns to Carrie, an evil smile spreading across his face. 'How long has it been, my dear? When did the dinosaurs go extinct?'

Carrie sits up straight and blinks, her mouth forming a perfect 'O'. 'I don't know, dear, but they clearly missed one.'

Kaye cackles and we move on to where there is a girl getting ready. Her hair is whipped up on top of her head in a messy bun and she's using the smallest brush to paint green vines extending from her hairline across her face.

'Our resident conceptual, this is Anne Drogyny.'

She looks up at me and I blink. 'Oh.'

'Oh?' She fixes me with a look of pure disgust. 'Does

221

it look that bad?' She goes back to her mirror and paints another line.

'No, I just . . .' I don't know how to word this because even I know that it makes me sound ignorant. 'I was expecting Anne Drogyny to be a guy, that's all.'

Anne takes a deep breath, putting her brush down. Kaye backs away a little. I know I've put my foot in it, but I'm not a hundred per cent sure how.

'You think that gay men have the monopoly on drag or something?'

'No, not at all, I—'

'Because you don't,' she snaps. 'Women can do drag, Michelle Visage says what she does is drag, Elvira says what she does is drag.' She sighs. 'You watch *RuPaul's Drag Race*, right?'

'Yeah.'

'That barely scratches the surface,' she hisses. 'There are trans queens and AFAB queens out there who would blow your freaking mind.' She sits back in her chair. 'I mean, look at me – I'm a bio queen. Did I blow your mind the other night?'

I shrug. 'You did, actually. I've never seen anything like . . . well . . . most of you,' I say, looking around. And it's in that moment that I really understand what she means when she says *Drag Race* barely scratches the surface. In this room alone there are acts that I never imagined I would see at a drag show. I thought it would be all lip-syncing, but there are dancers and singers and conceptual art pieces. The way that Anne is painting her face right now – you could put her in an art gallery.

'There are people who don't think The Duchess is a proper queen, just because she's trans.'

'The Duchess?'

'The very same!' I flick my eyes in the direction of the new voice to see a black woman standing by a table covered in make-up. She's a little shorter than me, wearing a pair of skinny blue jeans and a figure-hugging maroon top that shows off every curve and swerve. 'Lovely to meet you,' she says, shaking my hand.

'Lovely to meet you too.'

'The Duchess is my drag mother,' Anne says. 'Raised me from a baby drags to what I am now. You'll never see a lip-sync artist like her, never hear a singer like her – she is the real damn thing.'

'Leave the boy alone,' The Duchess says. 'You watch *Drag Race*, right?'

I've already answered this question once and responding feels like a trap. 'Yes.'

She puts a hand on my shoulder. 'Think of *Drag Race* as your gateway drug,' she says. 'The beginning of the rest of your life. Are you coming to the show tonight?'

'Yes,' I say. 'Two weeks ago for my birthday was the first time I'd ever been to a drag show.'

The Duchess smiles. 'Then you have a lot to learn. But you can learn a lot at Dragcellence. Keep your eyes, your heart and your mind open, and who knows what you'll find!' She kisses me on the cheek. 'It was lovely meeting you. Enjoy the show.'

Anne has gone back to painting her face. She eyeballs me in the mirror. 'Sashay away, race chaser. I'm still mad at you.'

'I-I-I'm really sorry. I didn't mean to—'

Kaye grabs my arm and ushers me away. 'She's not really mad. She just needs to cool off,' he whispers. 'She has that speech ready at the drop of a hat for anyone who dares to question what she does.'

I look at Kaye. 'Do people do that often?'

Kaye raises a glued-down eyebrow. 'All the damn time. And it's not fair because she's fierce.'

'You're kidding.'

'Trans queens and AFAB queens don't get the love they deserve amongst the LGBTQIA+ community,' Kaye says. 'And don't get me started on drag kings. Where the hell is their TV show?'

Kaye leads me across the room to a dining table with a small, round, lit mirror on it. Without even looking, he grabs a stick of purple glue and runs it over his eyebrows again.

'So, Robin, I'm glad you actually came,' he says. 'When you didn't show up on the dot, I thought you might have changed your mind. A lot of people think they want to be drag queens until they realize how much work it takes.'

'I'm not afraid of hard work.'

'You're a theatre kid so that doesn't exactly surprise me.' Kaye flicks opens a fan, the *thworp* sound echoing through the dressing room, and starts fanning his brows. 'So, you say you've been painting. What are you painting with, how often are you doing it and *please tell me* you're taking care of your skin.'

'Um . . . mostly drugstore stuff,' I say a little sheepishly, seeing the plethora of brand names on the table in front of him. Fenty, NYX, MAC, bloody hell.

'Nothing to be embarrassed about, sweetheart,' Kaye says, putting on another layer of glue before *thworping* his fan again and fanning away. 'You've got to start somewhere and better to practise with something that doesn't cost you the earth. How often?'

'Whenever I can,' I say, tugging my phone out of my pocket. 'And I think I've been getting better.' I swipe through a few of the photos and even I'm a little bit pleased with how I've come on.

'While you're practising,' he says, 'it might be an idea to use a straight edge for your contour. It will get it a little more even and a lot more severe. If that's what you're into. And, like I said last night, eyeshadow primer is your friend.' He rummages through his make-up bag and grabs one. It's still sealed. He hands it to me. 'Try this and call me in the morning,' he says in an unmistakably Mae West voice.

'Kaye, that's so kind. You don't have to——'

'Don't speak too loudly. They can't know I'm nice,' he growls. He takes my phone off me and looks through a few more of the photos. 'Have you found a style you like?'

I shake my head.

'That will take time,' he says. 'You don't have to stick to just one look, but if you find something you like then it can't hurt, of course. If it's something you can do quickly, even better. You never know when a gig is going to appear and it's nice to be able to do a thirty-minute face.'

'Thirty minutes?' I repeat. The faces I've been doing take me the best part of two hours. How the heck could you get that down to thirty minutes?

'Don't look so alarmed, sweetheart – it's all practice,' he says, applying one last layer of glue before covering his brows with powder. 'Now, the key to brows is to press down, hard, though I imagine you've watched enough tutorials to know that.'

I nod.

'Sometimes it's worth doing an extra layer if you have time.'

'Or just use spirit gum, it's a lot easier!' Pristine booms from next to me.

'Don't confuse the boy, Pristine,' Kaye snaps, applying another layer of glue and more powder. 'Let him get used to the glue first, then we'll talk about spirit gum.'

'Ooh, look at her. She gets herself one drag daughter and decides it's her way or the highway.'

'I'm just trying to keep it simple, stupid.'

Pristine Gleaming *thworps* a fan and starts to fan herself. 'Well, each to their own, darling, but I'm a sweaty bitch and a sweaty bitch needs to make sure her brows are a hundred per cent covered.' She spins slowly on the spot and walks back to her station, continuing to add to her impressive face.

'We'll talk about spirit gum another time,' Kaye whispers. 'Look, the first thing I should probably tell you is that there is no correct way to do this.' He gestures to himself. 'It's all about what you feel most comfortable in, what makes you feel your best. Every queen looks different and that's what makes all of this so exciting. Look at how many freaking tutorials you've done, every single one of them showing off a different face. You just need to find one that suits you.'

227

It's only now that he points it out that I can really see it. No two queens really paint the same face. There are similarities, of course, but they all have their own way of doing it and their own look that evolves and gets perfected over time.

'So, why do you want to be a drag queen?' he says, putting on some primer as he starts to get ready. 'We've already established you're a performer . . . kinda.'

'Well, I messed up getting into drama school this year,' I start, with an attempt at breeziness. 'It's all I wanted and it's gone, just like that. And the thing that brought me out of that funk was seeing this show a couple of weeks ago. Seeing all of you up there doing your thing brought me back to life, I guess, and it was a kind of performance I hadn't even considered for myself. But it was inspiring and exciting, so different to what I usually do . . .' I lower my voice so Pristine doesn't hear. 'Musicals and stuff.'

'Well, honey, it ain't no walk in the park,' Kaye says. 'There's a lot more to it than looking fabulous. Sure, I look gorgeous, you don't need to tell me . . .' He trails off, waiting for me to chime in.

'Oh, you look gorgeous. I thought it went without saying.'

He raises an eyebrow. 'Well saved. But you also need to *perform*. The singing thing you did—'

'I'm way better than that, I swear.'

'Thank *God*!' Kaye says. 'Otherwise there's no *way* anywhere would take you. Where did you audition?'

'Everywhere.'

'Like . . . ?'

'The Arts Centre, Hillview, LAPA . . .' I trail off. But that dream is gone for now. I don't even want to think about applying again next year.

'Look, rejection sucks,' Kaye says. 'But it's part of the business. You aren't the first kid to be rejected from drama school and, sweetie, you won't be the last. You ain't so special. I got rejected two years on the bounce.'

'You did?'

'Uh-huh,' Kaye says. 'Got in third time around. Hillview alumni, honey.' He shrugs. 'Maybe you weren't ready.'

'But I *felt* ready. I did everything I possibly could and—'

'Get out of your head,' Kaye says. 'You're probably getting in your own way most of the time. Now, what you need to do is apply that same discipline you had with your performing to your drag. It is an art form, so you better get to learning if you want in.'

'OK.'

'My advice is to absorb as much as possible,' he says. 'Paint as often as you can, watch a lot of drag, breathe it all in and you'll discover so much about yourself and the kind of drag you want to do. Find the performance forms that excite you, either here or online or at other clubs. You may even surprise yourself.'

As he talks, Kaye paints. Foundation, blend, highlight, blend, contour, blend. It's amazing watching his face transform into Kaye Bye's – the high cheekbones, the overdrawn lips – it's astounding. And she's beautiful.

'Stick around and watch the show,' she says. 'It should be a good one. Dusty Rhodes is coming down from Liverpool, and, honestly, wait until you hear them sing. You're going to die. Oh! And, if he actually bothers to show, Just Jeff will be here. Now *that* is a king that will blow your mind. Andi Vaxxx will also be here, a trans man who was a queen before he was a king and is honestly the most beautiful porcelain prince you will ever see in your life. We have a packed bill tonight.' She stands and walks over to a row of wigs perched on top of mannequin heads. She chooses a big, blonde one with wavy hair and puts it on. 'Then you can come back tomorrow, if you like. We'll paint a little more, talk about what kind of performer you want to be, see what we can do – how does that sound?'

'It sounds great,' I say, a little breathless. 'I . . . I . . . I'll be here.'

I finish watching Kaye get ready, then head downstairs to watch the show.

I take a few videos and shoot them over to Nat: Pristine lip-syncing to a Whitney Houston ballad and tearing the roof off the place. Dusty Rhodes, wearing a full tux and a harness, singing songs they'd written themselves that left everybody more than a little speechless. Just Jeff looking like a five foot two lumberjack with a beard that I could only dream of and lip-syncing to 'Soliloquy' from *Carousel*. Pristine heckled the whole way through, but was crying by the end. Andi Vaxxx wore a crown and deservedly so. He did a burlesque act and it was honestly hard to keep my eyes off him. He's beautiful. Like. Stunning. It's hard to believe that I didn't even know this place existed a few weeks ago.

My phone buzzes in my pocket – Mum.

> Everything OK? Thought you'd be home by now.

I check the time. Shit. It's a rare day that Mum gets home before I do.

> Just on my way. Class ran over.

I squeeze through the crowd and out into the night, pedalling like mad to make it back in time to have conceivably been at a dance class, but I'm already buzzing at the thought of being back tomorrow night.

'How was the class?' Mum asks as I walk in the door. She's sitting at the kitchen table, her nose stuck in a book, a pair of glasses on the end of her nose. 'It's late.'

'I know,' I say, a little out of breath from the bike ride. 'We just lost track of time. Every time I finished it was like "let's do it once more" and then it was ten. Wild.' The lies fall off my tongue so easily and I sort of hate it.

'Well, I'm glad you went back,' she says. 'I know you were worried about it, but it's fine now that you're there, right?'

I nod. 'How was your evening?'

'Really nice, actually,' she says, dog-earing the page she's on and putting her book down. 'I had some soup, read my book, listened to the music you hate — it was nice. I never have the place to myself. It's a novelty.'

'True.'

'I'd better make the most of it. You'll be here all the time when school's over,' she says, but her smile slips when she sees my face. 'Oh, Robin, I didn't mean—'

'I know what you meant, Mum,' I say, walking into the kitchen, grabbing myself a glass of water, trying to not let the thought of the future ruin my right now. 'You'll have me tomorrow night, though, right?' I say. It's the best way to ask without arousing suspicion.

She sighs. 'Alas, dear heart, no,' she says. 'There's an extra shift going, and I jumped on it. Forgot you were off tomorrow; it would have been nice to see you. Maybe at the weekend?'

'Yeah, maybe at the weekend,' I say, washing my glass up and putting it back in the cupboard. 'I should probably get to bed,' I add. 'Unless you want to talk or something?'

'No, you head off to bed. You must be shattered,' she says, ruffling my hair. 'You need to get this cut, by the way. It's out of control.' She looks me in the eye and kisses me on the cheek. 'Unless *you* want to talk? Is there something on your mind, you seem a little . . .' She trails off.

'A little what?'

'Elsewhere,' she says. 'Not your usual bubbly self after a dance class, that's all.'

'Oh.' I blink. Have I been rumbled? 'I think my brain's just feeling a little full, that's all,' I say. 'Dancing, schoolwork, you know? It's all a bit full on.'

'Ooh, on that note—'

'Oh God.'

'What?'

'You seem excited, why do I get the feeling this is going to be something that's going to make me want to bury myself in a hole and die?'

She snorts. 'No, no, this has nothing to do with my

exam-results-collection performance,' she says with a wink. 'I had a call from Mrs Finch. She's a delightful woman, not at all icy and demanding, so breezy.'

'Mum . . .' I warn.

'Tell me I'm wrong,' she says with a grin. 'See? You can't. She's awful. Wouldn't let up until I gave her *all* the dates I was free from now until the end of eternity. But we have a meeting in, so that's going to be fun. We'll braid each other's hair, drink milkshakes, talk about which boys we like and then we'll discuss your future and why she thinks I'm a terrible mother for letting you choose your own path.' She sighs a contented sort of Disney Princess sigh. 'We're going to have such fun.'

I shrug. 'Rather you than me.' I kiss her on the cheek. 'Goodnight, Mum.'

With Mum working tomorrow night, I can go to Entity again. Just for a little while, to see Kaye, get a few more tips and be back before Mum. Maybe this time Natalie can come with me. It was fun on my own, don't get me wrong, but it's definitely less awkward to be in a bar with friends. This is turning out to be a tiny bit perfect. First stop Entity, next stop the world.

TWENTY

I wake up to messages from Connor that I don't want to respond to.

> Robin?

> Robin, I'm sorry.

> Can I see you later?

I ignore them, having a quick breakfast with Mum before heading out to school. I can still feel the excitement of last night buzzing around my body, even if I did stay up a little too late watching drag performances on YouTube. I can feel myself soaking it up, falling further and further down the rabbit hole.

'I can't believe I've been here for a whole three seconds and you haven't asked me about Dragcellence yet,' I say to Natalie as she steps out of her door.

'Christ, are you going to be this unbearable always?' she says. 'If I'd known I was going to turn you into some kind of monster I wouldn't have got you to come to Dragcellence in the first place.' She's grinning broadly and deliberately withholding her interest.

We start towards school and I can feel the tension bubbling up in me, the excitement. I want to freaking explode.

'Come *on*, Natalie, you're killing me,' I say.

She laughs. 'Fine, fine, fine, how was Dragcellence last night? What you sent me looked incredible.'

I take a deep breath. 'It was amazing. So different to last time. I *wish* you'd been there.'

'Who knew Southford had such a glittering drag scene on a school night?' she says. 'I wanted to come, I really did, but the whole family were there and, frankly, I'm the best one. The night would have been a disaster without me.' She shrugs. 'It is *such* a burden being me sometimes. So, how was everything with Kaye? She didn't try and smuggle you into the back of a van and sell you for MAC Cosmetics, then?'

'Clearly,' I say. 'She was great. She introduced me to the other girls and then she let me watch her paint. It was honestly amazing.'

'How does she do it?'

'Totally different to what I do,' I say. 'I mean, she had her own way of doing it, which I guess is the point, right?

You look at how everybody else does it and then you figure it out for yourself. Like, figure out what works for your face.'

'Which is why you've been painting every night ever since we got your make-up,' Nat says. 'Does she have a name yet?'

I shake my head. I've been writing ideas down whenever I think of them, little notes in my phone or in the back of my notebooks, but nothing has screamed out to me.

'Maybe when I see her fully done up I'll know it, but right now I can't figure it out.'

She shrugs. 'I'll start thinking some up.'

'OK, and I'm sure Kaye will help if I ask,' I say. 'I'm going back tonight.'

'What?'

'And you're coming with me!'

'Robin—'

'It's fine, she invited me back,' I interrupt. 'There isn't a show or anything, but she said she would help me learn how to paint my face. So, I'm going and you should definitely come because if Kaye paints me I am going to be devastatingly beautiful and I need someone else to see it so I don't forget.'

'Baby, I love how excited you are over all of this, but I can't drop everything and come to Entity tonight,' she says.

'Holly and Eric from my law class are coming over to work on a presentation which counts towards our final mark . . .' She trails off and takes a steadying breath. 'I still need to get the grades for uni. It's important to me.'

I nod, trying not to let university talk get me down. 'You will! Queen Mary awaits!' I say as brightly as I can. 'And I'm sorry – I'm just trying to throw myself into this. What if this could be the thing for me next year?'

'Maybe you don't need a thing for next year.'

'Of course I do,' I say. 'Come on, you've got Queen Mary, I've got absolutely nothing without LAPA.' I try not to let the mood drop, try not to let that horrible feeling take over me. Try to take Kaye's advice and get out of my own way.

Natalie looks at me and opens her mouth, but quickly closes it and faces forward, keeping her gaze on the direction we're walking in. There are words dancing around her head trying to find a way out.

'What?' I say.

She takes a breath. 'Don't take this the wrong way.'

'Why do I get the feeling I'm about to?'

'Do you not think you're getting maybe a little bit obsessed?' she offers.

I don't know what to say. This was her idea in the first place. I never would have even gone to Dragcellence if it wasn't for her. She was desperate for me to do drag and now she's changing her mind?

'Look, maybe obsessed is the wrong word, but you've gone from obsessing about your musical-theatre course—'

'Obsessing?'

'As in being upset about it—'

'Because I didn't get in anywhere and everyone around me is going to university, Nat,' I say. 'I'm terrified about not having anywhere to go in September and feeling like a total failure.'

'I'm glad you've found something that makes you happy, OK? I really am,' she continues. 'But don't you think it's a bit much to go three nights in a row?'

'No.'

'OK,' she says flatly. 'I'm just worried, that's all.'

'About what?'

'We don't know Kaye,' she says. 'We don't know what she wants or what she's getting out of this and I don't want her to end up hurting you or anything, OK? That's all I'm saying.'

'Then come with me,' I say. It's not an invitation, not really. My voice is shrill and I can feel myself going on the defensive. It's more a challenge than anything else.

'I can't,' she says. 'Give me a couple of hours to work tonight with Holly and Eric, and I'll get rid of them and you can come over and we'll catch up. We've not had a proper girls' night, just you and me, in ages!'

'Good morning!' Seth chirps, jogging to catch up with us.

'Morning,' I say, my voice cracking. Which is great. I love that for me.

'It'll be fun,' Nat says. 'Promise.'

'I know, but Kaye invited me back and I want to go.'

'You're going back to Entity tonight?' Seth says. 'Can I come?'

Natalie looks at him sharply and then back to me.

'I mean, sure,' I tell him, turning to Nat. 'Come on, you were worried about me being alone there, now I'm not alone. Seth will protect me.'

'It will be my honour,' he says.

'I'm going straight from school and have my bike so—'

'That's OK,' he says. 'I'll drive and meet you there.'

I look him up and down. 'You have a car?'

'Is it automatic?' Natalie asks with an eye roll.

'Hyyyyyyydromatic,' Seth replies obediently. 'It's at my grandparents' house, but I can go home and drive to Southford. I'll probably end up beating you there.'

'Is that a challenge?' I ask.

'Maybe,' he says. 'Though I don't know what the winner gets.'

'I have to get to registration,' Natalie says as we make it

to the front gates. 'So do you, Robin – wrap this up.' She starts walking away. 'Bye, Seth.'

'You really want to come?' I say.

Seth puts a hand on my arm and I immediately stop talking because he's knocked all the breath out of me.

'I've said yes, Robin,' he says. 'I want to come. Drag stuff interests me, so I want to see it. And it doesn't look like you're messaging me any time soon so . . .'

Ah, crap. Rumbled.

'Kaye said to get there for five so come for then, and I totally meant to message you, but—'

'Cooper! Registration! I can feel myself ageing.' Natalie is standing over by the school entrance.

'Thanks,' I say to Seth. 'Are you heading this way?'

'I'm that way,' he says, pointing off towards the science block. 'I'll see you later.'

'Bye, Seth.'

He walks away and I can't help but watch him go. I hate that I'm getting caught up in this.

'Cooper!'

I jump and run to catch up with Natalie.

I practically sprint out of school at the end of the day, pedalling as fast as I can so I can get home, get dressed, pack my make-up and get to Southford. When I get there, Seth is walking up to the doors of Entity. He's had time to get changed into something different, a casual tee and a pair of dark jeans. He even looks like he's done his hair, or at least had a shower. He had loads of time and I've just ridden here like a total maniac.

He looks at his wrist as I approach. 'You took your time.'

'Do you want to come with me or not?' I ask, feeling incredibly sweaty and hideous next to him.

'Yes, of course, sorry,' he says, but he's smiling. I like that I make him smile. My heart does a little flip. Calm down, Robin. Calm down.

I knock on the door and Kaye quickly appears as his boy self.

'Good afternoon,' he says, looking from me to Seth. 'Who's this? Bodyguard?'

'No.'

'Boyfriend?'

I wish.

'No,' I say, perhaps a little too quickly.

'I'm Seth,' Seth says, reaching out a hand to shake Kaye's. Kaye takes it with the tips of his fingers and curtseys.

'Charmed,' he says. 'OK, boys, come on in.'

He leads us into Entity, grabbing us a couple of cans of soda on the way past the bar before guiding us upstairs to the dressing room.

Seth's eyes are wide as he looks around, reading the messages written on the walls, breathing the whole place in.

'This is amazing,' he whispers.

'Speak up, boy. You're allowed to give compliments to my home,' Kaye snaps, still smiling.

'I was just saying that it's amazing in here,' Seth says. 'Those messages on the wall, was that one from Raja?'

Kaye nods and smiles. 'Ah, we have someone with a keen eye and a pretty face,' he says. Seth's cheeks turn a little red. 'Raja came here many, many moons ago.' Kaye turns to me. 'Winner of—'

'Season three of *Drag Race*, wow,' I say. Raja was here. Natalie is going to *die*!

'Well, she came along, did a few numbers.' He sighs and looks wistfully off into the distance. 'Wonderful, wonderful queen. Of course, this was while I was still a baby so I didn't look nearly as beautiful as I do now. Even people who are completely stunning look like trolls next to Raja. I looked like a troll who'd been dragged out of a bin.'

'I'm sure you looked fantastic,' Seth says.

'Flattery will get you everywhere, dear boy,' Kaye says with a smile. He turns to me. 'Now, let's get you painted, shall we?' He glances back at Seth. 'Are you here to watch?'

'Yeah,' Seth says. 'I'm a huge fan of drag. I used to go

to loads of drag shows in London. Yet to see a night here though.'

I look at him and smile. He likes drag, he likes me . . .

Shut up, Robin.

'You'll have to come down. We put on a fantastic show,' Kaye says. 'Bring him next time,' he says to me. 'He'll love it.'

'You really will,' I say, wishing I had the courage to ask Seth out, to take him with me to somewhere like this, to anywhere, really.

We set ourselves up at Kaye's workstation and he grabs me my own mirror. I take out my make-up and let him go through it. Seth takes a seat nearby.

'This is good stuff to start with,' Kaye says. 'The make-up you use doesn't have to cost the earth — it's just about what you do with it. Don't feel like you need to go out and buy an influencer's palette because you think it will make you look beautiful. Skill makes you look beautiful — the product just helps. Do your research.'

He starts to paint me, only doing half my face, me trying to pay attention to every step so I can follow him, repeating what he is doing on the other half.

'Wow,' Seth breathes next to me. I'm painfully aware of how close he is to me.

'What's up?' I murmur as Kaye paints on an eyebrow.

It's not how I normally do my brows, it's how Kaye does his, and the arch is high and severe. I look sort of domineering and powerful in a way that I don't achieve when I do my own make-up.

'It's amazing,' Seth says. 'Like, it totally changes your face. If I saw you in the street, I don't think I'd recognize you.'

'I am not going day walking,' I say. 'Please, in Essex? I'd be killed.'

'Carry yourself like a queen and you will be treated as such,' Kaye says. 'Though even I wouldn't day walk and I'm many years into the game. Get an Uber. It's radical self-care.'

Seth laughs and I start to laugh too, but Kaye takes hold of my head to keep me still. I screw up the eyebrow, and I mean I really screw up the eyebrow. It looks nothing like Kaye's at all.

'I'm so sorry,' I say, looking closely at the mirror. 'This is awful, it's—'

'They're sisters, not twins,' Kaye says. 'I mean, this is more of a really distant cousin, but don't be so hard on yourself. It's a new look for you. The eye is good.' He grabs my head and turns me to face Seth. 'Look at the work he's done on that eye — they are practically identical and stunning.'

We've used pinks and purples from a cheap palette I got from the drugstore. They're not super pigmented so we've really had to work to get the colour out of them, but it looks good. I mean, really good.

Seth smiles. 'It's . . . it's really amazing,' he says, looking closely at my eyes.

'Say more things, Seth. I may not have to use blusher at this rate,' Kaye says.

'No, I mean it. You look so, so beautiful,' he says. 'I mean, not that you didn't before, but this is obviously a . . . I mean it's different – it's . . .'

There's a loud banging downstairs.

'Well, this is beyond rude. Who the hell could that be?' Kaye asks, letting go of my head and interrupting what is probably the best moment of my entire life. I could kill him.

'What?' I ask.

'I'll go get the door. You do the lip while I'm down there.'

'What? No, I'll wreck it!'

Kaye rolls his eyes. 'Fine.' He turns to Seth. 'You do it.'

'OK.'

'OK?' I repeat. 'Have you done this before?'

'He's following a line that I've already done, not defusing an atomic bomb,' Kaye says. 'I won't be long.'

Kaye vanishes out of the room, the door swinging open

and inviting in the smallest snippet of Britney Spears before slamming closed again. But for the muffled sound of the punters downstairs, the room is silent and I am staring at Seth.

'So,' he says. 'Do you want me to do it or not?'

'I feel like if I say no Kaye will have me kicked out of here,' I say. 'So yes. Do it. Please,' I add quickly.

It's not just the nerves about Seth doing my lips – it's how close he is going to have to be to do it. He picks up his chair and turns it round, the back of it facing me. He grabs the lip pencil and takes a seat in front of me, leaning his arm on the back of the chair.

'You're going to need to stay still,' he whispers, his voice coming out a little gravelly.

'Duh.'

'Which means no making snarky comments,' he says.

'Rude—'

'What did I say?'

'Sorry.'

He raises his eyebrows at me and I pull a fake zip across my mouth.

'Much better,' he says.

He's so close to me I can feel his breath on my face, and I'm staring into his eyes while he draws a careful line around my lips, overdrawing them just like Kaye has on the opposite side. He has the most beautiful eyes. They're sort of sparkly, even in the limited light and the longer I look at them, the more I think I could probably look at them forever and never get bored.

He grabs the brush that Kaye used and puts the lipstick on my lips, careful to stay within the lines, biting his bottom lip as he concentrates. Once he's topped it off with the gloss, he looks up into my eyes and I wonder how long Kaye has been gone and whether or not she'll be back in a second. There is a part of me that doesn't want her to come back at all because my eyes are locked on Seth and it feels like something is about to happen.

'You really are beautiful,' he whispers.

I shrug. 'When I'm like this, sure.'

'No,' he says. 'I mean it. You are beautiful, Robin.'

The door swings open, a blast of a Pet Shop Boys song making Seth pull back so fast it's a wonder he hasn't gone through the wall. Kaye looks at us both curiously, then smiles.

'The lips look lovely,' he says, but he's smiling much too broadly to be just referring to my lips. 'You'll have to do them yourself at some point, unless you can afford to hire the boy to be your make-up artist. What *are* you doing in two weeks?' he adds.

A man stumbles in behind him. He's wearing a pair of

tartan skinny jeans and a giant black coat. To say he looks dishevelled would be an understatement.

'You're right, darling, he is beautiful,' the man says in a voice that is unmistakably Carrie's.

'What's going on?' I ask.

'This one is in a tizz because she had someone cancel on her and there doesn't seem to be a queen in all of Southford who isn't booked and blessed,' he says. 'So I suggested you.'

'Me?'

'No, Seth,' he says, rolling his eyes. 'Of course you!'

'But I don't have an act yet.'

'I know,' Carrie says. 'Unless you're about to pull out something similar to your performance at the open mic.'

'You saw that?'

'Unfortunately yes.' Carrie eyes me carefully then turns back to Kaye. 'This doesn't seem like a good idea. She's too green. I'll have one of the queens do another number. I'll—'

'She'll be fine.'

Carrie looks over at me again and walks towards me. I instinctively back away.

'You think you can do this?'

Kaye is nodding at me behind Carrie's back.

'Yes,' I say. 'I've been practising a lot and—'

'You said you don't have an act.'

249

'Painting, I mean,' I say.

'You can't just stand up there and be pretty,' Carrie says. 'Not at Dragcellence. People come from miles around to see a show here. This is big.'

'I know,' I say. He's more than a little intimidating.

'One shot,' he says. 'That's all I'm giving you. And don't think for one second this is something I would do lightly. I'm doing Miss Bye here a favour. A thousand girls would kill for that slot—'

'But you don't have a thousand girls waiting for it,' Kaye interrupts. 'You have Robin. And Robin can do it.'

Carrie looks at Kaye and then back at me. He points a perfectly manicured finger in my face. 'You have one opportunity to make a first impression, or you're through,' he says. 'Don't fuck this up.'

'Have you finished playing the pantomime villain, dear?' Kaye asks, mock yawning. He may be happy to rip into Carrie, but all I can do is quake. Carrie says his goodbyes and walks out, slamming the door behind him.

'You must be mad,' I say. 'I don't have an act, Kaye.'

'Plenty of time for that.'

'I don't have a name.'

'Did you or did you not hear me say two weeks?' Kaye groans. 'It will be bloody hard to come up with something that quickly, but not completely impossible. You're just

250

going to need to work hard.' He looks me up and down. I must look panicked. 'Look, do you want to do it or not? Because I've just stuck my neck out for you here – it's my head in the smasher.'

'Kaye, I—'

'You can't hide forever,' Kaye says. 'You've been through some shit, I know, but you can't just never perform again. The only time I've seen you do it you were complete shit, but it was still blindingly obvious you've got talent.'

And that's precisely the reason I'm nervous. Suddenly I'm performing again and I don't feel ready for it, not in the slightest.

I stare at myself in the mirror, at the face half done by me, half done by Kaye. I look all right. But it's not about look, it's about performance, and I have nothing. I have less than nothing. I have the shattered nerves of my last performance and my failed auditions.

'Robin?' Seth says. 'You should do it.'

I turn to him. He's smiling. 'I should?'

He nods. 'Of course! It's an amazing opportunity.'

'Maybe . . .' I say. 'But—'

'Yes, yes, yes, dear, you don't have an act,' Kaye says. 'We will figure all that out. You'll come here, we'll make time, I'll get you dressed, teach you everything you'll need to know.'

'But two weeks isn't a long time.'

'Robin, you're a musical-theatre girl,' Kaye says. 'It's performance. You've got a lot of it in you already – you just don't know it yet.' He looks me in the eye. 'You keep saying you're worried about next year, what you're going to do, all that, so why not this? This is a paid slot, Robin. If the performance goes well, you could earn yourself a pretty penny next year as a queen.'

'Really?'

'Look at me!' Kaye says. 'I did it.'

'You did?'

'You think you're the only theatre boy to turn drag queen?' Kaye scoffs. 'Honey, you ain't that special. I failed auditions, I messed up bad, but I picked myself up again, created Kaye, tried again. All you can *do* is pick yourself up and try again. To let it all go after one failure is a disservice.'

'You mean that?'

Kaye rolls his eyes. 'Yes! Christ, Robin, what did I tell you? Rejection is part of the deal. You either let it kill you, or let it make you stronger. That choice is up to you. Now, are you going to take this opportunity or not?'

I turn to Seth. 'Will you come?'

'I'll be first in line,' he says like it's nothing, but really it's everything and my heart can't cope with it.

'This is all very adorable, but do I take that as a yes?' Kaye asks.

I turn to him. 'Yeah,' I say. 'Yeah, let's do it.'

Shit. Suddenly I'm performing again. I'm filled with the anxiety that I'd pushed away after the failed auditions, after falling flat on my face here a couple of days ago.

'Good, that saves me upsetting Carrie any more,' Kaye says. 'Right, no time like the present. Get up.'

'What?'

'On your feet, kid, we've got work to do, magic to make, all that shit.' Kaye walks over to another door, pulling out a rail of costumes in every colour of the pride flag. 'Ta-dah!'

'Maybe this is happening too fast.'

'Maybe you forgot we have two weeks, not two years, now get up!'

At Kaye's instruction, I start getting undressed, incredibly aware that Seth is sitting on the other side of the room. This isn't exactly how I pictured this evening going.

I take my shirt off and Kaye approaches with a black corset that he wraps round my waist. I pull it together at the front, hooking the fastenings until I can hardly breathe.

'Brace yourself, kid,' he says. And in one swift motion, he pulls on the ribbons and tightens it. The air is pushed out of me, my organs screaming as they get bullied into new positions. 'You OK?'

'Just about,' I manage. 'It's a little tight.'

'Beauty is pain.'

'Pain is one thing, death on the other hand—'

'All right, all right, a little looser,' Kaye says. 'Violet Chachki she ain't.'

'That's fine with me,' I say as Kaye lets the corset out and I feel like I can breathe again.

'Put these on,' he says, handing me a pair of beige shorts, padding in the hips and the butt.

'Really?'

'Yes, really.' He starts rummaging through a rack of shoes. 'These too – you've worn a heel before, right?'

'Uh, New Yorkers at my dance school.'

'New Yorkers?!' Kaye spits. 'Christ, boy, you've got a lot to learn. You think you're the ish because you can twirl in a New Yorker – you wait until you try it in a stiletto heel. Size?'

'Ten.'

'Wow,' Kaye says. 'Man feet. Good for you. Or in this case, not so much. You'll have to borrow from Carrie.' Kaye grabs me a pair of black stiletto heels and three pairs of tights. 'Get these on, and, Seth, come help me pick out a dress.'

Seth raises an eyebrow at me on the way past, hurrying to the costume rail with Kaye, rummaging through while

I pull the shorts up, then all the tights and slip the heels on to my feet. It's a struggle to balance at first. He's right when he says the New Yorkers are easier to walk in. Going from a three-inch heel to what has to be a six is no mean feat. But I walk a little, hearing snatches of conversation from Seth and Kaye as I wander, remembering to pitch forward, using my arms to keep my balance as I did in Emily's class.

I catch sight of myself in the full-length mirror hanging on the back of the door. I'm standing taller. Even I can see it. After hiding myself for so long, shrinking my shoulders, trying not to be too visible when out in public, here I am standing tall because in a six-inch heel, you don't really have a choice.

'Oh, darling, you're going to love this,' Kaye calls. 'What are you doing?'

I turn round to see Kaye holding a blue dress, the top of it a nude illusion covered in so many stones it's practically glittering in front of me.

'I was just looking.'

'Wait until you see the finished product,' he says, beckoning me over. 'Seth, put some music on.'

'Absolutely,' he says. 'Any requests?'

'Robin?' Kaye asks.

'Anything, I don't mind.'

'Darling, if you could try to be a little more assertive?'

I sigh. 'Something dancey,' I say. 'Pop, the queerer the better.'

'That's a good girl,' Kaye says. 'Now, step into this.'

I do as I'm told, stepping into the dress, putting my arms in, letting Kaye do up the zip behind me. Katy Perry starts to play from Seth's phone.

'Now, to complete this little look,' Kaye says. 'She looks like a blonde, doesn't she, Seth?'

Seth looks over, a wide grin on his face. 'I think so, yeah.'

'There's a good boy.' Kaye heads over to his dressing table and takes a huge, swept up piece of blonde hair with a dark root off a mannequin head. He hands me a wig cap and I obediently put it on, bending down so he can put the wig on my head. It's heavy, any false movement threatening to send me off balance.

I draw myself up to my full height, running my hands over the new body Kaye has put me in, the new waist he has cinched, the new hips he's enhanced, the stones sparkling in the limited light with every slight movement.

'My darling daughter,' Kaye says. 'It's not perfect, but it's a start. Prance a little, enjoy the song, enjoy the moment, dance around, feel yourself.'

I want to, but I can feel Kaye's eyes on me, and Seth's eyes, and I start to wonder if I'm making a fool of myself.

256

'Honey, no,' Kaye says. 'Get out of your head for a second. *Find her.* Find where *she* is in you. Let all of this go.'

'I can't,' I say. 'I . . . I don't know how to—'

'Don't worry about us; don't worry about him,' Kaye says, waving a hand in Seth's direction. 'Take a breath, close your eyes if it helps and just let the music take you.'

But I can't, and I can feel myself shutting down. I don't want to do this any more, I just—

The song changes and I recognize the song before the words even start. Lady Gaga. 'Just Dance.' I've never fallen so fast for someone as I did for Lady Gaga and this song, and now it's running through my body just like it did when I first heard it.

'Come on,' Seth says. 'Dance with me.'

'Seth, I can't. I—'

'No!' Kaye shouts. 'No more can'ts, Robin! Just dance.'

'Very funny!' I shout back.

'Come on,' Seth says, taking my hands. 'Close your eyes if it helps.'

So I do, and he's holding my hands and we're dancing, just j-j-just dancing. And maybe it is gonna be OK.

I open my eyes and Seth is smiling at me, grinning so broadly it's like his face is going to split in two.

'Yes! Yes! That's what I'm talking about!' Kaye calls, but it sort of vanishes because here's Seth and here I am and we're just dancing like there's nothing else happening in the world. The music is in my veins and I can't stop myself from singing along as I go, and I'm performing, in a way, and it's all for him, and a little bit for Kaye, I guess, but my eyes are fixed on Seth.

Then I stumble over my own feet, tripping and almost falling forward. Seth lets go of my hands and suddenly has his arms wrapped round my newly cinched waist. I look down at him, because I'm taller than him now and he's grinning, a little out of breath, his eyes twinkly as ever.

'You OK?' he whispers.

'Yeah,' I say. 'Thanks.'

'Pleasure.'

The song finishes, fading seamlessly into Britney Spears, and I don't know what playlist this is, but Seth somehow has my music taste down. And we're still dancing. Another few songs go by – a Judy Garland classic, Ariana Grande, Troye Sivan – each song creating a different mood, a different feeling. I've lost track of how many songs we've gone through, how long Seth and I have been dancing, when Kaye turns the volume down.

'Did you feel it?' he asks. He taps my chest. 'Did you feel it here? Because that's what this is. You of all people should know what that feeling is, that rush you get from performing.'

'It's hardly—'

'No,' Kaye says. 'That's what that was. There wasn't an audience of thousands, there wasn't a standing ovation or a fucking red curtain, but that was a performance. You're discovering who she is, what she does.'

'But what if I'm not ready in time?'

'You'll be ready,' Kaye says. 'Readiness is a state of mind as much as anything else and I'll do everything in my power to get you there. I promise. Just keep coming here. We'll arrange it. Every day. We'll make it work.'

'Thanks, Kaye.'

He looks away from me.

'What?'

'Do you hear that?' he asks.

'What?'

'That infernal buzzing,' he says. 'I knew I could hear something when the music was on but I thought it was my age. Thank God, I thought I was losing my marbles. Can one of you shut it off?'

I look at Seth. He goes and checks his phone then shrugs.

I walk over to the sofa where I've left my bag. My phone has fallen out. It's vibrated itself on to the sofa cushions and I see that it has gone ten thirty and my phone is flooded with messages and missed calls.

'Oh shit,' I say.

'What?'

'My mum.'

'Your mum?' Seth sounds concerned.

'Your mum?!' Kaye does not.

I scroll through my phone. Message after message asking if I'm still at dancing, if I'm on my way home yet, to message her when I get this, and then calls. So many calls. Holy shit.

'I've missed a lot of calls. I think she's home.'

'Didn't she know you were here?'

I shake my head, feeling suddenly sheepish in front of Seth, in front of Kaye.

I step out on to the stairs and dial Mum's number. She picks up immediately. I can hear she's in a state; her breath is short. She is panicking, or at least has been.

'Robin?'

'Hi Mum,' I say. 'What's up?'

'What's up?' she shrieks. 'What's up? Robin, I've been calling you for the last half an hour. I got home at half nine expecting you to be here, and when you weren't I called you and you didn't answer, so I called Miss Emily at the dance school and she said you hadn't been there *all week* so what's up at the moment is that I thought my son was dead.'

'Mum, I'm sorry I—'

'Come home,' she interrupts. 'Come home, now.'

I go back into the dressing room to see Kaye stood

there with a packet of make-up wipes. He nudges my chin so I look up. I must look upset because he's smiling at me, clearly trying to make me feel better.

'Get that stuff off your face and go home,' he says. He hands me a piece of paper with a number on it. 'If you can, come back before Dragcellence tomorrow and we'll do more of this. Otherwise, let me know when you can.' It feels ominous, like he knows how much trouble I'm in before I do. 'Just message me, OK?'

I nod and Kaye kisses me on the cheek.

'Is she mad?' Seth asks.

I nod. 'Furious.' My voice is shaking. I've been caught out and I have no idea what I'm going home to.

'Get your make-up off,' Seth says. 'I'll drive you back.'

'But my bike—'

'We'll come back for it, Robin,' he says. 'If your mum is worried, we just need to get you home, yeah?'

I nod and Kaye undoes the dress and helps me out of the corset. I take a seat and start to take off the make-up, wiping off what is probably the best face I've ever had, but for the briefest moment before I swipe the make-up wipe across my face I see her. For the first time since I started doing this, I see my drag-self looking back at me. I have a horrible feeling it will be a long time before I get to see her again.

TWENTY-ONE

When Seth pulls up outside my house, I realize I haven't spoken all the way home, not a single freaking word. I thank him and get out of the car.

'Do you want me to wait?' he asks.

'It's probably best that you don't,' I say. 'I don't want my mum to yell at you too. That would be way too embarrassing.'

'I'll pick you up in the morning,' he says. It's not a question.

'Thank you.'

Seth drives away and I look up at the house. All the lights are on and I can see Mum's outline in the window. She must have seen me because she disappears into the house. I'm in trouble.

As I walk the path to the front door, I try to think of an excuse that would be valid. She knows I've not been dancing. She's probably been in touch with Natalie and I have no idea what she will have told her. The silence in the house is utterly terrifying. The air is thick with tension that

I practically have to swim through just to make it to the kitchen where Mum is waiting, leaning on the countertop.

'Mum, I'm so sorry.'

'What for?' she asks.

'For staying out late and not messaging you. I just lost track of time and—'

'But not at dancing,' she says. 'You told me you had a dance class tonight. But I called Miss Emily and she told me she's not seen you since Monday. So, where were you?'

'I was—'

'And I want the truth,' she says, keeping herself as calm as possible. 'No more lies, Robin, please. I can't—'

She looks over at me and sees something. She crosses to me and slowly turns my face into the light.

'I don't even know what to say right now,' she says. 'Why do you have make-up on your face?'

I hurry over to the mirror, watching the specks of glitter twinkle back at me as I turn my head from side to side. Shit.

'I was at . . . Entity,' I say, trying to keep my voice even. 'There's a drag queen there who—'

'Entity?' she says. 'In Southford?

'Yes, Mum, but—'

'After everything we talked about?' she says. 'You know how worried I was when you went there for your birthday.'

'Which is why I didn't tell you. I—'

'Oh, you thought you were doing me a favour?' She laughs. 'Well, thank you, Robin, thank you very much.'

'What?'

'You lied to me!' she says. 'I know our situation is unusual. There are people at work who think it's bizarre how much I trust you, but that trust comes from the truth universally acknowledged that we don't lie to one another. It comes from the fact that when you say you're at a dance class, I know you're at a dance class, or when you say you're going to be at home, you are home.'

'I didn't want you to worry, so—'

'So when you don't answer my texts and I call your dance teacher and she tells me you haven't been there all week, how am I supposed to react?' she says. 'When you continue to not answer my calls, what am I supposed to be apart from worried? I didn't know where you were! Greg didn't know where you were! I didn't want someone knocking on my door in the middle of the night telling me you'd been beaten up again. I didn't want some stranger who drove you home tonight, whoever *that* was, having to explain to me what had happened to you because you were too broken to do it yourself.'

'I . . .' I don't know what to say to that. The simple thing would be to tell her the truth, but she's already worried. I think she already knows. To say it out loud . . . I don't know if I can.

'I feel like I'm losing you,' she says. 'We don't lie to each other, Robin; we don't do that. You're supposed to be a good kid, a grown man. If all had gone well, in a few months' time, you'd be out in the world doing your own thing, but here you are lying to me, behaving like a spoiled, thoughtless teenager.'

That hurts.

'I'm sorry,' I say. It feels like it's all I have.

A silence falls between us. It's like a crack in the ground, so wide and getting wider still, each of us on either side of it.

'You will come home every night after school,' she says. 'Whether I'm working or not, you will be here. You will message me to tell me you're home. I'll have Alice next door check in or something, I don't know.'

'What about dance classes?'

'That shouldn't matter, considering you've not even been going,' she says, her tone measured, so calm it's almost frightening. 'No going to clubs on school nights. You will be home by four thirty, no exceptions.' She looks up at me, her eyes red. She looks like she's about to cry. 'I thought I had lost you tonight, Robin. I was out of my mind with worry. I called *everybody* I could think of. I was moments away from calling the police because I thought something had happened to you, and I can't have something happen to you, Robin, not again, OK? I can't have you coming home black and blue and bleeding. I can't take it. So it won't happen.'

'So you're shutting me away?'

'Robin—'

'You're going to turn me into some kind of recluse because you're scared?'

'Damn right I'm scared,' she says. 'I don't expect you to understand what I'm feeling or be happy about what I'm doing, but I have to put my foot down.'

'You can't do that, Mum! I have to have a life!' I shout. 'I'll lose my mind. I've already lost LAPA, if I lose this—'

'There are other things you can do than working in a club, Robin. You can teach, you can—'

'Mum, you're not listening to me!' She's jumped to the wrong conclusion and I want to correct her, but what's the use? She's taking it away from me anyway.

'No, you're not listening to me, Robin,' she says. 'This is my decision and my decision is final. When you're out of school, you can do what you want, but until then it's my way and I don't want you going there any more.'

'Mum, please—'

'Robin, end of conversation.'

So I go. I run upstairs, rage, upset, anger, panic, a million and one things coursing through my entire body. I slam the door, because it feels like the only thing I can do right now. It's probably the first time I've ever slammed a door in my life and it feels kind of cathartic so I open it and slam it again. I slam my drawers, the door to my wardrobe, I punch my duvet, my pillows, I cry and I cry and I cry because I've probably ruined the only thing keeping me sane, the only glimmer of hope I had for next year.

I can't go back to Entity and it feels like my world has fallen apart.

TWENTY-TWO

I don't see Mum when I get up the following morning. I get ready, I shower, I eat breakfast, I make my lunch, and when she doesn't surface before I have to go I just leave. I consider shouting 'Goodbye' up the stairs, but there is a hollowness in my chest that tells me not to. So I don't.

I wait outside for Seth. My heart skips when his car rounds the corner and I wonder if Mum is watching me as I get into the passenger seat.

'Good morning,' I say, finding the energy to offer him a smile that he returns, though there is a sympathy behind his eyes like he knows that things haven't gone well. Maybe he can sense it.

'What happened?'

'You don't want to hear it.'

I turn the radio on. He turns it off.

'I've seen you cry, Robin,' he says. 'I think we're good to talk about bad days.'

I sigh. 'You're sure? It's a doozy.'

'Try me.'

I sigh again and proceed to tell him what Mum said. How I know she worries and how I lied anyway. It sounds awful coming out of my mouth. God, I really messed this up.

'So, what are you going to do?' he asks as we drive past my dance school that I can't go to any more, past the rival school.

I shrug. 'It will blow over eventually – by which point Kaye will probably have moved on to someone else because I've stopped showing up.'

'The way he did you up last night was beautiful,' Seth says.

'I wish I'd got a picture or something,' I say, a smile tugging at my mouth. 'Thanks for the lips, by the way.'

'Don't mention it,' he says. 'Robin, you can't just stop going. I know it's bad, but you just can't.'

'What are you suggesting?'

'Well, we need to go and get your bike anyway, right?' he says. 'So, why don't I drive you there today?'

'Did you not hear me when I said that my mum is keeping tabs on me?' I say. 'The neighbours are going to be checking up on me and everything. It's like freaking house arrest or something. Besides, there's no way I can get to Southford and back here before my mum would want me home.'

'So, we don't go after school,' he says, a sly smile on his face. 'When are your free periods today?'

And I realize exactly what he's suggesting and suddenly want to collapse or something. I've never cut school in my life.

'Seth, are you out of your mind? We can't—'

'Who says we can't?' he interrupts. 'You register in the morning, you go out on a free period, you come back – who will know?'

'Seth, I can't. I have exams—'

'This is Mrs Finch in your head,' he says. 'I hate that. Look, you didn't care when you were skipping classes for auditions, why is this any different? This is your life.'

'Yeah, Seth, it's my life. I can't have you fucking up yours too.'

He scoffs and shrugs. 'Don't worry about me. My life is pretty messed up as it is. I want to help. I've never seen anyone light up like you did when that music hit you.'

'Really?' I say. And I know what he's talking about. I could feel it in that moment – that tiny little spark that I always had before a show, during a performance, it was there again like it had never been away.

'I have no reason to lie to you,' he says as we pull into school. While he's parking the car, I can't help but think that maybe he's right. This isn't even a skipped class, it's a free period, and who cares about a skipped free period? If Kaye is free, it couldn't hurt.

'I'm free after my psychology class,' I say. 'I don't have a class until after lunch.'

Seth smiles. 'Then we'll go then.'

When I get out of the car, I see Connor. He's not too far away, watching as Seth and I walk towards school. I take a few deep breaths, wishing him away, not wanting to have to deal with him this morning of all freaking mornings.

'Would you look at that,' Seth says, nodding in Connor's direction. 'You ready to tell me about him yet?'

'Long story,' I reply.

'Boyfriend?'

I freeze. I don't even know how to answer that.

'I promise I'll tell you all about it, but I can't right now.'

'Robin, if you need me to—'

'I'm OK,' I say. 'I'll see you later. Meet you out here?'

He looks disappointed, but nods before heading towards school.

Connor walks up to me. 'Robin—'

'Please just drop it, Connor,' I snap, trying to speak quietly. I'm still trying to protect him, even when he is coming to talk to me somewhere way too open. 'I can't do this right now. I've got too much shit going on and I just can't deal with it so—'

'Do you want to talk about it?' he says, and I look at him. That warm, welcoming smile. The kind of smile that makes

272

me feel like I'm not alone and that maybe I am worthy of love even if it is from someone who calls me a . . . a . . .

'Not with you. Can you go, please?'

'Robin—'

'You heard him, Connor. Just go.' Natalie is behind him and her timing is so perfect I want to cry and kiss her wonderful, wonderful face.

Connor gives me a last, pleading look, then walks away, back towards the school, back to wherever his friends are, back to his other life, the one that doesn't have me in it.

'Impeccable timing,' I say. 'How do you do that?'

She shrugs. 'It's a gift. What are you doing in the car park?'

'Got a lift with Seth.'

She widens her eyes.

'It's honestly not what you think,' I say. 'But thanks for rescuing me.'

She shrugs and we start to walk towards school.

'What's going on? Has something happened with Connor?'

'I haven't really slept,' I say. 'Had a big fight with Mum,' I add.

'Right. Did you tell her about Entity?'

I nod. 'I had to.'

'And she was pissed.'

'I sort of deserve it,' I say. 'I mean, I've lied to her enough. But she went way overboard. She's not letting me go to dance classes. Or Entity. Basically, my drag career is over before it's even started. But I'm going with Seth today and—'

'Hold on, hold on, you're going anyway? How? Why?'

'I have to pick up my bike and Seth said he would drive me over.'

'But when?'

'I have a free period after psychology,' I say.

Natalie stops walking and eyes me carefully. 'Robin Cooper.'

'What?'

'Skipping school.'

'I'm not!' I protest. 'It's a free period. If I'm not free to do what I want, then that's false advertising.'

She laughs. 'I have the most beautiful image in my head of you explaining that to Mrs Finch.'

'She'd kill me.'

'She'd decapitate you and put your head on a pike outside her office.'

'Extreme.'

Natalie shrugs. 'So you're going?'

I nod. 'I have to, Nat. Last night Kaye offered me a slot performing,' I say. 'Paid. In drag. And . . . I have to

274

rehearse. I can't not, it's too big of a thing.'

Natalie nods, pouting her lips, thinking. 'I'll cover for you.'

'What?'

'If anyone asks where you are, I'll cover for you. But just this once, OK? It's a slippery slope to delinquency.'

'I don't deserve you.'

'You really don't,' she says.

'Thank you,' I say. 'OK, enough on me, how was your night?'

'No, not so fast,' she says. 'I need to know what the hell is going on with you and lover boy. He's making the puppy dog eyes at you and trying to talk to you and you're giving him nothing.'

'I am not giving him nothing.'

'You are giving him absolute nootch,' she says. 'In the dictionary next to the word nootch is a picture of you and the faces you were just pulling at Connor. Giving him absolutely nothing. Have you two had a fight or something? Have you broken up?'

'OK, first of all, if nootch makes it into the dictionary, I owe you some coin,' I say. 'And maybe I'm giving him nootch, but maybe it's because he deserves it.' I start walking again but she stops me.

'Robin, seriously, tell me,' she says.

I sigh. 'Can we walk and talk? I honestly can't look at your face while I tell you this.'

'Sure.'

As we walk towards school, I fill her in on everything that happened outside Entity. Everything from the way Connor looked at me, to Ryan and the rest of his friends showing up, to what Connor said to me, to the hug with Seth. She's dumbstruck.

'Please say something,' I say. 'The silence is horrible.'

'I just can't believe he would say that to you. And I can't believe you didn't tell me.'

'Yeah.' I shrug. 'Well. It's embarrassing.'

She stops dead and grabs hold of my arm. 'Robin, *please* tell me you're not making excuses for him in your head.'

'Nat—'

'No, for fuck's sake, Robin, you can't just let him say that to you and then go back to making out with him. That's not cool,' she barks.

'I'm not, I swear, but—'

'Argh,' she groans. 'Look, Robin, I love you so much OK? You're my best friend in the whole universe. Do you have any idea how much it kills me to see you with someone who doesn't treat you right?' She slides her hand down my arm and locks her fingers with mine. 'You're so great, and Connor has been such a prick. First not coming out for your birthday, then ghosting you and now *this*! He hangs out with pricks and he is treating you like an experiment and I won't have it.'

I want to remind her how he is when we're alone. How sweet he is, how he seems like he cares for me in those moments, how happy he has made me, but I know that won't cut it. I'm not even sure that cuts it with me any more.

'Have I totally lost you to the depths of your own head?' she says.

'I'm . . . I'm thinking that I don't really know what to do about the whole situation,' I say. She opens her mouth to speak, but I keep going. 'I don't want to talk to him or confront him about it. And we haven't really spoken since it happened so it doesn't feel like there is much to say. He thinks I'm disgusting and he called me a . . .' I don't even want to say it myself. It just doesn't seem right to put the word out into the world. If I were braver, I'd reclaim it, but I don't feel brave enough.

'Then let me talk to him. I'll give that asshole a piece of my mind.'

'Please don't,' I say. 'I just want it to go away.'

'Well, sweetheart, at the moment the only thing that isn't going away is Connor because you're not talking to him about it,' she says. 'Get rid of him. I promise you there is someone better out there.'

'Are you talking about Seth?'

She shrugs. 'I don't know. Maybe. I'm still not sold on him yet.'

'He's really great, Nat,' I say. 'Seriously.'

And I think back to what so very nearly almost happened last night as he painted my lips, and I'm about to tell Natalie about it when I realize I need to do some damage control.

'Can we not tell Greg? About the Connor stuff?'

'Sure,' she says. 'Why?'

'You know what he's like,' I say. 'He's so protective and I don't want Connor to get the wrath of Greg. He hates Connor enough as it is.'

'*The Wrath of Greg* sounds like a terrible movie that I definitely want to watch,' she says. 'But sure. We can keep it between us. Though I don't know if Greg has a wrath, so you might not need to worry.'

I shrug. She has absolutely no idea. I'm sort of glad about that. 'Well, still.'

The bad feeling sinks to the pit of my stomach, weighing me down as we continue our walk into school. I need to find the power to finish things with Connor before it's too late, before either Greg or Nat find out things that I don't want them to find out. That's the last thing I need right now. I've already lost Mum. I can't lose them too.

*

I spend the rest of the morning watching the clock, waiting for the moment when Seth and I can leave school and drive to Entity. I messaged Kaye and explained the situation, and he said he could meet us there during my free period. My heart was pounding so loudly in class that I'm surprised no one heard it.

As I pack my stuff up at the end of psychology, Natalie puts a finger to her lips and shushes, dramatically winking at me before I leave. I blow her a kiss before I run outside and meet Seth, jumping into his car.

'You ready?' he asks. 'Last chance to change your mind. The second we're off school property we're technically playing hookie.'

I take a deep breath. How much do I really want this? Enough. 'Drive.'

TWENTY-THREE

'Wait, you need to go back. Kaye wanted you to do what?' Greg asks, his eyes wide, his mouth agape.

'It's called tucking,' I say.

'It already sounds painful.'

'Well, it wasn't exactly a barrel of laughs,' I reply.

On Saturday afternoon, I had to get myself out of the house. All I'd had from Mum was silence and I just couldn't take it any more. So Greg and I headed over to Natalie's and I tried to explain the concept of tucking . . . badly.

'So how do you . . . ? I mean, what do you . . . ? Does it even . . . ?' Greg is squirming, crossing and uncrossing his legs as if I've just asked him to do it.

'There are a lot of ways to tuck and basically I wasn't about to put tape on my dick so we needed to find another way and the way we found was . . . . better,' I say. 'I mean it's not the most comfortable thing in the world, but the feeling goes away after a while. And you only start to feel the pain again when you *know* you're getting out of drag.'

'So you've tucked?' Natalie asks. 'You've actually done it?'

'Yes,' I say. 'I said a prayer to our dear lord and saviour Britney, shoved my balls up inside my body, pulled on a pair of tucking pants and . . . well . . . that's probably way too much information.'

'I've just heard way more than I ever want to hear about your balls,' Greg says. 'No offence.'

'Well, you did ask,' I reply, laughing.

I hated that I couldn't stay to watch Dragcellence. Pristine and The Duchess sent me videos of the guest performers they had (a queen called Angela Mansbury who did a full Mrs Potts routine and Dory Ann Slay, a slam poet who tore the roof off the place), but it just wasn't the same.

'Subject change?' I request. My phone buzzes. Seth asking what I'm up to. I quickly reply and put my phone back down, ignoring the messages from Connor sitting unread in my inbox.

'How is uni stuff going?' Greg asks Nat. Nat looks suddenly uncomfortable.

'Nat, I'm honestly fine. You can talk about uni – I'm not going to fall apart, I swear.' I've been trying my hardest not to think about LAPA and my drama-school prospects. The focus has been so much on Dragcellence, and the fact that I'm performing, that it slips to the back of my head. Which is where it needs to stay until application season comes around again and I go into a stress-induced panic. If I even decide to apply again.

'This isn't about that,' she says. 'I'm . . . I'm sort of . . . God, why is this so hard to say?'

'What's going on?'

'I'm reassessing my options,' she says, sounding a little bit like Mrs Finch.

'What do you mean? You're still going to Queen Mary, right?' I say.

'Well . . .' She trails off and looks away. And now I'm confused because that had always been the plan. For three years it had been the plan. She would go to Queen Mary and I would go to LAPA. They were the dream schools. They always have been.

'What? It's the dream, what's changed?'

'You.'

And now I'm looking at her like she's out of her mind.

'Come on, Robin, you know why I picked Queen Mary,' she says.

'Because you wanted to go there.'

'Yeah,' she says. 'But, also, no. It was because I thought we were going to be near one another, and we could live together. Durham is—'

'Durham? I thought that was where your dad wanted you

to go,' I say. 'You always hated the idea of—'

'No, I didn't,' she says. 'Maybe then, but it's a really good school. And, yeah, Dad has bored me to pieces about it, but maybe if I'd had a chance to really think about my options—'

'What's that supposed to mean?'

'Come on, Robin, I don't want to fight about this, but you bulldozed me with your ideas of us being together next year, and now that we're not I get to do what I want to do.'

'Oh.' Guilt crashes over me like a wave. 'I never meant to—'

'I'm not trying to make you feel bad, OK? It's just that I need to think about me now,' she says. 'I need to think of my own plan. I don't even know what you're doing next week, let alone next year.'

'Excuse me?'

'Don't take this the wrong way, Robin. You're just off doing a different thing and that's great because you're happy, but I need to know that I'm making the right choice for me.'

'I thought you *wanted* to go to Queen Mary. I thought you *wanted* to be together next year,' I say. 'I'm sorry for being such a burden.'

'Guys, don't do this,' Greg says.

'Christ, trust you to make this dramatic and all about you, Robin,' Natalie says.

'I'm not. I just didn't realize that me being a failure was such a freeing experience for you.'

'Oh for fuck's sake.'

'What?'

'Not everything revolves around you,' Natalie barks.

'Maybe my failure is the best thing that happened to you, huh?'

'You know what? Maybe it is!' Natalie says. 'Maybe you not being good enough to get into the top uni in the country is great, because I did. And I'm glad you haven't because it means I can go and do that without hurting your precious feelings. I'm free to do what I want.'

My phone buzzes at my side, and I see it's another message from Seth.

'Proving my point,' Natalie says, going back to her work.

A silence engulfs us and it isn't long before I'm making my excuses and leaving, Greg following close behind, running out into the street to catch up with me.

What she's saying makes absolute sense, but there's something else buried in it and I can feel it gnawing at my soul. Everything is changing. I hate that.

'So she hates me,' I say as Greg catches up. 'Have I been that awful? I'm sorry Greg, I—'

'She doesn't hate you. She's just figuring things out. And now the drag thing is happening and she feels like you're off doing your own thing and she doesn't matter so much.'

'But she *does* matter,' I say. 'She matters the most. God, I'm such a dick.'

'Nah,' he says. 'You're just going through your own stuff. Getting rejected from LAPA was really freaking hard for you so you're, I don't know, I guess you're so distracted by the drag stuff that it can come off that you don't care as much, which I know isn't true, but I'm just saying it, OK?'

I sigh. 'OK. It's the performance, though.'

'Huh?'

'It means a lot to get that slot in Dragcellence,' I say. 'It could be big and I really want it to go well. We don't have a lot of time and . . . I'm scared of failing again.'

'I get that,' Greg says. 'I really do. Just be careful with Natalie. I think she feels like she's losing you to this.'

'She's not. It's just—'

'Where your focus is right now – I know,' he says. 'But be careful.'

'I just need it to work,' I say. 'Like . . . God, I hate that I'm putting pressure on it, but if this goes well it could stop next year feeling so shit after you all leave.'

We walk a little further in silence, me pushing my bike, Greg wandering along beside me.

'You know,' he says, 'we'll actually be close to each other next year.'

'What?'

'I changed my mind for next year,' he says. 'Stuff isn't great at home and, well, Southford is as good a uni as Edinburgh for maths and this way I get to stay with Archie . . .' He trails off. 'So, you know, you won't be totally without friends or whatever. It won't be shit. I'll still be here.'

I stop and put my bike on the ground, wrapping my arms round Greg. He tenses up a little at first, but quickly returns the hug.

'What's this for?' he asks.

'For being a friend,' I reply.

On Monday morning, Seth is waiting for me at the bike sheds and it makes me want to die. His face bursts into a smile when he sees me and I hop off my bike and hug him. It feels right to be with him again. The weekend without him was borderline unbearable.

'Good weekend?' he asks.

'Horrible,' I say. 'I'm messing everything up.'

'How?'

'Natalie this time,' I say. 'We got into a fight.'

'So fix it.'

I laugh. 'Wow, didn't think of that. Thanks, Seth.'

'Do you want to talk about it?'

I shake my head. 'Not really. I'll figure it out, I guess. How was yours?'

'Fine,' he says. 'I had stupid amounts of homework to do. And I had this guy messaging me all weekend, couldn't shake him off no matter how hard I tried.'

'Why do I get the feeling you didn't try as hard as you think you did?' I say, nudging him as we walk. I take a moment. 'It wasn't too much, was it? If you want me to stop messaging or you're busy or—'

He grabs my hand and it stops me dead. 'You're OK,' he says. 'The messaging was fun. It's not like I had anything better to do.'

'Oh, the compliments,' I say. 'My cup runneth over.'

'God, why do you get me all tongue-tied?' he says. 'I just mean that . . . like I . . .' It's weird seeing him flustered. Seth doesn't do flustered, Seth does effortlessly cool Danny Zuko realness and this side of him is . . . interesting. And fifty shades of adorable. 'I liked messaging you. Please keep doing it.'

'Noted.'

As we walk towards school, I notice Connor looking over at me from his pack of friends. I can see that he wants to approach, I can see it in the way that he looks at me, but we both know that he won't because it's too much of a risk to try to talk to me out in the open.

'What are you doing with Kaye today?' Seth asks conspiratorially. When we saw Kaye on Friday we established when the best times were for us to come to Entity. At the time I felt really good about it, but after what happened with Natalie it feels like it's not such a good idea.

'Look, Seth, I know you offered and I really appreciate it, but—'

'OK,' he says. 'So we can meet out here at twelve, yeah?'

'Yeah,' I reply. I can't say no. Not to Seth nor to this opportunity. I have to take it.

'What's up?' he asks as we walk into school.

'Am I doing the right thing?' I ask. 'Am I becoming too obsessed?'

'Where is this coming from?' he asks.

'The fight with Natalie . . .' I say. 'Part of it was that I am ditching everything for drag right now. And I feel bad. Like I'm being selfish.'

Seth shrugs. 'Maybe you need to be selfish this time,' he says. 'You're not just doing this for fun – this could be your career.' He checks the time. 'Come on, we're late. If you don't want to go, Robin, we don't—'

'No,' I say. 'No, I'll see you at twelve.'

Natalie spends the morning being pissed at me for what happened on Saturday no matter what I do or say to try to smooth things over. She's even more annoyed when I walk out of a free period to head off to Entity. But she doesn't say anything.

The week continues like this; I take every opportunity I get to be driven off to Southford by Seth, learn something off Kaye and then rush back to school for class. On Tuesday, we try different dresses, some where I'm tucked, some where I'm not, to see what works for my body shape. On Thursday, Kaye has a few of her Dragcellence family members show me what they do, how they perform, giving me ideas. If Seth isn't free, I'm off in one of the dance studios at school, practising in a pair of heels. Priya has been sending me videos from the classes, new combinations to learn. Along with those I repeat exercises I've done in my dance classes at school, praying no one walks in and catches me.

By the time the weekend arrives again, I've spent three out of the past five days with Kaye and I've only really seen Natalie and Greg at lunch or during classes, which makes me feel like a bad friend. Greg is trying to be as supportive as he can, but I can see it in Natalie's eyes when she forces herself to say 'hello' or 'goodbye' to me. But it's my choice, isn't it? The show is in a week and I don't feel anywhere close to ready. This could be a chance to actually do something next year, to perform and get paid for it rather than waiting for my next opportunity to come along. I have to do it.

TWENTY-FOUR

Sunday night rolls around and I've spent the day in my room, catching up on work, watching drag on my computer and texting Seth. Things with Mum are improving. She doesn't know I've been going to Entity, so she doesn't hate me so much any more. We're just not talking like we used to. There's a barrier there and I don't know if it's her or me.

I'm about to go down for dinner before Mum heads off to work when my phone buzzes. I half expect it to be Seth again, but it's a name I've not seen for a while.

Connor.

> I'm outside. Please talk to me.

There is a burning in my chest. He can't be outside right now, not while Mum is here. It's too much.

> Mum is in. I can't. Tomorrow?

The three dots appear so quickly that I know if I looked out of the window right now his face would be lit up in the dark by his phone.

You won't talk to me tomorrow. Please. You can't keep doing this.

I know he won't go away. And there is a part of me that is curious about what he thinks he can say that will make this situation any better.

I sneak downstairs, past Mum in the kitchen preparing dinner. I close the door to the hallway and open the front door. He's right there, looking so unbelievably crushed that a wave of guilt threatens to drag me under.

'Hello,' he says, like it's the heaviest word in the world.

'Look, Connor, you can't be here right now,' I say. 'My mum is in and you know she doesn't know about us so . . .'

'What us?' he says. 'I've not spoken to you in ages and . . . I miss you.'

'OK,' I say. I hear the Natalie voice in my head, the one that tells me to end it, the one that tells me to get him off my doorstep and to never come back. 'But what you said to me, Connor, it—'

'It was only because Ryan was there and—'

'No, Connor,' I say. 'You were there when it happened last time and you were about to let it happen again. That really hurt me and . . . I'm not going to keep doing this. It hurts me too much. I care about you, I do, but for my own sanity I just have to stop this.'

'Is this because of Seth?'

'Seth?'

'The one you keep getting driven around by,' he says.

'This has nothing to do with him,' I say. And I mean it. Even without Seth, I know that this is what I need to do. 'I'm doing this for me.'

'Robin, don't do this,' he says, and he looks like he might cry, which makes me feel like some kind of monster. 'You can't, Robin, I need you. We can work this out . . .'

'Connor, no,' I say.

'Let's talk about it,' he says. 'Come on.' He reaches his hand out to me and it takes every little bit of willpower in my body not to take it and run out into the night in my pyjama shorts with no shoes on. 'Let's go.'

'I can't,' I say, though what I really mean is that I don't want to. And there is something at least a tiny bit freeing in that.

'Robin, are you at the door?' Mum calls. I can hear her approaching. Connor looks torn. He doesn't know whether it's worse to face my mum or to give up on this entirely.

'Connor, she's coming to the door,' I say. 'Just go. You don't want to do this.'

'I do, Robin, please.'

'I don't have anything else to say,' I say. 'I can't be with you any more, Connor. So you don't have to do this. Just go and—'

He reaches forward and grabs hold of my wrist. 'Come on, Robin, just come for a walk with me. After everything we've been through, you can't just—'

Mum opens the door to the hallway and stares daggers at me. She looks at Connor's hand wrapped round my wrist, at the tears blooming in my eyes.

'What's going on?' she asks.

'Connor was just leaving,' I say, trying to pull my wrist free. His grip is tight. He won't let go.

'No, I'm not. We're just talking.'

'This doesn't look much like talking,' Mum says, her voice firm. Suddenly she seems worried, and I don't blame her; this doesn't exactly scream 'healthy relationship'. 'What's your name? Connor?'

'Yes.'

'Will you let go of my son, please?'

'But—'

'Oh, believe me, Connor, that wasn't a request.' Connor can't see the signs because he's known my mother for all of two seconds, but she is about to unleash some kind of horror on him like none he has ever seen before. If he knows what's good for him, he'll run fast and run far. 'Either you let go of my son, or I will make you let go.'

He releases my wrist and takes a step back. 'Robin, please, I just—'

Mum steps in front of me. 'I think the conversation was over some time ago, Connor,' she says. 'Now run along.'

'Mrs Cooper, please, I—'

'Connor,' she says. 'Go.'

He peers around her to look at me, but I can barely bring myself to meet his gaze. My eyes are full of tears and he is just a blur at this point. But I see him walk away and I see Mum close the door and, without even thinking about it, I sink to the floor.

'OK,' she says softly, her mood moving from murderous bear to mother hen in the blink of an eye. 'I don't know Connor, do I?'

'No.'

'Is he a friend?'

'Um . . .'

'More than a friend?'

'Well . . .'

She sighs. 'I might need more syllables. I might be a mum, but I'm not a mind reader, much as I wish I was,' she says. 'Do you want some tea?'

'It's late.'

'It's tea, what are you, eighty?' I look up at her and she's smiling. She walks to the kitchen and I hear her fill up the kettle and put it on. I also hear the clattering of biscuits falling on to a plate, so I know she's already figured out what the situation requires. She might not be a mind reader, but she's pretty close.

'OK,' she says, carrying the two mugs of tea to the dining table. 'At the risk of setting you off singing, I'm going to say, let's start at the very beginning.'

'I've heard it's a very good place to start,' I say.

'You know, I've heard that too!' she says. 'Sit.'

I peel myself off the floor and join her.

'Are you sure you want to hear this?' I say, taking a sip of my tea. 'It's long and I don't think I come off particularly well in it.'

'Sweetheart, you've not come off particularly well at all recently, so I wouldn't worry about it too much,' she says, taking a biscuit. 'Go on.'

'It started in detention—'

'You had a detention!'

'Yes,' I say, impatient. 'In September, come *on*, Mum, you know that.'

'Why did you have detention?'

'Because I told Mrs Finch to bite me.'

Mum nearly chokes on her biscuit, unable to keep the

smile off her face. 'I don't remember that. Why did you do that?'

'I don't remember — it was something about auditions I think, but she wasn't happy about it.'

'Was I?'

'You high-fived me after I did it,' I say.

'I did?'

'Seriously, Mum, some consistency in your parenting would be so good every once in a while,' I say.

'Don't push it,' she says. 'Carry on.'

'We were in detention, the teacher had abandoned us to go and do some printing or something, so we were left alone,' I say. 'We'd never really spoken before. I thought it would just be a lot of awkward silence, but then he started asking me about gay stuff.'

'Gay stuff?' Mum says it like the absolute vaguery that it is. 'What's gay stuff?'

'He asked me how I knew I was gay, stuff like that,' I reply. 'And I told him that I just knew, because I did.'

'Christ, Robin, this is starting to sound like the start of a porn film.'

'I don't want to know how you know that,' I say. 'But he asked if I'd kissed a boy and I said I hadn't, so he asked if I wanted to kiss him, and one thing led to another and we started kissing and he gave me his number and then we've pretty much been sneaking around kissing and . . . doing other things for the past six months.'

'Wow.'

'Yeah.'

'And I didn't even notice!' She sits back in her chair and takes a sip of her tea. 'Maybe I've been working too much because you'd think I'd notice something like that.'

'Honestly, Mum, I was waiting for the day that I came home and you said, "So, Robin, who the fuck is Connor and when do I need to buy a hat for the wedding?" you know?'

'OK, first of all, I do *not* sound like that,' she says. 'But why do I get the feeling that this isn't the whole story?'

And she says she isn't a mind reader.

'Well, because it isn't,' I say. 'He's nice and everything, when we're together, but when we are at school it's all hush hush and no one is allowed to know.'

'He's in the closet?'

'So far in the closet he's in Narnia,' I say. 'And I don't mind that, it's his choice if or when he decides to come out, but he doesn't talk to me at school and he doesn't really treat me all that well when we're there because his friends are pricks and . . .'

'And what?'

And I'm crying again because this story just sucks so much.

'And I didn't tell you because it was his friends who beat me up over the summer,' I say. 'He didn't do anything, like, he didn't hit me or hurt me or anything like that, but he didn't stop it either.'

'And you dated him?'

'He apologized,' I say. 'His family is homophobic and awful, so are his friends, and . . . he was sweet.'

She raises an eyebrow. 'That's not all, is it?'

'He and his friends saw me outside Entity and he called me a faggot,' I say. 'When we were there last Monday night, he saw me in the street and his friends came over, and he didn't stand up for me. He just watched it happen and he even kind of joined in and if it wasn't for Seth . . . I mean, shit, I need to start saving myself one of these days, huh? If it wasn't for Seth stepping in, it might have happened all over again and . . . and it just . . . I don't know, it sucked. Like, I really liked him or I thought I did, and for him to do that to me when we'd been together for six months and so much had happened and . . .'

I trail off as I see Mum's expression. She's utterly horrified. And I am too, but there is still that bit of my brain that is coming up with excuses for him and I need to shut that off. I need this part of my life to be over.

The tears are rolling down my face now. I hate that he makes me feel this way.

'He was my first everything,' I say quietly. 'Like, absolutely everything and . . . I don't know, I wish I hadn't given it away to someone who just doesn't deserve it.'

'You had sex with him?' Mum asks. I can hardly believe I am sat at our dining table, crying and talking about sex with my mum. I want the earth to swallow me up.

I nod.

'Were you safe?'

'Mum!'

'Were you?' she asks. 'Look, I don't want gory details. I just want to know that you used a condom – it will give me peace of mind.'

'We did, yeah, every time,' I say. 'They scared the shit out of us at school about STIs – there was no way we weren't. I just feel so stupid. I gave him so much headspace and it was all for bloody nothing.'

'OK, Robin, I love you, but you do have a flair for the dramatic,' she says. 'Nothing is ever for nothing. Practically everything happens for a reason, even some of the shit stuff. This has taught you to expect more from people, and to not spend so much time on the ones who just aren't worth it. You deserve someone who treats you like a prince, not like some dirty little secret. You are no one's dirty little secret, Robin.' She takes a breath. 'As for the virginity stuff, well, virginity is a myth invented by the patriarchy to make women feel bad. It's now making you feel bad because HELLO, the patriarchy affects everyone, including men. So you slept with him,' she says. 'The saying is, you've got to kiss a lot of frogs, but you're obviously taking the study a little further than that.'

'Gross.'

'You're welcome.'

She moves around the table, sitting down on the chair next to me. 'Look,' she says. 'Men can be absolute shits sometimes, yourself included. But don't let him get you down. If he tries to talk to you at school tomorrow, tell him to piss off. Or get Natalie to do it – she'll probably enjoy it if he's been treating you like shit. Or Seth. He doesn't sound like a fan either.' She pauses and eyes me carefully. 'Do I know Seth?'

'No,' I say. 'Seth's new.' And that seems to be enough for her not to press it.

'What?' she says. 'What are you thinking?'

'It's just that . . .'

'Go on.'

'Connor is really going through it too, Mum,' I say. 'He's so scared of what his friends would say if they found out, of what his family would say and—'

'No, Robin, stop this,' she snaps. 'Stop making excuses for him, OK?'

'But, Mum, he's not a bad guy, I swear.'

'That's no excuse. He should have stepped in, he should have said something, not just let all that happen to you,' she says. 'Both times. Whether he knew you or not, what happened to you was wrong.'

'But, Mum—'

'Don't "but, Mum" me, Robin, come on! I raised you better than this!' she says, banging the table. 'What he did to you is not excusable on any level. He's allowed to not be out and to come to terms with his sexuality in his own time, that's his prerogative, but to have you sneaking around and feeling this way, and to not even defend you from his friends, and then to call you a . . .' She takes a breath. 'You know, if he was still at the door, I would tear his head right off.'

'I know, that's why I told him to go,' I say.

She sighs. 'No more excuses for him, OK? He's going through his own shit, sure, but that doesn't give him carte blanche to treat you this way. You're worth way more than that.'

She stands up and wraps her arms round me, kissing the top of my head. 'It'll be OK, my love,' she says. 'You've been through the shit and you're still alive. Shake him off and move on. There is a lovely guy out there waiting for you, and if he doesn't give you the absolute world then don't give him the time of day.'

TWENTY-FIVE

Seth rushes over, practically breaking into a small run, his satchel bashing against his leg as he approaches. Wow. I have a boy running towards me. Past me would lose his mind if he knew that.

'How are you doing?' he pants, a little out of breath as he reaches me. He leans on the wall near the bike sheds while I lock up. His cheeks are red, and there's the tiniest bead of sweat clinging to his forehead. How can he make sweaty look sexy? I don't understand it. It must be a perspective thing.

'I'm OK,' I say. 'Everything with Mum is . . . a lot. Stuff happened last night and we actually talked, which was nice and . . .' I trail off. 'You don't want to hear about that. I'm sorry.'

'What? Yes I do.'

'Come on, Seth, I feel like all I do is talk about me,' I say. 'Everything I have is drama and ridiculousness. Let's talk about something else.'

When I've locked up my bike, he pulls me into a hug and I breathe him in, hugging him back.

'What's this for?' I ask.

'You look like you need a hug,' he says. 'And I give good hugs, so it just makes sense.'

'So, it's a service you're providing?'

'Free of charge for you, Robin,' he says, letting me go. He's so corny it hurts me.

'Oh my God, this is getting boring now.' He points over to the tech block where Connor is standing with his friends, a cloud of smoke encircling them. Some vape, some smoke weed, either way they're a cluster of bad smell and I don't want to be near them. 'Head honcho of the Robin Cooper fan club.'

'I *really* don't want to get into this right now,' I say. I know I need to talk to Connor today, but not now, not like this. I'll get him alone and I'll break it off with him, but right now I just need to get inside.

We walk by Connor and his friends. I try not to look. And I mean I really try, but there's that little connection sparking up again. So I look and he's staring right at me, his eyes all big and pleading, seemingly not afraid to hide the fact that he's looking at me from his friends, which is dangerous. I'm not about to let him do that, so I turn away, and keep walking, round the corner and towards the school, keeping my focus on Seth because that feels safer.

'Robin?' I'm not expecting to hear Connor's voice so I

actually jump a little, which is kind of embarrassing. I turn to see him, alone. 'Robin, come here. Talk to me.'

I look around, trying to see if a couple of his friends have followed him round the corner. Some are watching him and my entire body is tense. He's staring at me so intently it actually scares me a bit.

'Connor, don't do this,' I say quietly. 'Not here. Think about it.'

'Please,' he says, advancing on me. I step back. 'What do you want me to do? I've said I'm sorry, I've come to your house—'

'He came to your house?' Seth asks.

'This doesn't concern you,' Connor growls.

'I think it does,' Seth says, stepping forward. I can see his fists clenched at his sides and I'm scared.

'Whatever,' Connor grumbles, turning his focus back to me. He's so close right now I can feel the heat of his body. The energy coming off him is chaotic and unstable, like not even he knows what he is going to do next. 'Robin, I don't know what you want me to do, but you can't keep ignoring me.'

His friends are still there and I don't want him to say something he can't take back.

'Connor, this is over. Stop it, OK?'

He reaches forward and grabs my arm. I see Seth stiffen

next to me. 'Robin, we can work this out. Why won't you give it a chance?'

I try to pull free. Seth is staring at Connor's hand gripped round my arm. I don't want this to escalate, I *so* don't want this to escalate. 'Connor, let go of me,' I say, trying to keep my voice steady because if I sound even the slightest bit distressed Seth will probably step in.

Connor grabs hold of my other arm and pulls me closer to him, his breath on my face, hot, wet, stinking of cigarettes. His grip is so tight I'm wincing, tears threatening to squeeze from my eyes. 'Robin, I—'

'That's enough,' Seth announces, grabbing hold of Connor and practically dragging him off me. 'He asked you to let go – he clearly doesn't want to talk to you – maybe you should just go.'

Connor pushes Seth hard in the chest. 'Who the hell are you to tell me what to do?'

Seth stumbles but recovers and pushes Connor back. He trips over his own feet, almost falling to the ground. 'Robin won't stand up to you, but I will,' Seth says. 'Now back off.'

'Make me.'

'I think I just did,' Seth snaps. I'm shaking. I don't want anyone getting hurt because of me, least of all Seth. 'Now walk away.'

His friends are approaching now – they know something

is up. Other students are gathering too, sniffing a fight from a mile off.

Connor steps towards Seth and he pushes him again, harder this time so Connor actually lands on the ground.

'Don't get up,' Seth shouts. 'And stay away from Robin, OK?'

Connor stays down and Seth turns to walk away, but before I have a chance to breathe a sigh of relief, Connor is back on his feet and has launched himself at Seth, the two of them gripping each other and wrestling to the ground.

'Stop it! Both of you, stop!' I shout, trying to pull them apart.

Connor ends up on top of Seth, managing to land a punch on Seth's face. The crowd gasps and I hate that this is turning into some kind of sideshow. I grab Connor and haul him off Seth, finding some kind of strength I didn't know I had as he stumbles away from us both. But that only gives Seth a chance to get back up, throwing himself at Connor and smacking him in the nose with a right hook. I swear I hear a break; I know I see blood and Connor stumbles to one side to lean on a wall.

A few moments later, Connor starts towards Seth again, and I can't let this go on. I hurry to stand between them.

'No more!' I shout, putting a hand up, as if that would stop a raging Connor. 'That's enough.' I walk over to Connor, keeping my voice as low as I can. 'I'm not doing this any more, Connor. You're not ready for any of this, OK? And I don't want you making a scene and outing yourself because of me. I don't want you to do that.'

'But, Robin—'

'No, Connor, look, there's an alternate universe where everything in life is perfect and maybe you and me work out, but in this timeline it's not happening,' I say. 'You need to figure out your shit, but you need to figure it out without me. We're through. Don't ever come near me again.'

I turn round and see Seth nursing his hand, wincing. He's still staring Connor down, like he wants to rip him apart. His jeans have what I think is a new rip in them and there is already a bruise blooming beneath his eye. I walk over and brush the gravel off him, and he's still staring at Connor as I do it.

'I'm so sorry,' I whisper. 'You didn't have to do that.'

'You were seeing him?' he asks, disgusted. 'Why didn't you say something?'

'I'll explain later,' I say, and I turn back to see Connor walking away. The crowd disperses and Connor heads back over to his friends. I should hate him right now, but I just hope he's going to be OK. I hope they didn't hear too much. 'We need to get you some ice or something. Come on, I'll take you to the medical room.'

'Can we not?'

'Seth, you've been punched in the face. You need ice or—'

'Somewhere else?'

I don't get it, but I don't need to get it. He's just saved my face at the expense of his own. I owe him.

We head inside, past reception, past the medical room and to the bathroom. It's empty, everybody in class getting registered by now. I grab a couple of paper towels and wet them, channelling my inner primary-school nurse.

I pass them to Seth who gingerly presses them to his eye, wincing a little on first contact. The wince is the tiniest stab of guilt.

'So, why not the medical room?' I ask as I pass him another paper towel for his hand.

'Thanks,' he says. 'My record is bad enough as it is. I don't think breaking someone's face is going to go down too well. So . . . thank you.'

'Don't mention it,' I say. 'Besides, shouldn't I be thanking you?'

He shakes his head and we head back outside, taking a seat on a bench near the entrance to the school. It's a little cold, and the dregs of students heading into school for registration are huddling into their jackets. The late ones, the naughty ones. Christ, when did I become one of them?

'You don't have to stay,' he says as he gets comfortable. 'Don't you have classes?'

'Oh, I definitely do,' I say, pulling my jacket around myself. 'But taking care of the boy who got a black eye and broke a guy's nose for me feels like it should be a priority.'

He laughs a little, so at least I know he isn't totally mad about this whole situation.

'So, explain what's going on with stoner boy?' he says.

'It's long.'

'Well, what a great way to start a story.' He raises the only eyebrow I can see suggestively and smiles. Gosh, he's got quite a smile. Wow. He leans back on the bench. 'Come on. If you're going to stay, you need to keep me entertained.'

I'd hardly describe everything that happened between Connor and I as entertaining, but it might make a good anecdote one day when it stops hurting like hell. I sit next to him and start at the very beginning, explaining absolutely everything to Seth. Almost everything, there are some things that should remain private.

'That's messed up,' he says flatly. 'All of it. You didn't need to lie to me.'

'It wasn't my secret to tell,' I say.

'You're a good guy,' he says. 'You could ruin his life, you know?'

'But what does that make me, huh? It's not my place.

He's got a tough family life and shitty friends, not that I'm making excuses for his behaviour or anything like that . . .' I trail off. 'But he's had his own shit going on. It's nobody's choice to decide when someone comes out. If they ever do . . .'

'Your mum is right that you deserve better. If I'd known all he did to you, I probably would have hit him harder.'

And now I feel sad. I'm mourning the loss of something that was definitely over the second he called me *that word*, that should have been over before it began. Dating a guy when his friends have kicked the shit out of you a few weeks before isn't a good move, but once it started I just couldn't finish it. I'll miss . . . whatever the hell it was we had. I think I'll miss being needed by someone. Even though he only needed me when it suited him.

'OK,' I say. 'So long as we're telling stories, maybe you should tell me why you're here.'

'What?' he says. 'I got punched in the face. Why do you think I'm—'

'Yeah, OK, smart guy, stop deflecting,' I say. 'It's a few months until exams start and you've popped up out of absolutely nowhere. What's that about?'

'No comment.'

'Seth.'

'It's long.'

'Well, what a great way to start a story,' I tease. 'Come on. You know all my trauma – it's only fair.'

He laughs. 'Trauma for trauma,' he says. 'If you're looking for a fair trade, I might have you beat.'

'Well, it's not a competition,' I say. 'But feel free to fill me in so that I can make an assessment.'

Seth shuffles and leans back. He takes a breath. Whatever he's about to tell me, he's not all that keen on letting it out.

'I don't know whether to laugh about this or not,' he starts. 'But everything that happened out there right now is the reason I'm here.'

'I'm not following.'

'I got kicked out of my last school for fighting,' he says. 'Someone outed me, I still don't know who, and I wasn't really ready. So there was a group of guys who took it upon themselves to make my life hell, every damn day. Then it reached a point where I couldn't take it any more. I kicked the shit out of a guy and nearly put him in hospital.'

'What?' I knew Seth was a bit of a badass, but I never thought for a second this would be why he was here. 'And what happened after that?'

'Well, everybody saw me hitting this guy, so plenty of witnesses, plus all of his buddies going against me and . . .' He trails off and shakes his head. 'And I got expelled.'

'Even though he was bullying you?'

'The school didn't see it that way,' he says. 'I didn't report the bullying so I didn't have a leg to stand on. I got expelled and my parents sent me to live with my grandparents. Took me away from my friends, from my brothers, and now I'm here. Why do you think I don't give a shit what anyone at this school thinks?' He laughs.

'When did this happen?'

'Just before Christmas,' he says, a sheepish smile creeping across his face. He's brave-facing it with the best of them right now, determined not to crack, but I can see that it still hurts. He's really been through it. 'Merry Christmas to me.'

'Shit,' I say. 'That sucks, I'm sorry, Seth.'

He shrugs. 'It might be about to happen again, you never know.'

'Oh, Seth, no, I won't let it,' I say.

'Shit happens.'

It's a much better outlook than the one that I have when it feels like my life is falling apart. My first port of call is to crawl into a ball and wallow. And my life isn't even that bad – at least I still have my mum.

I lean my head on his shoulder. 'I'm still sorry, though,' I say. 'I wouldn't wish that on anybody.'

'Even Connor?'

'Not even Connor,' I say.

He sighs. 'Me neither.'

'So what classes are you taking?' I ask. 'I get you for English, but nothing else. Where are you all day?'

'I messed up my exams last year,' he says. 'When people are bullying you, they can really get in your head and I royally failed everything, apart from English, so I'm being held back. I'll finish my English exam this year and finish the rest next year. It means I'll be at uni a year later, but I was going to take a year out anyway. I figured there's no harm.'

'No, I guess not,' I say, though I'm totally thinking the opposite. I seem to have done nothing but panic about the prospect of a year out. He makes it sound so easy. But I guess he doesn't have a choice. 'You're very zen about all this.'

He shrugs. 'You can plan for things as much as you like, but life will always throw a curve ball. You have to keep going. There is something good that comes out of practically every shitty situation. You found drag. I found you. Whatever happens, you have to find a way to make it work. Otherwise what's the point?'

He smiles and I smile back and I just want to cry looking at him. He's going to be here for another year and so am I. So is Greg. I'm not going to be totally alone. A sunny side to every situation.

'Thanks, by the way,' I say, realizing that he's sitting here with a black eye in the making and I've not even thanked him for going all knight in shining armour on me. 'You didn't have to step in like that.'

'Well, I sort of did,' he says. 'He wasn't about to let go of you; it would have been pretty shitty of me to walk away.'

'But you got punched.'

'I don't mind taking a punch for you,' he says. 'It was a calculated risk. I've been punched before, but I just couldn't stand him being like that with you. I really thought he was going to hurt you and I just . . . You don't mind? You're not freaked out?'

'No. What he was doing was a lot and . . . just thank you.'

'Don't mention it,' he says.

'Robin?' I look up to the school entrance and see my mum there ready to open the door. She's not looking like herself: her hair pulled up into a sensible-looking ponytail, her make-up business professional, her outfit smart casual. The category she's walking in is Woman in Total Control of Herself and she is serving. 'What are you doing out here?'

'I'm uh . . . well . . .' I can't find the words.

'Are you in trouble?' she asks, raising an eyebrow.

'No, not at all, I—' I stop myself. 'Connor tried to talk to me today and he got a little . . .' I trail off. There's no way to say this without it sounding really bad on Connor, which I guess it is. 'It got a little physical and Seth, this is Seth—' I gesture to him, Mum flicks her gaze to him, her eyes widen briefly when she sees the state he's in but then she turns to me again. 'He stepped in and got Connor to leave me alone, but Connor punched him and here we are. I didn't want to just abandon him. It seemed cruel when he basically saved my face.'

She cracks a smile, but quickly hides it away. 'Well, thank you for saving my son's face,' she says, still trying to hide her smile. 'It means a lot to him. He's only got one . . . most of the time.'

'Ooh, she's on fire this morning,' I say. She curtseys. 'Wait a second, what are you doing here?'

'Meeting with Mrs Finch,' she says. 'That's why I'm dressed like the alternate-universe version of your mother.'

'Does it help if I tell you that you look nice?'

'Only mildly,' she replies with the slightest of smiles. 'I'll see you tonight? We can talk about this meeting later. I imagine it will be juicy.'

'Don't get thrown out of school.'

'Oh, you stop that,' she says. 'You know I don't like to make a scene.' She raises an eyebrow at me and walks inside.

I let out a heavy breath.

'That wasn't so bad,' Seth says. He pulls his phone out of his pocket. 'We're officially late, by the way.'

My turn to shrug. 'If I'm late to register, I'm late to register. I have a free this morning anyway and this feels more important. You feel important,' I add, trying to stop that throw-up feeling from overtaking my whole body.

'Really?'

I nod. 'Yeah.'

'So, what's the plan for today?' he asks.

'Huh?'

'We're heading out on your free period, right?'

I nod. 'Yeah,' I say. 'I'll register and then we'll just go. We're getting an act on its heels today. I don't know what it's going to be, but we're going to try some shit.'

'What time do you need to be there?' he asks, and I smile.

'Kaye said around ten would work.'

'OK, ten it is,' Seth says.

'Will you be OK to—?'

'Yeah.'

'Because I can reschedule or something.'

'Shut up,' he says. 'I'll be all right. You can't miss this. I won't let you.' I lean my head back on his shoulder and settle in there for a while, basking in the silence. 'You need to go and register,' he says.

'I don't want to,' I reply. 'It's way more fun here.'

'The sooner you do that, the sooner we can just get out of here,' he says.

'OK,' I say, not moving an inch.

'Robin.'

'Seth.'

'This is nice.'

I smile and get up and head to registration. I get there just in time to see Greg and Natalie walking out of the room and into the corridor. Nat breathes a heavy sigh.

'Where the hell were you?' she says. 'I messaged you. Seth broke Connor's nose. Did you see? Are you OK?'

I mean, it's not great, but at least she's talking to me?

'I'm fine, Seth's fine—'

'Did you tell him about the faggot thing?' Natalie asks, and I turn to her so sharply it takes Greg less than a second to jump on it.

'What faggot thing?' Greg interrupts.

'Shit.'

'Nat?' Greg turns to her, his face thunderous.

'Sorry, Robin,' she says.

'What thing? What happened? Are *you* OK?' he asks me.

'I'm fine,' I say. 'It's Seth who's got a bruised face. And it doesn't matter what happened, because it's over now. It's done.'

'It totally matters,' Natalie says. 'Before Robin sang at Entity that night, he bumped into Connor outside and Connor called him the f-word and said he was disgusting. That's why he was so messed up.' She looks at me. 'You told Seth and he decked Connor, right?'

'Wrong!' I say. 'Connor was getting physical, I told him I didn't want anything to do with him any more and . . .' I trail off as I see Greg's face. He looks so hurt. Worse than that, he looks angry. And I can see what he's going to do before he does it.

'Fucking hell, Robin,' Greg says. 'What's the matter with you?'

'Huh?'

'It's like you're looking to destroy your own life,' Greg says.

'Greg,' Nat says. 'It doesn't matter. It's over – it just doesn't matter.'

'It does matter,' Greg groans. 'It all matters because it's just another lie on top of all the other lies.'

'No, come on, Greg, it's done. Finally. We can move on. Let's go to the common room and cool off.' Natalie turns to me. I hesitate.

'Well, actually, I was—'

'Robin, what the hell?' Natalie interrupts.

'What?'

319

'Entity again?'

I open my mouth to speak, but stop myself.

'You can't keep doing this. Look, I covered for you this morning because I thought you were late, but now you're pissing off to—'

'I'm performing on Friday.'

'You're going to screw up your exams!'

'This is an opportunity, Nat. Come on, everything has fallen apart for me, and Kaye and drag—'

'I'm sick of hearing how everything has fallen apart for you, Robin! You've become so self-centred I can hardly cope!' she barks. 'I'm so stupid. I spend so much of my time thinking about you it's a wonder I even have my own life. Not that you answer your phone to me. Ever.'

'Well, after what happened at yours last Saturday, can you blame me?'

'Robin, Nat, let's not go here again, please.'

Natalie turns to Greg. 'Wait, what do you mean, other lies?' she asks. 'You said there were other lies – what other lies?' She turns to me. 'What is it?'

'Do you want to tell her or shall I?' Greg asks.

'I don't think it's necessary.'

'I do!' Natalie snaps.

A crowd has started to gather in the corridor, people queueing up outside classrooms, and I can feel their eyes on us, watching us as we fall apart.

'So do I,' Greg says. 'Remember Robin's dancing accident during the Summer of Fun?'

'Greg, please don't do this.'

'Robin got beaten up,' Greg says.

'What?'

'It was Connor's friends who did it. Robin was waiting for me in Southford, they saw him and they attacked him for no reason,' Greg hisses, and I can see a vein popping in his neck, his hands fists at his sides. 'He was there and didn't do anything.'

'We weren't dating at the time so—' I whisper, wary of the crowd we seem to have gathered.

'So you lied to me?' Natalie says.

'If I hadn't have got there when I did, who knows what could have happened.'

'You *both* lied to me?' Natalie says, shaking her head. 'What the fuck is wrong with you? Why wouldn't you tell me?'

'Robin asked me not to—'

'Really?' Natalie says furiously. 'Are you so pathetic that just because Robin asks you to do something you do it? He's not your little brother, Greg – he's not a child – you should have done the right thing.'

'Nat—'

'And you.' She rounds on me. 'We're supposed to tell each other everything. If I'd have known, yeah, I probably wouldn't have been thrilled that you were dating him because he's clearly got issues, but I'd also be worried about you.' She turns to Greg. 'Weren't you worried about him? I mean, fucking hell, Greg—'

'How has this turned into my fault?' Greg asks.

'Because you let him stay with Connor! You said who knows what would have happened if you hadn't been there – were you not worried about what could have happened when they were together?'

'Of course I was!'

'Then why didn't you do anything?'

'Because he asked me to keep it quiet,' Greg says again. 'I was trying to be a good friend.'

'Being a good friend would be stopping him from being with that twat in the first place,' Natalie snaps. 'Not that Seth's any better.'

'You're starting on Seth now? Seriously?'

'Come on, Robin, he's a loser,' she says. 'He doesn't care about school, he doesn't care about you—'

'You don't know if he cares about me or not,' I interrupt. 'You don't even know him.'

'You've known him for two weeks, Robin – *you* don't even know him.'

'I know that he's been looking out for me,' I say. 'I know that he's been trying to help me get through this shitty part of my life and—'

'Shut UP, Robin.'

'What?'

'SHUT UP!' Natalie shouts. A murmur runs through the crowd of people watching. 'I don't care any more. I'm sick of it.'

'What?'

'I. Don't. Care,' Natalie says slowly. 'We're supposed to be best friends, but you obviously don't give a shit about anyone but yourself.'

'Natalie, I can explain—'

'There's nothing to explain,' she says. 'In a few months' time, I'm off to start a new life without you anyway, and you're obviously perfectly happy with your shiny new toys, so I'm just going to leave now, make it easier on both of us.' She turns to walk down the corridor. This is exactly what I was afraid of happening.

'Natalie, wait, don't.' I move to follow her, but she turns to face me one last time.

'Don't follow me, Robin. I'm done,' she says.

'Nat!' Greg calls.

'Piss off, both of you!'

The crowd that has gathered looks at me and Greg before

they start to disperse, whispers passing between them.

I turn to Greg, who looks torn between following her and staying with me.

'Greg—'

'I don't want to talk, Robin,' Greg says.

'But, Greg, I—'

'Just don't,' he says. 'I need to think, OK? You've really fucked up this time.'

TWENTY-SIX

Seth drives me to Entity and I find myself checking my phone every few minutes. I'm here, but I'm totally not present and he can tell. Jared, the bartender, lets us in and tells us that Kaye will be late, so Seth and I head upstairs. It's so quiet. The sort of quiet that means my brain is working overtime.

Seth appears in the doorway. 'Robin—'

'Sit down,' I say.

'Why?'

I smile. 'Do you trust me?'

'Of course I do.'

'Then have a seat.'

He sits at Kaye's workstation and I grab a chair to sit opposite him. I take out my brushes and my make-up, waiting for him to ask me to stop, but he doesn't, so with a careful hand, I start to paint his face.

'What are you doing?' he asks.

'Painting you,' I say, gently using a bit of yellow to cancel out the colour of the bruise blooming below his eye. 'Do you mind?'

'No,' he says. 'You going to tell me what's up?'

I sigh. 'I had an argument with Natalie, and also with Greg, so at the moment it's me and you against the world. How about that?'

He shrugs. 'I think that could work.'

I sigh. 'I feel like shit.'

'Is that why you keep checking your phone?' he asks.

I nod. 'I sent an apology,' I say. 'I'm waiting to hear back.'

'It'll be OK, you know?' he says.

But I really don't know that. I don't want to cry about it right now, so I double down on the painting.

'So, you gonna tell me what happened with them?' he asks.

'I don't know if I want to,' I say. 'They already think I'm a bad person – I don't want you to think that too.'

Seth sighs. 'Start talking,' he says. 'You're painting me – I can hardly respond right now.'

I explain what I did, trying to ignore the tiny winces he gives every now and again. I don't know if I'm touching the bruise or touching a nerve. I'm not sure which is worse.

'Oh, Robin,' he says.

'What?'

'You know what.'

'Yeah,' I say. 'I'm a total fuck-up.'

He shrugs. 'You don't need me to tell you that lying is

bad,' he says. 'You also don't need me to tell you that your friends are reacting like this because they love you and you hurt them.'

I stop painting. 'Then why are you telling me?'

He raises an eyebrow. 'Maybe you need to hear it out loud,' he says. 'You need to fix it.'

'I know.'

'ASAP.'

'I know.'

'You can't paint your problems away,' he says, which makes me smile.

'Watch me.'

I contour him, I highlight him, I give him a blue eye with a heavy wing because I think it will suit him and I'm right, and then I start to paint myself. The silence between us is so comfortable I just want to sit in it for a while, him watching me as I make a start on my face, as I transform into someone new. I wish I knew how to make it right. I don't know if I can now.

'I know, I know, I'm late,' Kaye says as he enters the bar. He stops when he catches sight of me and Seth. 'Well, well, well, what do we have here?' he asks.

'Thought it would be worth getting into full paint while we waited,' I say. 'I didn't know how long you'd be so—'

'So that's why Seth is fully painted and you've only just finished your eyeliner?'

'Yeah.'

'You look good,' Kaye says to Seth. 'Have you considered drag?'

Seth snorts. 'God no. Happy consumer and observer. I could never do what you guys do.'

Kaye curtseys. 'Not all are given such gifts,' he says, then turns his attention back to me. 'Finish your face and get to the stage. We've got work to do.'

I finish painting and head downstairs with Seth, who is looking properly handsome in his paint. Kaye has turned on all the lights in the bar, but it looks seriously different in the day time. The artwork is still there, the tables, the colourful walls, but there's definitely something about it that feels a few shades wrong. It doesn't have any life in it, only the remnants and echoes of the energy I normally feel when I'm here. Layers of it, from last night and from decades ago.

Seth sets himself up at a table near the back of the room, pulling a sketchbook out of his bag. I head to the stage.

It's bigger than I remember. Last time I was on it, I was focusing on not falling apart in front of a room full of people.

'Have you had a chance to think about what you want to do?' Kaye says.

I have. Well, sort of.

'I would love to sing,' I say. 'But after what happened last time I don't know if I could do it without having some major trauma flashbacks.'

Kaye rolls his eyes. 'Sweetheart, with lines like that you were born to be a queen.' He leans against the bar. 'What do you want to be doing, then?'

'Well, I thought that maybe I could lip-sync,' I say. 'It seems like the sensible thing to do. And easiest I guess?'

Kaye stands back up. He looks around himself, perplexed, like he is searching for something to beat me over the head with. I'm trying to figure out what I've said wrong here.

'What?' I say.

'You think lip-syncing is your easiest option?' he says. 'You still have *so* much to learn, sweet boy.'

'Why? What have I said? They do it on *Drag Race* all the time and—'

'You need to stop speaking before I smack you over the head with a bar stool,' he interrupts, holding up a perfectly manicured hand. 'You want to do a lip sync because you think it's easy?'

I look over at Seth who pulls an 'I don't know' face and goes back to his sketch pad, still totally listening, waiting to see if I manage to fit my foot further into my mouth. I don't want to make it worse, so I just stay quiet.

Kaye sighs and hoists himself up on the bar. He crosses

one leg over the other and looks over at me.

'There is a great tradition of lip-syncing that goes way beyond doing it for your life or your legacy or the house down boots mama werk yes gawd.' He tongue-pops and it is quite possibly the loudest noise I have ever heard in my life. I actually wince. His mouth must be cavernous.

'So, tell me about it,' I say.

'It's about more than knowing the words to the song,' he says. 'It's more than just putting a frock on and mashing your mouth around the lyrics for three and a half minutes.' He stops, looking a little off into the distance. 'Well, it can be. It depends who you ask.'

He hops off the bar. 'It's exactly like when you're singing something. It's about *connection*. A song can be so carefully chosen that it takes you right back to a particular moment in time and you present that onstage in front of an audience and give them a piece of your life, as it were. The best lip syncs I have seen are the ones where the artist is connected to what they are miming to, where they are living that moment, which is in itself a representation of the past, in the present. And in that moment it takes on a new meaning depending on who is watching, where it's being performed, how people are impacted by watching it. Do you understand?'

'Yes,' I say dumbly. 'I mean, I think so?'

'So it's more than just picking a song that you like, Robin,' he says reverently, his voice hushed. 'You can do it that way, absolutely, and there is so much fun to be had, but let's dig a little deeper. Let's find a song that speaks to your soul. And it's possible you'll have to do it a hundred times over before you find the right one, but you're looking for something that you feel connected to.' He looks up at me hopefully. 'What song do you want to try?'

I start running through song choices in my head, trying to find one that might speak to me in that way, that might give the effect that Kaye wants. I look over to Seth who is pretending to work, but still stealing enough glances over here that I know he isn't working that hard. All I can think of are musical-theatre songs, a few pop songs here and there.

'Hey, don't tell me all your ideas at once,' Kaye says. 'Take your time, please.'

'Sorry,' I mumble. 'I can't think – there's too many songs I—'

'You know this isn't about being perfect, right?' Kaye says. He says it so flatly, so simply, that it almost knocks me off balance. 'You're allowed to try things out, play around, fuck it up and fail. That's the whole point of this, of performance. It's not supposed to come out perfect first time round. Even when you actually do the thing in front of an audience, you can let yourself discover things.' I must look at him a little blankly because he rolls his eyes. 'Look, you're a dancer, right?' I nod. 'Well, you didn't just walk in there on your first day and triple pirouette or jump into the splits or whatever,' he says. 'You had to work at it. And you're a singer, right?' I nod. 'Well, you didn't just wake up with breath control and placement, you had to work at it. You're an actor, right?' I nod. 'Well . . . acting was never my strong suit, but I bet you don't know *all* the acting techniques. You wanted to go to drama school so you could keep working on your craft. What would be the point in going if there wasn't anything to work on?'

'So I'm allowed to be wrong?' I say. It doesn't sound quite right to me.

Kaye laughs. 'The more wrong you are, the more we have to play with,' he says. 'Give me everything you've got and we'll see where we are. Give me your phone.'

'What?'

'Come on,' he says. 'I'm going to put on a song and you're just going to perform it.'

'You can't do that – what if I don't know the words?'

He shrugs. 'We'll find one that you know,' he says. 'Casual reminder, Robin, that this is supposed to be fun!'

I sigh and get my phone out of my pocket, opening Spotify and handing it to him.

My whole body is shaking. I'm nervous as Kaye walks

over to the sound system. There is a distinct, electrical hum as the speakers click on, a pop as he plugs in my phone, and I realize I'm not breathing, and I need to breathe.

And a song starts to play.

I've heard it a million times before, but not for the longest time. I couldn't tell you the last time I voluntarily listened to it. But I know it so well. 'Born This Way' by Lady Gaga. Her voice has already started and I'm not doing anything.

'I wasn't ready!' I shout over the music.

'Pick it up!' Kaye calls back. 'Come on. You know it?' I nod. 'Then do it!'

The beat is there, familiar, like it's already imprinted on my soul, the music transmitting from the speakers and running across the room to infect my body, my brain.

My mouth starts to move. Without thinking about what I'm going to do next, I perform to the empty room, to Kaye and Seth.

Don't be a drag.

Just be a queen.

When I'm done, I'm sweating, I'm breathing heavily, I can still feel the echoes of the song dancing on the tips of my fingers, the words still fizzing on my tongue. In that moment, I was her, and I was living it and even now it's over I can still feel it in myself.

I look at Kaye.

'Shit,' Seth breathes. I look at him. He's smiling. He's smiling so much and I can't believe that I've had that effect on someone by lip-syncing.

I look back to Kaye. I don't know what I want him to say, or what I want him to do, but to see him standing there smiling is maybe just enough.

'It's not perfect,' he says. 'But I think you know what I mean now, don't you?'

And I think I do. Maybe someone smarter than me could put it into fancier words, but it's more than a song – it's a feeling, it's a moment. A lip sync is lived by the performer and, possibly, by the audience.

'Not perfect by any stretch,' a voice says from the door. I turn to see Carrie standing in the doorframe. I wonder how much of it he has seen. 'But you might be all right.'

'Really?'

'I wouldn't get your hopes up,' he says. 'You think you can whip him into shape before Friday?'

Kaye smiles. 'Of course.'

'Pride cometh, dear.'

'He'll be ready,' Kaye says. 'Don't you worry your ageing little head about it, Carrie. You'll have him for your show.'

Carrie walks over to me, weaving his way through the tables to the stage. I'm really towering over him right now, not just in the heels, but on the platform.

'The paint is good,' Carrie says. 'But paint doesn't make a performance. Remember what I said.'

'Don't fuck it up?' I say.

'Don't you dare,' Carrie says. 'See you Wednesday night, my darling,' he calls to Kaye as he leaves.

'It's a start,' Kaye says. 'Everybody has to start somewhere. Find a song that speaks to *you*, that means something to you, and we'll work on it. Don't let Carrie get in your head. Let him spur you on . . .'

'Kaye—'

'Don't call it a comeback,' he says. 'Shake off the fear of the last time you were on that stage and know that you've got this, OK?'

I nod.

'Now get back to school,' he says. 'You've got classes, haven't you?'

'Gosh, you're such a mum.'

'Don't start that now,' he says. 'You're making me sound old. Now, get back to school and work hard or you're grounded.'

Even as we approach the school, dread fills the pit of my stomach. We walk in and I can feel eyes on me and Seth, people that no doubt saw what he did to Connor or have heard about it through the grapevine. I'm obviously guilty by association and their eyes on me is . . . a lot.

When I get to the common room, Greg and Natalie are both in there. Natalie is at one of the desks with Holly and Eric from her law class. They're deep in conversation, but Natalie still looks up briefly when she sees me. And Greg is sitting with people that I don't even know, people who are probably in his science classes. There's a brief moment where his face brightens and I swear he is about to talk to me, but he stops himself and turns back to his friends.

I look at Seth.

'Can we go?' I ask.

'Robin, you need to—'

'I don't know what to say,' I say. 'I can't right now.'

He nods and we walk out.

TWENTY-SEVEN

When I get home, Mum is parked outside, so I hurry in to see what happened between her and Mrs Finch. Mum probably tore her to shreds. There is still a weird sort of tension as I walk into the kitchen. But at least we're talking now.

'Hey, sweetie,' Mum calls from the kitchen. 'How was school? How's the pretty boy that saved your face?'

'Good,' I say, not a lie, but not the truth either. I seem to be doing that more and more lately. 'I didn't hear any screams or rumours of you getting dragged off school property by security, so I assume you didn't completely obliterate Mrs Finch?' I add.

Mum appears at the kitchen door. She has two cups of tea in her hand and passes one to me. The silence is unnerving. There is something about it that tells me this isn't the conversation I thought we were going to have.

'Do you want to sit down?' she asks, gesturing to the dining table.

'Sure.' I take a seat and she takes one opposite me, the

table between us, a barrier. Something is going on.

'So I spoke to Mrs Finch. We had a long chat,' Mum says. 'And you're right, she's sort of pushy and domineering and to start with I was totally against everything she was saying. I was kicking off – I was interrupting her – she said something about how fiery you are, and this is where you must get it from.'

That makes me smile. Even though in every TV show I've ever watched people are scared of turning into their mums, I think my mum is pretty cool, so I always thought it wouldn't be the end of the world if I did.

'Yeah,' I say. 'And then what?'

'She tried to push it, but I stood firm, told her that you knew your own mind, you worked hard and wanted to figure things out on your own,' she says. 'She didn't like that, but I think it was better it came from me rather than you. The only thing she disagreed on was that you work hard.'

I blink. 'What?'

'She told me you've been cutting classes.'

'I haven't.'

'You've been running out on your free periods with that pretty boy who saved your face?' Mum is waiting for me to say something. 'She doesn't think he's a good influence on you and—'

'No one seems to.'

'Regardless,' Mum continues. I can tell she's trying really hard to keep calm. 'You're sneaking off to that club, aren't you? What the hell are you thinking? Are you really going to tank your last year at school for the sake of a job in some gay bar?'

And I have a choice here. I can either continue to keep this from her or I can come out with it. With all the lying I've been doing over the past couple of weeks, all the hurt I've caused, maybe the best thing to do is just be up front about something for once.

'It's not just a job, Mum,' I say. 'I'm performing.'

'You're what?'

'I'm going to Entity because I'm performing there on Friday,' I say. 'It's kind of a big deal and it's the best I've felt about myself in a long time and—'

'No.'

'Mum!'

'No, Robin, I can't believe you would do this,' she says. 'I told you no, and you've disobeyed me. Does my trust mean nothing to you?'

'Mum, it's really important to me and—'

'And my trust isn't?' she says, and I can see that I've hurt her.

'I know I shouldn't have lied, but I couldn't let them

down, Mum. This could be a huge opportunity for me,'
I say. 'Next year I—'

'No, you're not doing it, Robin. While you're under my
roof, you play by my rules,' she says.

'Oh, don't be such a cliché!'

'Robin, I'm not having you go to that club every night,
while I sit at home and worry about whether or not you're
going to come back alive!'

'BUT YOU'RE NOT AT HOME, ARE YOU? YOU'RE
NEVER EVEN HERE!' And as the words leave my mouth,
I see them float across the space between us and smack her
in the face.

'Why do you think I'm not here, Robin?' she shouts.
'I'm not here because I am working my ass off to give you a
life. I'm the only one doing that. I'm paying for your dance
classes, I'm paying for your singing lessons, I'm making
sure you have every opportunity in life, and you don't even
notice!' She starts to pace around the table. 'Well, fine, if
that's how you feel. If you don't want to go to college next
year, you won't be sitting around on your arse while I pay
for everything.'

'I never expected to—'

'You're going to pull your weight, and you're going to
get a proper job,' she says.

'Mum, this could be a job! Just come on Friday and you'll

see what this could be, Mum! This could be—'

'No, it's not happening. Call them. Tell them you can't.'

'You're overreacting.'

'You're still not going.'

I open my mouth to speak, but don't have a response.

I turn round and walk out of the door, desperate for air, desperate for space, ignoring Mum's shouts behind me. This is all just too much.

I take my phone out of my pocket, the sudden urge to call Natalie disappearing when I remember we're not speaking. I scroll down to SB and delete his number. Time to get him out of my hair. I can't even be tempted any more. I scroll back up to Greg and press call.

'Hey,' he says. I didn't think he'd pick up. 'What's up?'

'I just . . . I needed . . .' I'm crying so hard I can barely catch my breath. 'I had another fight with Mum and I wanted to talk to somebody and I didn't know who to talk to. I can't call Nat right now, and I almost didn't think I could call you, but—'

'Why not, Seth?' And it's a stab. I don't want Seth to come between us, that's the last thing I want.

'I've known Seth for three weeks; I've known you since we were, like, five and we got paired up as "buddies" on the first day of school,' I say. 'I'm sorry, Greg.'

He sighs. 'Is that all you've got?' he says.

'I'm trying to make it right,' I say. 'I messed up. I mean, I really messed up. I never should have—'

'No, you shouldn't have,' he interrupts. 'Look, if that's all you're calling for, I've got stuff to do and—'

'I don't want to lose you, Greg,' I say. 'I shouldn't have lied. I shouldn't have kept all this from you when all you were trying to do was look out for me. I've been a shit friend.'

'You have,' he says, laughing a little. 'Like, seriously shit. I've tried to be supportive here, but, Robin, this is ridiculous OK? You're so . . . all or nothing. It was either all drag or none at all and it pushed me and Nat away. Nat more than me, I think, but still.'

'I'm going to do better,' I say. 'I really am. No more lies.'

'That's a start.'

'No more Connor.'

'About bloody time,' he says.

'I deleted his number,' I say. 'That's done.'

'And Dragcellence?' he asks.

'I'm performing on Friday night,' I say. 'If you're there it would mean the absolute world, but I understand if you can't be. I wouldn't blame you.'

'OK, I'll think about it,' he says. 'What about Natalie?'

'I'm going to talk to her at school tomorrow,' I say. 'I've tried messaging her, but she isn't responding.'

'She's mad.'

'Yeah,' I say. 'I'm going to talk to her tomorrow. I just want her to be happy.'

'Don't give up on her,' Greg says. 'She's mad at you, OK, but she loves you. She's mad at you *because* she loves you, which is a weird thing, but it is what it is.'

'I won't,' I say. 'I can't, she means too much to me.' Silence falls on the other end of the line. 'So you're not mad?'

'I'm less mad than I was,' he says. 'Just don't do this to me again, Robin, OK? No more lying.'

'I won't,' I say. 'Never again, I promise.'

I can hear him smiling. 'I have to go,' he says. 'I'll see you tomorrow?'

'I'll see you tomorrow.'

TWENTY-EIGHT

I spend the rest of the week scrambling to get everything learned. Seth is still taking me to Entity whenever we can, Kaye working on the number with me, making sure the movements are perfect. The dress we've found is one that matches the one she plans to wear on Friday, so we really will look like some 'Mother-Daughter, Toddlers-In-Tiaras eleganza!' Kaye's words, not mine.

Friday rolls round much too fast. Mum and I are barely talking. She has taken a couple of extra shifts, which means I get the house to myself, so I've spent the evenings practising, whether that's my lip sync or my face. I've even found myself thinking of other numbers, things similar to what Kaye has done at Dragcellence. Numbers that are songs mixed with spoken word, pop-culture icons with pop music. But my focus is Friday's number. I think I've finally nailed it too. The only thing that will be different is the audience, because *everything* changes when there is an audience.

The audience is what gives you that extra little rush of

energy. You never know if it's going to be for the best or for the worst, whether they're going to be kind or whether they're out for blood. It's impossible to tell. I hope they're feeling forgiving because as it creeps closer and closer to showtime, I'm a bag of nerves.

There's just one thing I have to do first. Before the end of lunch on Friday, I find myself hurrying around the school trying to track Natalie down. She's not in the common room. She's not in the canteen. I eventually find her in the library.

She is sitting with Holly and Eric again. They're deep in conversation and I don't want to be rude, but I want to talk to Natalie if I can. I don't want to just leave this hanging in the air.

I walk over to the table, trying to keep myself calm. Holly nudges Nat's arm and she looks up as I approach.

'Hey, Nat,' I say.

'What do you want, Robin?'

'I don't want to make a scene. I just wanted to see if we could talk.'

'Robin, don't—'

'Look, you don't have to listen to me,' I say, trying to keep the shake out of my voice. 'But I just want to say that I'm really sorry. I've properly screwed up. I lied to you, I wasn't there for you when you needed me and I've been a shit friend. And I understand if you never want to talk to me again or you don't want to forgive me. But I want you to know that I'm sorry and I love you.' I take a breath. 'That's all.'

'OK,' she says. 'Are you done?'

I nod.

'OK.' She turns back to her friends and they carry on talking. I don't know what I expected. I didn't expect her to outright forgive me, but I thought we might at least talk.

I turn round and walk away, not wanting her to see me cry, not wanting it to look like I'm trying to guilt her. That must be it, then. I might just have to let it go. Shit.

After school, I head home and rush upstairs, ignoring Mum, and jump in the shower. I shave, I play my song as loudly as I can, determined to get the lyrics perfect, so perfect that anyone would think I was singing live, determined not to let my car crash of an existence ruin the best chance I have to drag up my life. That's what Kaye does, that's what the best queens I've seen at Entity manage to do, that's what I want to do.

There is no way Mum is going to let me go out tonight, so the only thing I can do is walk out. She's already pissed at me.

I give myself a quick look in the mirror before I go,

barrelling down the stairs at top speed, knowing I need to be there as fast as I can.

'Where are you going?' Mum asks as I come downstairs. 'Robin Cooper, I said, where are you going?'

'You know where,' I say flatly.

'Robin.'

'What?'

'I told you that you weren't going to that—'

'Try and stop me,' I interrupt.

'Don't walk out that door, Robin,' she says. 'Don't do it. Don't do things that you can't take back.'

I know I'm overstepping, but right now I'm so desperate to find out what the heck I'm supposed to be doing with my life, if it's this or something else, that I'm willing to push everything else aside. My hand is reaching for the door handle before I second guess myself, and I'm stepping out into the night with the sound of Mum's voice echoing in my ears behind me. Then I'm on my bike and away.

It's not how I want to start my evening, and when I make it to Entity I'm crying. And I must look a wreck because I walk into the dressing room upstairs and Carrie double-takes.

'Good grief, sweetie, cheer up. It might not happen,' she says, going back to glueing down her eyebrows. But it already has happened, and I don't know how to say that to her. I don't know what to say to anyone.

'Typical drag queen, always late,' Kaye pipes up from his station. 'Come over here, sweetheart. We need to get you painted for the GODS before your professional debut.'

'Sure,' I breathe, dumping my bag down and heading towards him. I sit in front of the mirror and look at my face. My eyes are red and my skin is blotchy. I've missed a patch of stubble on my jawline so will need to get rid of that before I even start and Kaye is looking at me as if he's seen a ghost. 'What?'

'Sweetheart, I mean this in the absolute nicest way possible,' he says. 'But you look an absolute wreck. And I've seen Carrie after a full day at Drag World, eyelashes stuck to her forehead, wig all askew—'

'I can bloody hear you, you ungrateful hag,' Carrie calls out. 'Do you want your slot or not?'

'Do you think you can fill it?' Kaye snaps.

'A queen like you? Dime a dozen.'

'Oh, honey, that outfit tells me you should spend your dimes more wisely,' Kaye parries.

'If you two are done reading each other, there is a very upset little gay boy sat here who looks like he's about to pass out,' Pristine says, sitting to one side of me. She's almost completely painted so her face is covered in glitter and gorgeousness. Even up close she looks perfect.

That is a skill. 'What's up, sweet boy?'

I take a deep breath. I don't want to keep crying – I can't keep crying. I have to perform and it has to go well. This can't be another failure in my life.

'Everything's falling apart,' I say flatly. 'My best friend isn't speaking to me, my mum hates me, I don't know what I'm going to do when term is over and I just . . .' I can't catch my breath. I'm having a breakdown in a room full of drag queens.

Pristine places a caring hand on my shoulder. 'Why don't you go outside and take a few deep breaths and calm down?'

'She needs to get ready,' Carrie says.

'Well, there's no point in putting make-up on her face if she's just going to keep crying it off,' Kaye snipes. 'Come on, darling, all you're breathing in here is setting powder and hairspray. Your lungs will be coated. Let's get you outside, take a few deep breaths, steady yourself and then come back and get ready.'

I turn to Kaye. 'I'm really sorry. I'm not usually like this—'

'Tearful and dramatic?' Kaye says with a raised eyebrow. 'Darling, it's part of your personal brand. Let's go and sort you out then come back in here and get painted. You've got time.'

'Hardly!' Carrie calls.

'Down, boy!' Kaye barks.

Kaye leads me out of the dressing room, and down the stairs, the two of us heading for the alleyway where we first met. I don't know when it became my crying place, but somehow it makes me weep harder than I was before.

'Kaye, I don't . . . I don't know if I can do this,' I whisper.

'Right,' he says. 'Why?'

'Everything is just falling apart,' I say. 'Mum doesn't get it. She's scared for me, she wants me to do something stable and . . .'

'And you don't want to?'

'No.'

Kaye sighs, putting a hand on my shoulder. 'And you think the answer to that is quitting?'

'I don't—'

'Because what you need to be doing right now, Robin, is following that thing beating in your chest,' he says, poking a finger hard at my heart. 'You've been through some shit, OK? I understand that maybe more than most, the people upstairs too, but that isn't a reason to give up on yourself.'

'But it's so hard, it's—'

'And it isn't going to get any easier, kid,' he says. 'Life is full of shit like this, OK? Bad things happening, shitty people determined to drag you down instead of lifting you up. Sometimes you have to be your own biggest fan. That's

351

what I did. Have a little faith in yourself, Robin. Please.' Kaye sighs. 'Do you know how much it kills me that every time I think we're getting somewhere, I see the light go from your eyes? I see that fear, all that self-doubt creep back in.'

'Really?'

'Yeah,' he says. 'You do your number and the second it's over, I see you questioning, analysing, wondering what went wrong before you wonder about what went right. When you paint your face, you'll notice the little bit that's gone wrong before you'll notice how good you look.'

'Auditions really messed me up, huh?'

Kaye lifts my chin so I have to look him right in the face. 'First thing you need to do is stop crying, because you can't paint a good face if it's all damp and shit,' he says. 'Second is you need to find that little place in yourself that believes in you. If you want to perform for a career, you're going to go through the ringer on a weekly basis. Performers are some of the strongest people I know because if they let the rejection get to them then it's over. You need to believe that you're good enough. I do. Your mum does.'

I scoff.

'She does, Robin, otherwise she wouldn't have been paying for all your classes,' he says. 'Your friends believe in you. And here's someone else who does too.'

'Robin?'

I look up in the direction of the voice. Standing in the glorious light of the Essex sunset, is Seth. His blond hair is swooped over to one side, his dimples popping in his cheeks, his eyes wide with concern. I long for a day when Seth doesn't have to come to my rescue for the slightest little thing, but today is not that day.

'I'll be upstairs,' Kaye says. 'Sort yourself out and come up when you're ready.' He checks his phone. 'Which needs to be in the next fifteen minutes if you want to do a leisurely two-hour paint. Evening, Seth. Have a word, would you?' Kaye heads back into the club.

'Hello,' I say, trying to sound bright, but the quake in my voice gives away just how fragile I am right now. 'Lovely night.'

'What was that?'

'Motherly advice,' I sniff.

'Why are you crying?' he asks.

'Oh, the usual.' I sniff again. Tearful and dramatic sums it up pretty perfectly right now. Maybe I should put it in my Instagram bio. 'Sorry,' I add. 'I guess I'm just not feeling my best right now.'

'Well, I gathered that from the crying,' he says. 'How are you feeling about tonight?'

'That's just a whole other set of things,' I say.

He sighs. 'Without the theatrics.'

I look at him and see that his eyes are kind and genuinely worried about me. I mean, I'd probably be worried about me too if I saw me crying in an alleyway and not for the first time. But he's become my person in all this. He's the enabler, he's the one who has helped make this happen even when I was ready to throw in the towel. I wouldn't be standing here if it wasn't for him.

I throw myself at him, wrapping my arms round him as tightly as I can. He reciprocates quickly and I breathe in the calming scent of him.

'Come on,' he says. 'Talk, and talk fast – you have a show to get ready for.'

Just hearing that makes me nearly throw up.

'I'm nervous,' I say. 'It's sort of like stage fright but there's something about it that seems like there's a touch more pressure on it.'

'Why?'

'I'm about to find out if this was all worth it,' I say. 'And the last time I was onstage, it was a massive failure. And the time before that was auditions, where I put all the work in and did everything I could and I still failed. I'm sick of failing. I'm failing at everything. I just want something in my life to go right, something to . . .' I trail off because I can feel myself getting worked up again. 'Sorry.'

Seth puts his hands on my shoulders, forcing me to look him in his beautiful face, to stare into those sparkly eyes.

'You're allowed to have feelings,' he says. 'You're allowed to be nervous, but for goodness' sake, Robin, just believe in yourself a little bit, huh? You're really fucking talented, but you can't keep relying on other people to tell you that. I know you believe in it somewhere deep in your soul so will you just listen to that part of yourself and go in there and . . .' He hesitates for a moment. 'Slay the house down, boots or whatever the heck the phrase is.'

I laugh. And it helps. I laugh a little more and feel that vague darkness in my chest lift a touch. He's smiling too, and it really is the most beautiful smile ever. Like, I feel as if I should have to pay to see it; it's a walking work of art.

'I should probably go and get ready.'

'Probably.'

Neither one of us moves. His hands are still on my shoulders, his eyes still locked on mine, and there is that energy between us again. I know he feels it too – he has to. And then he's leaning in. And that magnetic pull, that spark that I feel around him, that buzzing in my entire body is pulling us together. And our lips are touching.

The world around me falls away, the club, the alleyway, the distant sounds of pedestrians, of traffic, of anything other than this one moment. His hands move from my shoulders to the small of my back and he's pulling me closer and I reciprocate, desperate to have my hands on him.

But I feel like I blink and it's over, the two of us standing there in the alleyway, our foreheads touching like we're characters in a film. He's smiling. I'm smiling. My face hurts from smiling. Smile, smile, smile.

'I need to go inside,' I say, breaking the magic, still struggling to believe that it actually just happened.

'I know,' he says, taking a breath. 'I'll see you after. Give them hell.'

I nod. He kisses me one last time, sweet and fleeting, and it gives me the energy I need to step back inside and go upstairs to get ready for the show.

Kaye is halfway painted now, her pink and blue eyeshadow popping like you wouldn't believe.

'What are you so happy about?' she asks.

'I'm ready,' I say.

'I'm glad to hear it,' Kaye says. 'Now for goodness' sake, paint yourself so we can get you corseted and on to that stage. You have two hours – is that enough?'

'Yes,' I say, faking confidence I don't really feel, trying to find the old me or maybe a new me, I don't know.

I glue down my brows, painting the bottom half of my face while I wait for them to dry, just like Kaye taught me. She's pretending she isn't watching me while she gets dressed, but I can see her looking over every now and again, seeing how I'm doing, making sure I'm not completely fucking it up. Her neck is on the line here and she isn't about to let me forget it.

Kaye has already set out a wig for me to borrow, a shoulder-length wavy number that moves from a blonde root down to blue ends. So, after applying Trixie Mattel levels of eyeliner, I decide to go with an orange and blue eye to try to compliment it. It's all working. I push past the point where it doesn't look right, where the face isn't quite complete, and start adding finishing touches, blush, highlight. Kaye helps me with my eyelashes because eyelashes are still really hard and, by the time I'm putting a little bit of gloss over my lips, I look like a completely different person.

'Now that is a face I can put on a stage,' Carrie says, appearing next to me in the mirror. She's ready to go, her wig so high that now she's in heels she's dusting the ceiling with it. 'You look gorgeous, hun. But who is she?'

'Huh?'

'What's her name?' Carrie says. 'I can't introduce you without a name.'

'I don't know yet,' I say, staring at myself in the mirror. It won't be complete until I put the wig on, but I look . . . pretty. A little graphic, a little bit inspired by Kaye, a little by the tutorials I've watched to death at home. But I don't know who she is. What is her name?

'Let's ask Mum, shall we?' Carrie says, straightening up. 'Oh, Kaye, my dear,' she coos. 'Your daughter is here and, though you've been through the pains of labour and shat all over the table, you've forgotten to name your child.'

'Maybe I don't need a name.'

'Oh fuck off, darling, everyone needs a name!' Carrie barks.

'Not forgotten dear,' Kaye says, now appearing in the mirror. 'My doubting little diva, queen of umming and ahhing over absolutely bloody everything. My darlings of Dragcellence, may I introduce to you, Miss Mae Bee.'

I look at my face in the mirror and see that it fits. She's right there, staring me in the face, her eyeshadow neon and popping like there's no tomorrow, lips so bravely overdrawn I look like I've had an All Stars level of fillers. Mae Bee. She's been there the whole time, just waiting for me to find her, to wake her up.

'How does it feel, darling?' Carrie says.

I smile and nod. 'Perfect.'

'Good,' she says. 'Now, don't forget what I told you. This is some once-in-a-lifetime bullshit right here, OK?'

'OK.'

'Don't be about to fuck this up.'

'I'm not.'

She eyes me carefully. 'Who are you and what have you done with the boy who walked in here in pieces two hours ago?'

I coquettishly bat my eyes. 'There was a boy here? I don't know what you're talking about . . . sir.' I wink. Carrie raises an eyebrow.

'You might be ready for this,' she says. 'What's the number?'

I tell her the song and she heads downstairs to get the crowd warmed up. There is a deafening cheer as she walks into the bar. Everybody loves Carrie.

Kaye helps me get my wig on, and Pristine helps me into the corset, and before I know it, I'm fully tucked with three thick pairs of tights on for good measure and in a pair of black knee-high boots with a six-inch heel, wearing a leotard and skirt.

Kaye takes my phone off the dressing table. 'Pose, darling,' she says. 'It's almost time for your gaybut' — she pronounces it to rhyme with "debut" — 'let's get some pictures to remember it by, huh?'

I do as I'm asked, posing, pouting, serving as best I can. She's about to put my phone down when I stop her.

'What?' she says.

'I need pictures with you,' I say, like it's the most obvious thing in the world because, to me, it is. 'You're my drag mother, right? This is your fault.'

'My fault?' she says, laughing, but there are tears in her eyes. And as she looks me up and down, taking in the work that both of us have put into this look, I can see that she's proud of what she's done. 'Well, when you put it like that, you'd better not go down there and fuck it up.'

'Careful,' Pristine says. 'That's almost a RuPaul-ism.'

'Shut up and take the picture,' she says. It's when I hear the applause downstairs that I realize Carrie has finished her first number and that I am next.

We all go down the stairs together, Pristine bringing my phone, determined to document this seminal moment in my own gay history. And I sort of love her for it. She seems to be as excited as I am nervous.

The bar is completely packed, just like it has been the other times I've been at Dragcellence. Everyone is focused on the stage where Carrie is working the microphone, but my ears are ringing and I can't hear her, the nerves taking over my entire body so my knees are actually shaking.

'You've got this sweetie,' Kaye whispers behind me, and I suddenly wake up to the noise in the room, to Carrie looking across to me, ready for the signal for me to tell them whether or not I'm ready. I give a thumbs-up and she turns back to her adoring crowd.

'My darlings, for the first time tonight at Dragcellence,

I would like to present a brand-new queen, the daughter of our very own Essex Queen, Kaye Bye.' There is a wild cheer from the audience. 'My darlings, please give a warm welcome for her Dragcellence and drag gaybut, Call Her Mae Bee!'

All eyes in the room turn to where Carrie has gestured, to where I am standing at the far corner of the room. A spotlight finds me and the music starts to play, the striking up of a band, the familiar beginning of 'Don't Rain On My Parade', and as icon, legend, queen, sensation Barbra Streisand begins to sing I start my walk to the stage, trying to recreate what I rehearsed.

I lock eyes with people on the way, their eyes wide, most of them smiling, some of them cheering, all of them parting like the Red Sea to give me a clear path. When I make it, the lights are bright but not so bright I can't make out a few of the people in the audience.

Seth is standing near the back, a drink in his hand, a smile on his face so broad it makes me want to work harder. I direct some of the song to him and he cheers. I spin and find someone else in the audience to focus on and almost stop dead when I see her.

Mum.

She's sitting with Natalie, Greg and Priya, each of them absolutely beaming. Mum has tears in her eyes, Natalie is smiling. They must know that it's me. Greg must have told Natalie that I was going to be here and . . .

I don't have time to think it through. I have to keep going, keep performing, keep mashing my mouth around to this glorious song.

There's the build-up.

I'm raising my arms as Barbra is belting 'Here I am'.

I tear off my skirt and throw it to Natalie, the crowd goes nuts, there is screaming, whooping, cheering, and I am lip-syncing and spinning around that stage like it's mine because in this moment it is. And before I know it the song is over and I am curtseying, Natalie handing me back my torn-off skirt as I totter from the stage and back over to Kaye and Pristine to the sounds of applause, to people chanting my name and if I could just live in one moment forever, it would be this one.

TWENTY-NINE

The rest of the night continues, Kaye and Pristine performing twice each, Carrie doing a number every now and again, the Duchess slaying the house down with some J. K. Rowling tweets mixed with 'Sorry Not Sorry' from SIX, and before I know it the night is over and people are leaving Entity or sticking around because, for them, the night is only just beginning. And I am hiding backstage, trying to work up the courage to go out and face my mum, face Natalie, face the people I've disappointed.

'Your public awaits,' Kaye says. 'Are you all right?'

I shake my head. 'There's a lot of people out there that don't like me too much right now,' I say. 'I don't know if—'

'Maybe they don't like Robin,' Kaye says. 'But Mae Bee? Mae Bee is a star. Let them meet her. Come on.'

I take Kaye's hand and she leads me back out to the bar. Through the crowd, I see Mum. She's standing up, Greg, Priya and Natalie around her, and I know she is looking for me. She is doing that weird meerkat thing that mothers do when they're trying to keep an eye on their kids in the playground or something. But it doesn't take her long to spot me. I'm six foot six and in a blonde wig with blue ends, for crying out loud. You can't miss me. She starts over to me, squeezing through the crowds to reach me.

I try to second guess everything she's going to say, ready for some kind of onslaught, mad at me for running out of the house to do this when she told me not to, mad at me for doing it in the first place. I'm about to come out to my mum for the second time in my life and my heart will not stop pounding.

I'm taller than her anyway, but it's only when she gets close to me that I realize just how tall I am in these heels. I'm an absolute giant. She looks like a Borrower.

'I don't even know where to start,' she says, unable to keep the smile off her face.

I wince.

'What?' she says.

'Are you . . . upset?' I say.

'Yes,' she says. 'Upset that you ran out of the house tonight like that. And that you only really told me half the story. Look at you, Robin.'

'Too effervescent?' I say.

'No, Robin, not at all,' she says. 'Look at you – you're the brightest thing in the whole damn room.'

'Thanks.' I'm trying not to get choked up. I don't know how waterproof this eye make-up is.

'I'm just surprised, of course I'm surprised. Happy for you. A little scared.'

'I knew you'd worry,' I say, averting my eyes, not wanting to look at her in case I start to cry. 'After what you said before I went out for my birthday I was worried. I didn't want you to freak out and take it away before I really had a chance to do this. But I'm safe here, Mum. Really.'

'Robin, I just . . . I don't want—'

'Wait.' I look around and see Kaye standing at the bar, flirting with Jared. 'Kaye, can I borrow you for a second?'

'My darling daughter, I'm a little busy right now.'

'It'll only take a second,' I say. 'I actually want to introduce you to somebody.'

I walk her over to my mum, who looks a little dumbstruck.

'Kaye, this is my mum; Mum, this is my drag mother, Kaye Bye.'

'Drag mother?' she says.

Kaye kisses Mum on both cheeks. 'It's such a pleasure to meet you,' she says. 'I just love your boy. He's . . .' She looks over at me and smiles. 'He's one of the good ones, a beautiful soul.'

'Thank you,' she says, looking from me to Kaye and back

again. She's confused. 'So, you're his drag mother? What is . . . what does that mean?'

'I have been Mae Bee's guide, mentor and person in charge of making sure she doesn't look busted and sully the good name of Dragcellence,' she says. Mum still looks a little lost, which makes Kaye smile. 'I'm here to look out for her, keep her safe.'

Mum smiles and I can see that there are tears welling in her eyes. 'Well, thank you,' she says. 'Thank you for looking out for my boy when I'm not there.'

'It is honestly my pleasure.' Kaye turns to me. 'Are you done playing happy families, dear?'

'You can go,' I say. She totters back to the bar.

'She's beautiful,' Mum says. 'You picked a good mum.'

'She's not a patch on you,' I say.

Mum takes a breath and pulls me into a hug, her head barely reaching my chest. I try not to laugh. 'If you want to do drag, do drag. It's theatre, it's performance, it's everything you want and, if it earns you a bit of money, it's better than doing something that you hate. You spend a lot of time at work – you might as well do something fun.'

'So you're OK?'

'Not a hundred per cent,' she says. 'But that's something we can talk about later.'

'I'm really glad you came,' I say.

'Of course I came,' she says. 'You know, considering we've known each other for eighteen years, you're doing a terrible job of knowing me. I know I said I wouldn't, but you were going to be here and . . . I wanted to see. I always want to see you perform, Robin. Whether it's you singing at a school event or in a school play, or doing this in a bar, it's me getting to see you in your absolute element and nothing makes me prouder than that. I'm proud of you, Robin Cooper . . . Mae Bee . . . whatever I'm supposed to call you. But please know,' she adds, 'if you ever lie to me again, I will knock you off those heels, do you hear me?'

I laugh. 'Loud and clear,' I say. 'Sorry, Mum.'

She blinks. 'What for?'

'For being shit,' I say, but it feels too general. 'You don't deserve that. I should have said something. We don't do secrets.'

She waves a hand at me. 'Look, most teenagers have a rebellious, parent-hating phase,' she says. 'You just happened to have yours a bit late. But I certainly would appreciate it if it could be done with now. I'd like my son back, if that's OK.'

'Yeah, sure,' I say.

'Promise?' She sticks out her hand, her pinky extended.

Pinky swear. 'Do you want me to come home with you?' I ask.

'Christ, no, not right now – you have your adoring public to attend to,' she says. 'But we'll order in dinner tomorrow maybe, hang out, watch a terrible film, OK?' She kisses me on the cheek. 'I'll see you when you get home.'

'You're not leaving are you?'

'Robin Cooper, I am not going to stay here and cramp your style,' she says. 'I'll see you tomorrow. I love you.'

'I love you too.'

Mum heads for the door and is quickly replaced by Natalie, Greg and Priya. Priya is holding Greg's hand. The tiniest detail, but I clock it and can't help but smile. Natalie looks uncomfortable. It's the first time I've seen her look anything other than joyful while she's been at Entity and I know it's my fault.

'I'm really sorry,' I say. 'I know it's not enough, but I am. I've been an awful friend.'

'Yes, you have,' she says. 'I've not been too good myself, but, honey . . .'

I chuckle. 'I know.'

Natalie throws herself at me and wraps me up in a hug. I hug her back, tentatively at first but eventually giving in to the full squeeze. Greg stands near us, looking a little nervous.

'I'm sorry,' I say into Nat's hair. 'I'm so, so sorry.'

'Good,' she says.

'No, Natalie, I fucked up, hugely,' I say as she pulls away. 'Look, no more secrets, OK? I just want my best friends back.'

'Connor is a prick, good riddance to bad rubbish,' Natalie says. 'But Seth . . .'

'Seth . . .'

'He might not be so bad,' she says. 'I'll reserve judgement until I get to know him better.'

'OK,' I say. 'That's wise.'

'I am very wise.' She shrugs. 'OK, we can fix our friendship starting tomorrow, but can we talk about Mae Bee now?'

'You were amazing,' Greg blurts. 'I mean, I don't know a lot about drag, but what you did was cool.'

'Honestly, babes, gagged,' Priya says.

'It was insane,' Natalie says. 'I can't believe that was the first time you'd done it with an audience. You had no reason to be nervous at all.'

'Adrenalin is a hell of a drug,' I say.

'If you don't start wearing your heels at dancing, I'm going to be *very* disappointed,' Priya says. 'You're coming back, right?'

'If Mum lets me.'

'Good.'

'You were fantastic,' Nat says. 'Seriously. And, look, maybe Ru is right. Drag, bringing families together.'

'VOM!' Greg says. Nat hits him on the arm.

'I really am sorry, Nat, I—'

'Let's not do this now,' she says, holding up a hand. 'You can start making it up to me tomorrow. Until then you can tell me what all the queens are like and what's happening with you and Seth.'

'Oh,' I say, looking over to see Seth hovering by the door. 'If we're not doing secrets any more, Seth and I are close now. Like. Really close.'

'How close?'

'Erm. We kissed.'

'ROBIN!' Priya shrieks. She hits me on the arm. 'You and Seth what?'

'We kissed.'

'Wow,' Greg says.

'Huge wow!' Priya says. 'I need details, full and frank details because—'

'Hey, Seth,' Greg says loudly.

Seth strides over, that trademark smile on his face.

'Hey.'

Priya turns back to me, trying to keep a smile from bursting across her face.

'Did you enjoy the show?' Greg asks.

'Yeah, it was amazing,' he says, turning to me and smiling. 'I have no idea why you were nervous.'

'He's ridiculous, isn't he?' Natalie says, rolling her eyes. 'Zero confidence, bundle of nerves, comes out and serves a lip sync with a reveal. I can't even.'

'I know, right?' Seth says. 'Congratulations.'

'Actually it's ConDRAGulations,' Greg says, with a sly smile. 'I've been doing my research.'

I laugh. 'I'm proud of you.'

'Everybody in here loves you,' Seth says.

I snort. 'Please, I did one number.'

'And it was incredible,' Natalie says. 'Accept it. People think you're good and you're allowed to be happy about it.'

And I am happy about it. There are people all around the bar that are looking at us, well, looking at me, and it's sort of wonderful. It tells me that I did a good job tonight.

'So,' Natalie says. 'Seth. What are your intentions with my Robin?'

'Oh my God,' I groan.

'It sounds like she's joking, but she isn't,' Greg says. 'So, seriously, intentions. We're very protective of him.'

'I know.'

Natalie hits him in the arm. 'Hey, I heard you broke Connor's nose. Nice. You beat me to it.'

'I've been wanting to do that for a while too,' Greg says.

'Not my finest moment.' Seth looks a little sheepish. 'But he was being an ass and . . .' He looks at me and he smiles, his eyes all wide and loved-up.

'He was hurting your boy?' Natalie teases. 'Knight in shining leather jacket.'

'Are we done with the third degree?' I ask. 'I don't want to talk about Connor any more. It's over. New beginnings.'

'New beginnings,' Natalie says. 'I like that.'

Natalie heads to the bar, Greg and Priya following close behind, their fingers entwined, leaving me alone with Seth.

'So, you really liked it?' I ask.

'Yeah, I did,' he says. 'You were amazing.'

'Seeing you out there helped,' I say. 'Like, a friendly face, it made the whole thing a lot easier.'

'Well, I'll make sure I come every time,' he says.

'Do we need to talk about what happened earlier?' I ask.

'Well—'

'Because I've been wanting to do that for a really long time,' I say. 'And if you ever wanted to do it again, well, you know where to find me.'

'Does now work?' He smirks.

'Now works fine.'

He smiles and takes a step towards me, kissing me softly on the lips. He has to get up on his tiptoes to do it but manages.

'OK, lovebirds, let's break it up!' Kaye appears at my side, her face a little severe. 'You can catch up with your friends later – now I need you to meet your adoring public.'

'Mama wants to show off her new little showgirl,' Pristine says. 'It's *very* Toddlers In Tiaras. You should have seen her while you were on, Mae – she was absolutely beaming.'

'How dare you!' Kaye snaps. 'Stop telling my girl how proud I am. I don't want her getting a big head. Say goodbye to this handsome little dish.'

'Bye, Seth.'

'Tell him you'll see him after.'

'Will you stick around?' I ask.

'Sure,' Seth says, turning to Kaye. 'She's all yours.'

'Thank you, my darling, what a nice little suitor he is,' Kaye says, leading me off into the crowd. 'Now that you're my daughter, do I need to have the talk with him?' she asks.

'No,' I say. 'I think he's one of the good ones.'

Kaye sighs. 'Then hold on to him tightly, darling. Lock it in now before he has a chance to run away. Ooh, here are some people you should meet . . .'

THIRTY

'Carrie won't shut up about you, darling,' Kaye says as we take off our make-up in the dressing room. I've lost track of what time it is. I must have been in it for a good three hours and my body aches. 'I think she may hire you again.'

'Well, that would be great considering I have nothing to do next year,' I say.

Kaye stops taking off her make-up and looks over at me. 'Did you enjoy tonight?' she asks.

And I know I've been a little bit flippant and said the wrong thing. I am trying to figure out how I can put into words what it felt like to be up there tonight. There is no feeling like performing. There is a rush that you can't really get any other way, a level of risk that you miss the second it's over. But as Mae Bee there is something else. Something that gives it a little bit more sparkle, a little bit more oomph, a feeling of *power*. I've never felt so powerful or fully in control of myself before, but, in that moment, there it was. The more applause I got, the more powerful

I felt, like some kind of oversized Tinkerbell in three pairs of tights and a six-inch heel.

'More than I can really say,' I reply. 'It was amazing and the second it was over I wanted to do it again, but then I realized I don't have any other numbers so I couldn't even ask.' Kaye smiles. 'So, if Carrie were to offer me another slot you'll find me in a dance studio somewhere working my absolute tits off to have the numbers ready for her. New stuff, spoken-word stuff like what you do. Maybe even singing.'

'Maybe even singing, eh?' Kaye says. 'Well, looks like someone has found their spark again.'

I turn back to the mirror and continue taking off my face, trying to hide the smile that is tugging at the corners of my mouth 'Something like that, yeah. Thank you, Kaye.'

'For what dear?' she says.

'For the opportunity, for the chance to—'

'Don't go into a big speech now, my darling,' she says. 'It's far too late and Mama's had too much to drink for any of that sentimental shit.' She pauses. 'But you're more than welcome. It's a pleasure to have you as part of the family.'

With that glow still vibrating in my chest, I finish getting ready, saying my goodbyes to Kaye and heading downstairs to the bar. It's a heck of a lot emptier now and, unlike when I'd walked in before and all eyes had turned to me, now

I'm just another gay boy in the bar. I happen to be freshly moisturized and my feet hurt like hell, but no one knows that it was me up there. That is, no one except the boy smiling at me from a table in the far corner.

I hurry over to Seth and plant myself next to him. He kisses me straight away, soft, fleeting, enough to startle me. I look around and see that no one is looking at us. I didn't need to do that, least of all here. I've spent so long having to check myself for the sake of Connor that I didn't even know what it was like to just kiss someone.

'That was an experience,' he says.

'What? The kiss?' I say.

'No, the drag, the performance, all of it,' he says. 'It was nice to see you up there doing your thing.'

I grin. 'Yeah?'

'Uh-huh.' Seth reaches over and takes hold of my hand and my heart thrills a little at his touch. Holding hands is seriously underrated. I could honestly do this forever. 'And it didn't end in tears this time.'

'What a novelty!' I reply. 'Thanks for waiting around. I thought you might have gone home or something?'

'Oh no, I had to wait to get my time with Dragecellence's new star,' he says. 'How is Mae Bee?'

'Mae Bee is tired,' I say. 'But Robin Cooper is wide awake.'

A bell rings behind the bar. 'Five minutes!' the bartender calls.

'Do you want to go somewhere else?' I ask.

'Sure,' Seth says, pulling on his jacket and standing up. 'Where did you have in mind?'

'I don't know,' I say. 'Just anywhere.'

I say my goodbyes to Carrie, Pristine, The Duchess and Kaye, all sitting at the bar out of drag, enjoying a drink as the evening winds down, and Seth and I leave Entity. We walk down the empty high street, drunk people swaying and singing, sober people swerving and keeping their heads down to avoid them at all costs. And we just talk.

We jump in his car and he drives until we find ourselves outside the school, which looks weird in the dark, strangely quiet and less significant than it seems in the light of day. And maybe it's his presence, or maybe it's the performance, but there is an odd sort of calm that washes over me.

It's something I've not felt for the longest time. Everything has felt so heightened and stressful, arguing with Mum or steering clear of Connor, or sneaking out to Entity so I can practise with Kaye. But now it's faded away and all that's left is me and Seth.

'What now?' he asks.

'I need to get home,' I say. 'There's always the chance my mum will be up waiting for me to get in to make sure I'm not dead. If she's still up, I'm going to feel so guilty.'

'Well, I'd best get you home, then.'

When we arrive, he gets out of the car and we stand on the street corner, lit by the white glow of a streetlamp. His face looks beautiful in this light, in every light, but I can see the tiredness in his eyes. He needs to get home too. But we're still standing here holding hands like the world will end if we let go.

'Thank you,' I say.

'What?'

'Thank you, Seth,' I say again. 'I don't think at any point through all of this I've stopped and said thank you for everything that you did for me. Driving me to Entity, sneaking around, picking me up when I was mid-breakdown—'

'That seems to be my speciality.'

'You're more than welcome to it, it happens often enough,' I say. 'But you've done far too much for me.'

He shrugs. 'It was an excuse to spend time with you, to get to know you better. I hope you don't mind that I kissed you earlier.'

'Mind?' I repeat. 'Seth, I've been wanting to do that from the second I laid eyes on you.'

'Slut.'

'Shut up!' I nudge him with my shoulder – it's an excuse

to make contact with him. It's a cheap shot I know, but it sends a little rush through me. 'I wanted to kiss you because you were pretty. Now I want to kiss you because you're one of the nicest people I've ever met.'

'Stop it.'

'I won't,' I say. 'You're really *nice*, Seth. You've got this bad-boy exterior but inside you're actually soft.'

'And it makes you want to kiss me?' he says.

I nod.

'All right, then.'

He leans in and I follow suit, kissing him softly on the lips under the streetlight. And it's different to every kiss I ever had with Connor. It's not urgent or fevered or being worried about getting caught: it's soft, it's sweet, it's safety. He lets go of my hand and wraps his arms round my waist, pulling me closer to him.

'Goodnight, Robin,' he says.

'Goodnight. Let me know when you get home safe,' I say, kissing him lightly again. 'And thank you again.'

'Stop thanking me.'

'I won't,' I say. 'I don't know how I'll ever repay you.'

'Another kiss will do.'

I give him one last kiss and he smiles.

'There, we're even.'

'Somewhere, Natalie knows this is happening and is

making vomiting noises,' I say. He laughs and it's the most wonderful sound in the world. 'Goodnight, Seth.'

'Goodnight.'

We part ways and I move through the darkness of my house and to my bedroom. As I crawl into bed, there is the briefest moment where I'm not sure I'll actually fall asleep, my brain buzzing, my lips still tingling from kissing Seth, but then the tiredness hits me like a wave, pulling me under.

When I wake up the following morning, my feet burn like they haven't for a long time. I guess without going to dance classes all the time I'd forgotten what it was like to have your feet absolutely wrecked by a performance. Heels are hellish. I felt powerful as anything when I was wearing them, but I am paying the price now.

I check my phone and see that I have messages from Natalie and from Seth, a couple from the girls at Dragcellence sending videos of my performance. I reply to the ones from Natalie first, they're mostly congratulatory messages for last night so I thank her and throw a few gifs her way. The videos of my performance can wait. I need to let the thrill of it all die down first before I see how unpolished I am as a queen. Polish will come with time. And that's fine. It doesn't have to be perfect right away.

Seth's messages are so cutesy I want to vomit and cry at

the same time. He's wonderful. I'm excited to see where that's going to go.

'I heard your alarm!' Mum calls up the stairs. 'Can you come down here? I'm having a crisis!'

'Give me a minute!' I call back, my voice a little hoarse. Seth and I talked a lot last night. We kissed a lot too. My mouth is like a freaking desert, which isn't cute. But Mum sounds in good spirits. Maybe now she knows my absolute last secret we can move forward. Secrets are poison. It was one thing to keep Connor from her, but to hide Mae Bee was stupid.

I pull on some clothes and head downstairs. I catch sight of my reflection in the mirror and see that there is glitter on my face. I wasn't even wearing glitter last night so how that got there is beyond me. There's a joke in there somewhere about queer people sweating glitter, but I'm too damn tired to make it.

When I get downstairs, Mum has dresses hung up and so much make-up spread out on the table that it looks like there has been a break-in. She is in something of a state.

'What's happened? Has your closet exploded?' I ask, stopping at the bottom step, not sure I want to walk into this level of chaos at – I check my phone – one o'clock in the afternoon? Jesus Christ, I have slept the hell in.

'Look, I didn't plan on bothering you with this, like, at

all,' she says, rushing around, examining dresses. Her hair is done, straightened to within an inch of its life and looking silky smooth as *anything*. 'But I'm going out this afternoon, possibly for the rest of the day, and I have absolutely nothing to wear at all.'

'Possibly for the rest of the day?' I say, raising an eyebrow. 'And who might you be doing that with?'

She scoffs and waves a hand at me. 'Nobody, just a couple of friends. I totally spaced on it until I got home last night so rain check on the trashy movie and takeout?' she says.

'I may still partake,' I say. 'I don't want to do anything today if I can help it. Honestly, everything hurts and I'm dying.'

'Tough work being a star?'

'Stop that,' I say. 'Just an awfully long time to be wearing heels. I don't know how you do it.'

She holds up two dresses, one black, one leopardprint. Mum went through a phase where leopardprint was her favourite colour and I think, in this moment, she fully regrets it.

'Black,' I say. 'But maybe with a colourful cardigan or wrap or something? Statement necklace?'

'Who do you think I am?'

'Someone who definitely has a statement necklace somewhere in her jewellery box. Come on, Mum, are you kidding me?' She rummages and pulls out a giant, burnt-orange necklace and it's so gaudy that I may steal it from her. 'Perfect.'

'Thank you,' she says, and sits down in front of a mirror, starting to do her make-up. I watch her carefully, the way she does her foundation, only lightly. The way she uses only the slightest hint of eyeliner, unlike her son who uses so much he looks like a panda even now. 'What are you doing?' she asks.

'Watching you,' I say. 'Getting tips.'

She scoffs. 'You don't need tips from me,' she says. 'You looked gorgeous last night.'

I smile. I can't help it. 'Really? You think?'

She looks over the mirror at me. 'Are you fishing?'

'Maybe a little.'

'I would tell you to tone down the eyeliner but I imagine that's a drag thing,' she says. 'Not something I would do.'

'You should try it,' I say.

'What? Drag?'

'Yeah,' I reply. 'Well, drag make-up. It's freeing. It can be big, bold and colourful, or understated and elegant, like what you're doing now.' She's doing a smoky eye and the whole thing is like second nature to her, like she's done it a hundred times before, a thousand even, and I guess she probably has. There is a blind sort of boldness to it: she knows what colours, she knows how much and she blends and blends and blends and, just like when I am doing my make-up, there is that moment where you think it's gone wrong, but it's not – it's just not finished. In a strange way, it feels like a metaphor for life. Everything looks like it's wrong and that it's falling apart not because it is, but because it's not finished yet. It's not a mess – it's a work in progress.

'You're more than welcome to do my make-up one day,' she says, applying a nude lip. 'But not right now. Call it payment for me backing out on our evening together.'

I scoff. 'Don't worry about me. I'll find something to do.'

'Maybe invite Seth over.'

'Mother—'

'Do I need to have the talk with you?' she says. 'Do I need to have the talk with *him*?'

'I'm not inviting him over,' I say. 'I owe Natalie a night in, I think. So as soon as you walk out the door I'm going to call her and get her over here. Girls' night.'

Mum laughs. 'Girls' night,' she says. 'Wonderful.' She looks over at me from the dining table, her face just about finished. 'I know we barely touched on it last night,' she adds. 'But I am proud of you, you know. For everything you're doing, finding something that satisfies your creative flair and maybe stops you being so sad about college.'

'Thanks,' I say. 'It does make me happy.'

'I can see that,' she says. 'You up on that stage was the happiest I've seen you in a *long* time.'

I shrug. Performing is joy. I mean, it's also fear and panic and wanting to throw up, but once you're out there and you're doing it, it is just joy.

'While we're being open,' she says. 'Anything else you want to tell me? Any more secret boys or second lives?'

'No. I swear that was it. You know everything now. Connor, Mae Bee, all of it.'

'Not quite everything,' she says, wiggling her eyebrows. 'I need to know more about Seth.'

'Oh, is that the time?' I say, checking my bare wrist. 'Shouldn't you be going?'

'Robin—'

'Mum, I will fill you in tomorrow, I swear,' I say. 'But he's nice. Like, really nice, and when we've been officially a thing for longer than twenty-four hours you can meet him properly. And not a moment before, because you'll probably say or do something embarrassing.'

She considers this. 'Well, that does *sound* like something I'd do,' she says. There is a car horn outside and she jumps, looking towards the window, smoothing her hair. 'OK, deal. But you are right – I do need to go.'

She hurries to the hallway and grabs her bag off the hook.

She gives me one last twirl, smiling. 'What do you think?'

'You look beautiful,' I say. 'Now, don't drink too much, don't do drugs and be home by midnight.'

'If you're about to lecture me about being home by midnight, we really are going to have to have a talk, Mr Stayed Out All Night, Still Has Glitter On Their Face.' She raises an eyebrow and smirks at me. 'See you later. There's money in the kitchen.'

'Love you.'

'Love you too.'

She hurries out of the door and bundles herself into a car, waving at me through the window as it pulls away.

I grab my phone and call Natalie, not expecting her to answer so quickly.

'What's happened? Have you already messed things up with Seth?' she groans. She's doing something else; I can tell from her tone of voice.

'Good morning to you too.'

'Good *afternoon*, you dirty stop-out,' she says. 'So, did it go well? Do I need to buy a hat?'

'You don't suit hats.'

'I *do* suit hats — how *dare you*!' she snaps. 'It's a turn of phrase and would have been a funny joke, but now you've wrecked it. What do you want?'

'Mum has run out of the house for a girls' day and

I thought you might want to come over for trashy films, takeout and a girls' night,' I say. 'I am fully yours.'

I hear her shuffling on the end of the phone, possibly putting down whatever she is doing. 'You have a house to yourself and you're inviting me over instead of Seth,' she says. 'Are you out of your mind?'

'No,' I say. 'Nat, I've been an awful friend and we haven't had a film night in . . .' I try to think of how long it's been but an actual figure escapes me. 'I can't even remember, so come over.'

'Invite Seth,' she says.

'Natalie, I—'

'Invite! Seth!'

'Natalie,' I say firmly. 'I'm trying to do a nice thing here and you're ruining it. Come over tonight. I'll queue up the worst films I can find on Netflix and we'll eat pizza and talk shit about them. It'll be fun.'

'Fine,' she says. 'But you should invite Seth, Greg and Priya over too. We need to assess if this boy is good enough for you.'

'You know him as well as I do.'

'We do not. You've been galivanting off to drag clubs with him for the last few weeks. I need to make sure he's not another Connor. Your track record with boys speaks volumes.'

'Natalie—'

'See you in a while. I have work to finish. Text me a time, love you bye.'

I sigh. 'Love you bye.'

She hangs up the phone and I text Seth and Greg, giving Natalie a time of 5 p.m. and everyone else a time of 7 p.m. so I get some alone time with her. And as I get ready for them coming over I feel calm.

It's that same calmness that I felt when I was walking around with Seth last night, that feeling that things are going to be all right for the first time since all the rejection. Things have evened out. It's not a mess any more.

And I don't know what tomorrow will bring, or the day after that; all I can count on is today, and today is a good day. One day at a time, I'll figure it out. Whatever the future holds, it is enough to just try. And maybe that's not so scary after all.

ABOUT THE AUTHOR

George Lester is a freelance editor, musical-theatre lover and drag nerd who lives with his wonderful partner in Twickenham. He semi-regularly posts videos online talking about books and writing (mostly). He is also a drag-queen under the name That Gurrrl.

ACKNOWLEDGEMENTS

I can't believe I am actually getting to do this thing. I'm writing this during the lockdown in March 2020. I hope that whoever is reading this is looking back on that time and thinking 'wow, that was weird, thank God everything is fine now and Donald Trump isn't the president anymore!' I have dreams kids, I hope I'm right.

Having a book published is a dream that I have had since I was, like, ten years old. I love books and I love telling stories. I was a bookseller and loved selling stories to people, and I was an editor and loved helping other writers hone their own stories. So the fact that I am sat here writing the acknowledgements for a book baby of my own is really special and I know I am going to forget somebody in this line up, for which I apologise. I promise you'll be in the next one. (Nudge nudge, wink wink.)

First of all, I need to thank the wonder and dreamboat that is Rachel Petty. You came to me with an idea, something that I'd never really felt I had the ability to write, and you combined two of my loves into one wonderful thing – I am eternally grateful for that. You also smashed this edit so fast

I cannot even cope. You're a genius and I adore you. Simran Sandhu, your insight on this book has been so incredibly valuable and I am so lucky to have you on Team *Boy Queen*. And Charlie Selvaggi-Castelletti, you were late to the party, but I'm glad you arrived – you're incredible. Kat McKenna, thank you for everything you have done for me in life and everything you have done for this book, to Amber Ivatt, girl you are killing it and I am so so excited for all the things we have planned! Jess Rigby, I am SO excited that I get to work with you on this!! No take backs!! THIS IS IT BABES! Rachel Vale, this cover slayed my entire existence. I screamed when it arrived. You are an icon. To Sales, International, Foreign Rights, Production and Art: you made all of this possible and I can't thank you enough for making this little gayboy's dream come true. (Also LOL you totally couldn't get rid of me!)

Sam Copeland, what a legend you are! It took us a while, but we got there. I don't know what I did to deserve an agent like you, I really don't. You always stick by me, no matter what I want to write, and you always push me to try things out. I'm so, so grateful to have you in my corner. This is hopefully just the start of a marvellous journey and I cannot wait!

Mum and Dave, you have supported me in every venture I have ever had. You have backed me, you have been there for me and (Mum specifically on this one) you will listen to me ramble on about my life on the phone for 45 minutes at a time and offer your wisdom. I cannot thank you enough for all that you do for me. Sam and Oliver, you're the best siblings a guy could ask for! And to the rest of my family who are always there for me, I know I'm not around a lot, but I love you all immensely!

Katy, Lani, DL and Marcus, the family. You heard about this before a lot of people and you backed me on it 100%, as you do with all the things that I do. I couldn't ask for a better collection of friends. You make me feel braver than I actually am and I have no idea what I would be without you. To the rest of my Mountview family, my angels and darling queens who show me nothing but love and support, you are ridiculously talented beans that I am SO DAMN LUCKY TO KNOW. I miss you every damn day and that's the tea. Keep killing it. Please.

Joe Parslow, my drag mother (whether you like it or not), I owe a lot of this to you and the knowledge you imparted on me and That Gurrrl. She wouldn't exist without you, and you can either take that as a compliment or not. Our tutorials that descended into general drag chats were eye opening and I can't thank you enough for the world you have given me by opening my eyes to all the drag in it. Sherrill Gow and Merryn Owen, this is also your fault, which I guess makes you my drag aunt and uncle? How extended can we make this family? I want to thank you for all the love and support you gave me during my time at Mountview. This is a bold choice and I wouldn't have been able to make it without you guys. I can't thank you enough.

To Leejay and Cat (it's not the front, but this is fine too right?), thank you for all you have done and continue to do for me in my acting life. Your constant support and love means the absolute world!

I don't want this to go on forever and ever, which it totally could because I have so much love for so many people so, I'm just going to do a little list if you will allow me; Victoria Walters, Kim Curran, Non Pratt, Lisa Williamson, Sara Barnard, Patrick Ness, Juno Dawson, David Levithan, L. D. Lapinski, the 2020 debuts who gladly listen to my neurosis in the group chat, I have huge amounts of love for each and every one of you for a multitude of reasons. I am so so grateful to know you and to have had your wisdom (and your incredible books) in my life.

To any drag fan who is reading this, PLEASE go and see some local drag and support your local queens! You will be AMAZED at the incredible performers you can find on your doorstep or, if not on your doorstep, a short bus/train ride away. And if you can't go and see a show, find them on Instagram! They will blow your mind, just as they did

Robin's and just as they continue to blow mine every time I see a new queen at a show. If you're a fan of *RuPaul's Drag Race*, let it be the gateway drug and lead you to more drag, more kinds of drag, it'll be worth it, I swear! *RuPaul's Drag Race* is amazing, but I promise you there is SO MUCH MORE!!

To every cheerleader I have met either in real life or digitally, every bookish-type human who has already read and reviewed this book, you have no idea just how much your support means to me. Every time I post something book related, I wonder if anyone will care and you always do. It means the absolute world to me to have your support and love through all of this. I appreciate you so damn much. Shantay, you ALL stay.

And finally, I need to thank Jordan for being my rock, not just during this book, but in my life. Through thick and thicc and thin, you have always been there for me and supported and backed me and I cannot thank you enough for that. You are at the start and the end of this book, because you hold it all together, just like you hold me together. I can hear you making vomiting noises and I don't care. I love you and that's that!!

Until next time,
George/That Gurrrl xx